for Anna Lee, A—, ———, Debbie, Mary Beth, Pat and Robin.

And also for Jeremy and Raquel.

Against All Enemies

AN ALLISON QUINN THRILLER
BOOK TWO

VANNETTA CHAPMAN

Introductory Quotes

"A complex network of cameras, infrared heat-source monitors, patrols, and investigative protocols deters, detects, and deals with criminal activity. Captains can warn difficult passengers, suspend shipboard alcohol privileges, or put ashore anyone that poses a threat to others on the ship. Brigs (jails) are available to secure troublemakers or even suspected criminals until they can be handed over to port law enforcement, but often 'cabin arrest,' with or without security staff posted in the corridor, suffices."
~Mike Howard
"Cruise Ship Security: How Safe are Cruisers?" GoNOMAD

"Cruise ships, by and large, don't have armed security guards. Contrary to people who want to believe that the ships are armed but the cruise lines don't want to tip their hand to the terrorists, there is in fact no hidden cache of weapons ready to be deployed by the cruise ship's security forces."
~Jim Walker
"Is Your Cruise Ship Prepared for a Terrorist Attack?" Cruise-LawNews.com

"It depends on the cruise line, but some cruise lines do have security personnel with guns on their cruise ships. Cruise lines may choose to arm security personnel in order to provide added protection against potential threats and to deter crime onboard."

~Olin Wade

"Does Security Have Guns On A Cruise Ship?" Remodelor-move.com

"I, Allison Quinn, do solemnly swear
that I will support and defend
the Constitution of the United States
against all enemies, foreign and domestic;
that I will bear true faith and allegiance to the same;
that I take this obligation freely,
without any mental reservation or purpose of evasion;
and that I will well and faithfully discharge
the duties of the office on which I am about to enter.
So help me God."

Chapter One

Allison Quinn's frustration accelerated toward the boiling point. She was sweating. The weather had to be in the 90s, though it was only April in Texas. When had it started reaching ninety in April? Her short brown curls were probably standing on end. She couldn't see them. She wasn't about to stop and stare at her reflection in a car's window. But she could feel them, frizzing around her head like a halo. Too much humidity. Too much heat. Sweat trickled down her underarms and the little bit of makeup she wore felt as if it were sliding down her face.

She stood in the middle of the Dallas Mixmaster and quelled the urge to pull her firearm and shoot something. Just the heft of it in her hand would go far in calming her agitation.

But today wasn't about shooting or even apprehending terrorists.

Today was about catching up to where they'd been and what they'd done, and then—most importantly—predicting what they planned to do next.

Shooting would have to wait.

Drivers of cattle trailers and 18-wheelers honked angrily at Mercedes, BMW, and Tesla drivers. Hyundai, Ford, and Cadillac

1

also made cars with self-driving features, but the bulk of the disabled vehicles blocking lanes on this fine April day were BMWs and Teslas. The backup stretched as far as Allison could see in both directions. Tempers flared, there had already been at least two punches thrown, and it wasn't even eleven in the morning yet.

Her newest partner, a young man sporting three earrings and long hair tied back with a band, hustled over. Malik Elliott was all enthusiasm and zero experience, which is why the powers-that-be had assigned him to Allison.

"Tell me something good, Elliott."

"TxDot and Highway Patrol are both onsite." He adjusted his designer glasses. "They're working on getting enough wreckers to move the disabled vehicles, but it's going to take some time."

The highway interchange connected Interstate 35E and Interstate 30. It had been constructed in the early 1960s and saw over a half a million vehicles per week.

"What sadist conceived a place like the Mixmaster?" Allison growled.

Elliott stared at the ground, trying to hide a smile.

She hated when he did that.

"What?"

"Nothing, Boss."

"Just say it."

"Hasn't been called the Mixmaster since 2017."

"Really?"

"Seven-hundred-million-dollar improvement. It's the Horseshoe now."

"The Horseshoe?"

"I didn't name it, Boss."

Allison tried, without success, to hold in a sigh. "Do you have any good news to report? Anything helpful?"

"The event is trending on Twitter. No one has tied it to cybercrime—yet. And Tesla stock has dropped 12 percent."

A trooper wearing a Texas Highway Patrol uniform

approached somewhat hesitantly. He looked old enough to be her grandfather and cranky enough to be her twin.

"Problem, Officer Sanchez?"

"I have a driver, a Mrs. Kincaid, who's insisting on talking to the person in charge. You are the person in charge, right?"

"Yeah. That would be me."

Allison instructed Elliott to get an update from the car manufacturer on exactly what kind of cyber breach had taken place, then she followed Officer Sanchez to where Mrs. Kincaid waited. Kincaid was elderly and impeccably dressed. By all outward appearances, she was also quite wealthy.

"Are you the person in charge, or is Officer Sanchez simply trying to hand me off to someone else?"

"Senior agent Allison Quinn, and yes, I'm in charge."

She didn't specify that she worked for Homeland Security, JCTF Division. In an attack like this one, the Joint Cyber Task Force, consisting of FBI and HS agents, worked hard to fly under the radar.

Allison held out a hand, which the woman shook with a surprisingly strong grasp.

"Nice to see a woman in charge."

Allison didn't respond to that. She'd worked with plenty of less-than-competent men and women. Allison assured Officer Sanchez that she would take it from here.

Once he'd moved out of earshot, Mrs. Kincaid stepped closer and lowered her voice. "Before my vehicle shut off, a symbol displayed on the screen."

"A symbol?"

"Yes."

"A malfunction symbol?"

"No. It was a tree of sorts."

Allison's pulse picked up a notch. Thirty thousand websites were hacked worldwide every day. It was estimated that three hundred thousand pieces of malware were written every day. DDoS attacks—distributed denial of service attacks—were expected to grow to fifteen million in the current year. Until that moment, until Mrs. Kincaid said the word *tree*, there had been no indication that this was anything more than your garden-variety attack.

But if she were correct about the symbol...

Mrs. Kincaid waited, one finely arched eyebrow raised.

"If I gave you a sheet of paper, could you draw me a picture of what you saw?"

"I can do better than that, Agent Quinn. I took a picture with my phone. Let me AirDrop it to you."

Quinn walked to the side of the highway, pulled out her cell phone, and punched the contact button for her boss.

Kendra Thomas answered on the first ring. "Talk to me."

"I'm sending you a photo just shared with me by one of the Tesla drivers."

"Okay."

"This symbol appeared on her vehicle's screen before everything shut down."

There was a moment's silence, then Thomas came back. When she spoke, her voice was resolute. Not surprised. Certainly not frightened. More like a general who was ready and prepared to enter the next battle. "It's them."

"That's definitely the symbol for the group that very nearly carried out an EMP attack in Seattle. They were also at least partially involved in what went down at the Grand Canyon. As you know, DHS is fairly certain they are a branch of the Anarchists for Tomorrow. Whether it is actually them or someone pretending to be them—"

"Circles within circles with these people."

"I recommend we elevate the current situation to a level three threat. This could be just the beginning."

Technically the DHS had only two types of advisories—

bulletins and alerts. Bulletins usually dealt with critical terrorism information not indicative of a specific threat. Alerts were more specific about the nature of the threat. The two types of alerts were elevated and imminent.

That was technically how terrorist events were handled.

The color-coded system of the post 9-11 era had been replaced in 2011, but within the JCT they still used a number system. Five was a vague threat with little actionable intelligence. One represented an imminent risk for persons or systems within the United States. Currently they were at a level four.

"Given the scope of damage here and the possible connection to the AT. . ." Allison stared out at the gridlock. "I believe it warrants a move to level three."

"Done." Thomas's voice was steady and definitive. She didn't waste time questioning the agents on the ground. She also didn't hesitate to inform them of the bigger picture when they needed to know. "We were about to deploy agents to Galveston on what we thought was an unrelated op. I'll coordinate and get back with you."

Thirty minutes later, Allison received instructions. "Galveston. Terminal 2, Pier 28. Leave Elliott in charge of the Dallas site."

Which said a lot.

If an agent with Elliott's lack of experience could be put in charge of a site, there was no further threat there. Allison had worked under Thomas in Seattle—an op that still caused her pain in her shoulder when the temperature fluctuated. A gunshot wound could do that to you. Thomas was decisive and efficient, and she did not broker fools. If she was sending Allison to Pier 28 in Galveston, then that's where the threat was.

Allison updated Elliott, then caught a ride on a helicopter, which was the only path out of the Mixmaster—or rather, the Horseshoe—other than walking. The copter took her to the downtown Dallas federal building where the task force had set up camp. There she requisitioned a vehicle. She drove the nondescript Chevrolet Tahoe out of the underground garage, passing the Sixth Street Book Depository as she made her way through downtown.

She hadn't been born when John Kennedy was assassinated in 1963, but she knew the details—both what had been made public and what hadn't. Unlike some of her co-workers, she didn't think the high-tech world they lived in had grown more dangerous or more deadly.

The world had always been dangerous and deadly.

Ask John Kennedy.

Ask Jackie.

You could go back in time all the way to Lincoln in the Ford Theater, and if you visited Europe, you could trace the history of violence back centuries. A brief study of history chronicled the violent state of humans and humanity.

What had changed were the tools of war.

The war itself—that had stayed the same.

And she, Allison Quinn, had taken a solemn vow to protect this country. To fight this war. Privately, she'd also vowed to catch the persons responsible for her father's murder.

Since the Anarchists for Tomorrow were apparently involved, with the current operation, she just might be able to do both.

Game on.

Chapter Two

I t took Allison nearly six hours to drive from downtown Dallas to Pier 28 in Galveston. It shouldn't have taken that long, but it did. Her first mistake was stopping at the notorious travel center Buc-ee's.

Her only family lived outside of the small town of San Saba. Aunt Polly would have warned her it was foolishness to stop at the world's largest convenience store for a pit stop. Allison didn't listen to the wise voice of Aunt Polly that popped into her mind. Instead, she allowed her fatigue and hunger to convince her it would be the quickest way to use a bathroom and grab some food that wasn't deep-fried.

The food was fresh and tasty.

The bathrooms were numerous and clean.

But the crowds put her back fifteen minutes.

By the time she was once again behind the wheel of her vehicle and belted in her seat, she was antsy to make up for lost time. She fought the traffic to the feeder road, took the onramp to the freeway, and floored the gas pedal on the Tahoe. That decision ended up costing her another ten minutes when she had to explain to the officer who pulled her over that she was on official business. He let her off with a warning that in Texas, if you didn't have flashers on the top of your car, you did not break the posted speed limit.

She wanted to argue that point.

Instead, she thanked him, set her cruise control one mile per hour over the speed limit, and tried not to think of what might be happening while she was in transit.

Nothing was happening.

Kendra Thomas would call if the situation had changed.

The traffic in Houston was as horrendous as she remembered. At one point she counted eighteen lanes from the feeder roads on the east side to those on the west. She popped out of the concrete jungle on the southeast side of downtown and sped past the slew of exits.

Clear Lake City—home of the Johnson Space Center.

League City—location of the grisly site where thirty murdered women were found in the 1970s.

Texas City—home of the United States' third-largest oil refinery.

She was sure there were good things about the Houston area, but her mind was focused on likely targets, the macabre past, the vulnerable infrastructure. She couldn't stop envisioning worst-case scenarios.

As soon as she drove over the causeway bridge into Galveston, Allison began to see signs for cruise line parking. She'd never been on a cruise. She had no idea what to expect. The overabundance of signage eventually directed her toward Dream Sail Cruises. Parked at Pier 49 were two monstrosities docked side-by-side. They looked to be nearly two hundred feet above the water and probably a thousand feet long.

How did they float?

What would a terrorist do with something this size?

The one on the west side boasted the name *Harmony of Dreams* painted on the side. Next to it was an equally large ship named *Fantasia Breeze*. Who came up with these names? They sounded like knock-off perfume brands.

"More like a nightmare than a dream," she mumbled as she pulled her vehicle into one of the Port Authority parking spaces. She wasn't Port Authority, but she also wasn't about to park six blocks away and wait for a shuttle. Gleaming in the sunlight next to her vehicle was a souped-up silver Corvette. Port Authority must be paying well these days.

Allison hurried toward the gangway where employees were loading crates of food and supplies, and she nearly stumbled when she recognized the other task force agent. She nearly walked back to the Tahoe. Donovan Steele was easy enough to spot—five foot eleven, athletic, and Black. The buzz cut he insisted on wearing sealed the deal. There was no one else quite like Donovan on the JCTF. He looked like he should be on a football field, not wearing a suit and chasing terrorists.

"This day just keeps getting worse."

She thought she said it under her breath, but Donovan turned and greeted her with a smile.

"I know you're not talking about me. How are you, Allison?"

He stuck out his big hand. Allison had no choice but to shake it. She had history with Donovan Steele. She owed her life to the man, but that didn't mean she had to like working with him. Her relationship with Donovan was complicated. It was not something she wanted to deal with today. Or ever.

She tried to plaster on a smile, or at least dim the glower that she was sending his way. "This must be big if Thomas sent us both here."

He pulled her aside, out of earshot should any of the Dream Sail Cruise employees be overly curious. For all they knew, one of the workers could be an AT terrorist pretending to work for Dream Sail Cruise.

"Thomas has deployed top-level teams to Miami, Palm Beach, Tampa, Boston, New York, New Jersey, and Los Angeles."

"And you just happened to be the closest senior agent to Galveston?"

Steele grinned his big, toothy grin. The man could star in an orthodontist commercial. "Maybe she thinks we work well together."

Allison refused to consider that.

"What happened up in Dallas?"

She filled him in, ending with a description of the AT symbol that appeared on Mrs. Kincaid's car display.

"That explains why Thomas upped the threat level."

"Actually that was my idea. What's going on here though? Hacking into a bunch of electric cars, I understand. It makes a statement. It's very public. It emphasizes our dependence on technology and our vulnerability because of that dependence."

"I suspect you're right there. Cyberbugs are not fans of EVs. They're too easy to hack into."

"But this? A cruise ship? What could the Anarchists for Tomorrow possibly be saying with a cruise boat?"

"The Kids in the basement..."

It was their endearing term for the men and women who fought cyberterrorism from a keyboard back at headquarters. Instead of being offended, the group had promptly ordered t-shirts with those five words as their logo.

Donovan waited for two men who had unloaded their dollies to walk past them. "The Kids picked up a text thread that had been buried behind lines of code."

"Didn't know they could do that."

"It's something they've started seeing in the last six weeks. Anyway, this text thread mentioned cruises, day of reckoning, and the roots of revolution."

"AT."

"Probably. Throw in what you discovered in Dallas, and it even seems likely. We have to at least check it out."

Allison turned to study the gigantic cruise ship. "Why this one?"

"Actually, it's both of them. Our analysts found, buried behind the text threads, two sets of numbers. When The Kids ran one of their programs on the data they found latitude and longitude along with..."

"Pier numbers."

"Yup."

"Why do we keep getting saddled with the genius terrorists?"

"Definitely more of a challenge than your average disgruntled American."

"In general, terrorists are not the brightest crayons in the box. Remember the guy who tried to light his shoe on fire on a transatlantic flight?"

"Richard Colvin Reid. I guess we're just lucky. We tend to get the gifted and talented sort."

"Okay. How long do we have?"

"*Fantasia* leaves at two tomorrow afternoon. *Harmony* leaves at four."

"I'll take *Harmony*."

"And I'll go with *Fantasia*. Has a nice Disney sound to it." He checked his watch. "Meet back here at eighteen hundred."

"Six. You mean six."

Again the flash of his grin and a short salute, then he jogged off toward *Fantasia*.

Jogged.

Like it would kill him to walk.

Allison was cranky and tired, and she had the sinking feeling that they were just getting started. But another part of her felt like a Beagle that had locked in on its first scent. They were close to whatever was about to happen. She was certain of that. Her instincts had never failed her.

She'd been forced to take a six weeks leave after what went down in the Grand Canyon. At first she'd fought it emotionally and physically. Then she'd slept, recuperated, tried to find her equilibrium. Finally, as time and Aunt Polly had worked their magic, she began digging into her father's past.

He'd worked for the agency's Cybercrime Unit during a period when most people hadn't even seen a personal computer. The idea that such machines could be used to create chaos sounded like something out of an apocalyptic novel. Her father had worked for the CIA during the day, and at night he had put in extra hours trying to understand the roots of the cybercriminal world.

Somehow, in the hours between those two things he'd managed to single-handedly raise his daughter. He'd been a terrific dad, and she missed him to this day. She mourned him still. He'd been taken from her too early, and she'd long ago vowed to find and apprehend the persons responsible for his death.

During her enforced time off, Allison had focused on that. She wasn't terribly surprised when she came across multiple references to fantasy wargames of the 1970s, then role-playing games from the 1980s, and finally black op groups, underground groups, and even dark web groups. They all had one thing in common—anarchy. And that trail of information, that scent, had ended when her father was killed in 1996.

He'd been close to putting the pieces together.

He'd nearly proven that the link between those computer whiz kids of the dawning computer age and the cyber terrorist groups being closely watched by the CIA existed.

Allison's plan—no, her life mission—was to pick up where he'd left off, to stop these people intent on causing mass murder and mayhem, and to capture the persons responsible for her father's death. Something told her that person was still alive, though Arthur Quinn's murder had been twenty-seven years ago. The approximate age of the perpetrator would be somewhere between forty-seven and...she supposed there was no top limit. Ninety? One hundred? Regardless, she would see the person put behind bars.

And today, that mission started on a cruise ship called *Harmony of Dreams*. Allison could almost feel her father smiling at that. She strode to the gangway on the right. Donovan had already disappeared into his ship. She flashed her badge at the attendant guarding the door, noting that there were no armed security personnel present. None that she could see, anyway. There were huge crates and pallets of supplies being loaded onboard. It apparently took a lot of people to resupply a cruise ship.

"I need to speak with your senior security officer, your head engineer, and then your captain—in that order."

The twenty-year-old with spiked purple hair stared at her as if he couldn't quite comprehend what she'd said.

"Pick up your phone or your radio and call the security department. If you can't do that, call your supervisor. Now."

He jumped at her last word as if she'd hollered. She hadn't hollered, but Allison was aware that she had a way of intimidating people. It wasn't usually something she did on purpose. She was simply very intense when focused on an op.

Ten minutes later, she was in the main security room.

The woman in charge of security was in her fifties, sported a trim physique, and had no-nonsense gray hair cut in a straight bob that fell just below her ears.

Allison was willing to bet that Becca Price still ran five miles a day and did fifty push-ups each morning to stay in shape. She obviously took her job quite seriously, which was a point in their favor.

"You're saying that our systems have been compromised?"

"No. I am not saying that. I'm saying that we have indications that one or more cruise ships at a U.S. port may have been or may in the future be compromised."

"Wow. Sounds like an attorney wrote that statement."

Allison smiled.

Becca Price was someone she could definitely work with.

"What is your reporting structure?"

"We have thirty guards onboard..."

"Armed?"

Price hesitated.

"I need to know what you have as far as resources."

"We don't like to talk about firearms on board a cruise ship since we spend a good amount of time in international waters, but yes... the guards have access to firearms should that be necessary."

"Okay. They have access, which means they are not armed on a day-to-day basis."

"A few are."

When Allison pinned her with a stare and simply waited, Price shrugged and said, "Six are armed at all times. The rest have access to both pistols and shotguns should it become necessary, which in my twelve years with Dream Sail Cruises has never happened."

"Noted. Who has immediate access to the firearms?"

"Only myself and the captain."

"Regarding your guards, what kind of people are we talking about? Ex-military?"

"Many are. We also recruit individuals with previous experience in the FBI, law enforcement, and corporate security."

"Incident reporting structure?"

"I report to the captain. He reports to the Coast Guard. While we're in dock, port security is also involved."

"The ship's manifest?"

"All passengers and crew are screened by U.S. Customs and Border Protection."

Allison already knew everything Price was saying. CBD was, in fact, a part of Homeland Security. What she wanted to confirm was that Price understood the reporting and command structure.

"You have a brig?"

"We do."

"Holding capacity?"

"Four. Again, we've never used it. Occasionally we have needed to confine a guest to their cabin, but it's never risen to the need for armed intervention or putting someone behind bars."

"Okay." Allison glanced around the small office. Price barely had enough space to open the drawers of the single filing cabinet without them banging into the desk. Allison supposed it was all the space the woman needed. There was enough room for the three chairs across from the desk. But you weren't going to fit more than four people into this space. It definitely wasn't big enough to hold a departmental briefing.

As if reading her mind, Price said, "We reserve a conference room for briefings. Would you like to meet with all security officers scheduled for this sailing?"

"Not yet." Allison's fatigue had dropped away as she tried to envision how and where a cyberattack would occur onboard a ship of this size. Being physically on the ship helped. She could mentally plan for obstacles and incidents. She could strategize how best to respond. In other words, she could do her job.

"What kind of situation are we facing?" Price asked. "And don't tell me that you're not at liberty to say. This is my crew, and I will not have them walking into it blind."

Allison admired that Price's first concern wasn't her job or her own ability to handle what was coming but rather the safety of the men and women working under her leadership. Perhaps that selfless quality was why she decided to be candid with the woman.

"Cyberattack."

Price shook her head, surprise coloring her features. "How…"

"We don't know."

"But…"

"The Joint Cyber Task Force—composed of personnel from the FBI as well as Homeland Security—has received credible evidence of an impending attack." She held up a hand to stop Price's next question. "We don't know where. We don't know when. This ship is one of many locations being monitored."

"You're experienced at this?"

"I am."

Price blew out a breath and ran a hand around the back of her neck. "I suppose I was imagining armed insurgents boarding the vessel in the middle of the Gulf, but a cyberattack…how would that even work?"

"The first thing they'd do is disable your communication and propulsion systems."

"Comms I understand, but why propulsion? What good does a ship stuck in the middle of the Gulf of Mexico do anyone?"

"Unclear."

"When?"

"We don't know."

"But it's impending?"

"We believe so, yes."

"Okay. What else can I do?"

"Take me to your head engineer. After that, we need to brief your captain."

An hour later, Allison was seated on the bridge with Price, McKinley and Ferguson. They were meeting in a sitting area off to the side of the main room. The room was carpeted in a nondescript blue carpet. Dead center sat a control area with chairs, monitors, radios, telephones...all manner of devices that Allison couldn't identify. Floor to ceiling windows, complete with giant windshield wipers, stretched across the bow of the ship.

Captain Brandon McKinley sat in the armchair—though *sat* was a bit of a misnomer. The man's posture was ramrod straight, and he didn't recline in the overstuffed chair so much as perch on the edge of it. McKinley was in his late forties, Black, former Navy. Unlike Donovan Steele, McKinley had taken advantage of being out of the military and allowed his hair to grow a quarter of an inch. He looked to be five foot ten, one hundred and seventy pounds, and in good physical condition. At the moment, he was piercing Allison with a glare as if she were to blame for the current state of affairs.

The head engineer would have been comfortable working with The Kids. Brock Ferguson had long hair pulled back with a band, one earring—which made Allison think of a pirate—and he couldn't have been thirty years old. He appeared to be mixed race, barely Allison's height of five foot, six inches, and he was showing the beginnings of a belly which was probably indicative of the fact that he stared at monitors most of the day.

Allison had carefully and succinctly laid out the situation.

"I will not put my crew, my passengers, or my ship at risk." McKinley's eyes were a deep brown, and his expression gave nothing away.

"Understood. However, I need to emphasize that there are over a dozen vessels being assessed at the moment from all the major U.S. ports." She'd given them a brief history lesson of the AT and their past tactics. "The AT won't hit them all. They'll want to make a splash—one place, maybe two—and they'll want it to be big."

"Meaning what?" Price asked. She still looked puzzled, as if she couldn't quite visualize how the hacking of their systems could result in chaos.

Allison came across that quizzical attitude fairly often. People were so used to the integration of technology in every aspect of their life that they couldn't quite imagine what would happen if someone unplugged the entire thing. They couldn't conceive— very few people, in fact, even understood—how much of their world depended on computers and satellites.

"Meaning that I suspect they would have people on board to document and live stream the event."

"How..." Captain McKinley shook his head. "If everything is down, how would that be possible? Say they have a suitcase EMP, which I can't imagine making its way through security, but say it does. If everything is down how would they live stream anything?"

"Their devices would be hardened," Ferguson explained. Of the three ship personnel before her, Ferguson was the one who was least surprised. On some level, he understood their vulnerability. Maybe he'd even worried about something like this happening on his shift. "It's easy enough to put a laptop in a hardened case. You can buy one on the internet for two hundred bucks."

"And it would have a satellite card," Allison added. "So the fact that your servers are down wouldn't affect their ability to live stream the event at all. Often the motivation of groups like this is simply to spread fear. Show a cruise ship sitting in the dark, in the middle of the Gulf, with no engines, and no navigation. It's a cyberpunk's dream."

Captain McKinley bounced the fingertips of both hands against one another. "Why don't we simply scuttle this cruise? No one has boarded. Now's the best time to do it."

"Several reasons—the most obvious being they might hit somewhere else, in which case you would have disappointed nearly three thousand passengers for no reason."

"It's more than that though." McKinley directed his unwavering gaze on Allison. "You're not worried about disappointed passengers. You want to catch these criminals. If we cancel, you won't have a chance to do that. They'll be in the wind."

Allison shrugged.

He wasn't wrong.

Instead of arguing, she said, "We're still at level three which means..."

"Imminent but unspecified threat. Yeah. I got that the first time you said it." He stared out at something beyond the floor-to-ceiling windows, something in the water, maybe something in the future. "How do you suggest we proceed?"

"Search the ship—top to bottom, bow to stern. Go in every stateroom, search every closet, check under every bed."

"All right. What else?"

"All those crates of supplies that are being loaded? Open them. Look inside. Anything that seems like it doesn't belong, anything at all that your people see that gives them pause, call me. Lastly, my boss has already been in contact with Port Authority. They'll be giving both the crew and the passengers a more-thorough-than-usual examination."

"I don't want the passengers spooked."

Allison glanced at Price, who rubbed her fingertips across her brow. Finally, she sat up straighter and said, "We'll tell them it's new machines. Apologize for the inconvenience. Offer a free drink coupon."

Captain McKinley nodded, stood, then motioned for Allison to walk with him. When they'd reached the bank of windows, he turned to her and stuck out his hand. "Thank you for updating us."

"Of course."

He let go of her hand, but he didn't step back. Lowering his voice, he said, "I expect you to continue to do so in a timely manner. Almost three thousand guests and twelve hundred crew will be on this ship tomorrow, Agent Quinn. It will be up to you and me..." He glanced over his shoulder. "As well as Price and Ferguson, to see that they make it back to this port safely."

Then he turned and walked away.

She'd been dismissed.

Allison almost laughed, but the early morning, long drive, and initial assessment had taken every ounce of energy she possessed. She nodded at Price and Ferguson, then exited the bridge and made her way down the long hallway and to the bank of elevators. From there, she could see all the way down to the promenade—a mall-like area filled with stores, cafes, and art displays.

And within twelve hours it would also be home to over four thousand souls.

Chapter Three

Donovan was watching for Allison as she came trotting down the gangway of the *Harmony of Dreams*.

He pointed at his watch and she gestured rudely.

He liked working with Allison Quinn. She was sharp, focused, and sexy. She also didn't give him an inch unless she was hoping he'd hang himself.

"Almost late, Quinn."

"Which translates to on-time. What did you learn?"

She was out of breath and pale. The circles under her eyes seemed darker than they'd been a few hours earlier. And still, she was a beautiful woman.

"What are you staring at?" She patted her hair down as if she expected to find something untoward there.

"Let's eat."

"What?"

Her incredulous tone made him laugh.

"Eat. Consume calories. Gear up for the battle ahead. People do it, Quinn. Some people do it several times a day." He'd put a hand on the crook of her elbow and was steering her toward their cars.

She jerked her arm away. "You do realize the mission clock has started on this one?"

"Yes, I understand where we're at in the grand scheme of things."

"Terrorists could be boarding the ships as we munch on shrimp."

Donovan stopped and glanced back at the ships, then grinned at her. "Looks to me like they've closed up the gangways for the night. Plus, if any terrorists do manage to get on board, it'll be easier to trap them there."

"You're entirely too cavalier about this."

"Uh-huh. Let's take my car."

She sighed and her shoulders dropped.

Allison Quinn could convey a dozen emotions with a sigh. Donovan could fill a book with her nonverbal cues. Instead, he put his hands on his hips and pretended to look offended. "What's your problem?"

"I just thought we could take my car."

"Is it that one?" He pointed at a Chevy Tahoe that he knew was government issued. Black. Cloth seats. Probably had a hundred thousand miles on it.

"Yes."

"Let's take mine." He nodded toward the birthday present he'd bought himself. Silver. Shiny. Leather seats and a Bose performance series sound system with fourteen speakers. Still had less than two thousand miles on it.

A smile twitched at the corner of Allison's lips.

"What?"

"Nothing."

"You're about to laugh. What? You don't like state-of-the-art vehicles?"

"It's a midlife-crisis car."

"It is not. Besides, I'm not mid-life."

"You're thirty-eight. Do you plan on living past seventy-six?"

"I do."

"In our line of work?"

"It's possible."

"Unlikely."

"I think you need a drink with your meal."

She didn't argue, simply dropped into the passenger seat of his silver Z06 Corvette and glared out the tinted windows. He'd pulled onto the main thoroughfare before she spoke.

"You do realize this car has an onboard computer."

"It also has 670 horsepower and can make zero to sixty in 2.6 seconds. Besides, all cars have onboard computers."

"We'd be better off if they didn't."

"And now you sound like my pop."

"Smart man."

"He likes you, too."

She tried to glare at him, probably hoping to squelch his good humor. "I've never had the pleasure of meeting your father."

"True, but I talk about you."

She groaned, raising his spirits even more. Yup. An op with Allison Quinn was just what his life had been missing.

"Seafood or seafood?"

She ignored the question and closed her eyes. He'd already decided where they were eating, so it was probably better that she didn't have a strong opinion on the matter. Donovan believed in treating himself to the local cuisine when possible. He'd even made a reservation.

When he parked, Allison opened one eye, yawned, and stared at the restaurant in front of them. Finally, she murmured in a resigned way, "Seriously?"

"Sure."

"A little fancy."

"You were hoping for Whataburger?"

"I was hoping for fast." She exited the vehicle and made a beeline for the front door of the restaurant.

"Now see, that's where you could learn from me." He jogged to catch up with her.

"Learn from you?"

"Right. Slow down a little. Enjoy the ambiance. Live a little, Quinn."

She didn't bother arguing, which meant that she was more tired than he'd realized. Pasta and protein would perk her right up.

She ordered the shrimp salad. He chose the combination platter which included charcoal-grilled Gulf shrimp, scallops, and snapper. As they waited for their food, they compared notes on the two cruise ships and found they were nearly identical in personnel and readiness.

"They have no idea what this sort of attack could entail." Allison reached for one of the hot rolls, broke it open, and then stared at it as the steam rose.

"Here. Put butter on it, then eat it."

"You certainly are bossy." But she smiled as she accepted the small container of butter and slathered half of it on the roll. When she'd eaten the whole thing, she sat back and sighed. "Lack of imagination—that's the problem. They can't really conceive what twelve hours off-line, twelve hours in the dark..."

"In the middle of the Gulf."

"Right. What that could do. Most people don't understand how distressed they would feel to be disconnected during an emergency."

"Do you think this is it?" Donovan wasn't making small talk. He sincerely wanted to know. He valued Allison's opinion and analysis. She was good at this—one of the best. "Do you think it will happen here, on one of these ships?"

Their waiter returned with their food. Allison waited until he'd offered fresh pepper, refilled their water glasses, and stepped away before she answered.

"On the one hand, why would they have an attack in the

Dallas area and then a second event three hundred miles away? That seems too easy. Like a misdirection. They might as well have sent us a map and a timeline."

"Maybe that's what they're thinking. That it looks too convenient, so we'll discount it."

"Circles within circles."

"Exactly."

The rest of the meal passed with chitchat about colleagues who had left the task force, new hires, the Kids in the basement, even Kendra Thomas.

"She certainly earned the promotion."

"And I respect that, but I'd rather be reporting directly to Reid Clark."

"Rumor is that your DHS boss is considering retirement after that heart episode in December."

"I heard the same."

"Don't look so glum. You'll still have me."

Which earned him the eye roll he expected.

"Seriously though, you look tired."

"Thanks, Donovan. A girl loves to hear that over dinner."

"When was your last vacation?"

"Aunt Polly's. Last fall."

"That wasn't a vacation, Quinn. That was required time off for your injuries. It's not the same thing."

"And now you sound like Reid."

"Excellent. Two against one. Maybe you'll start listening."

She sat back and studied him. "I suppose you're one of those people who takes an annual vacation to some exotic place."

"Let's see. I spent a week in February fishing in the Keys. December was home with my folks. And October, once we'd put all that happened at the Grand Canyon to bed, I took a week in the Canadian Rockies...hiking, golfing, that sort of thing."

"You enjoy that?"

"I do."

She shrugged as if she couldn't imagine. And she probably couldn't. Allison wasn't what Donovan thought of as well-rounded. She had two passions in life—fighting terrorism and apprehending her father's killer. When possible, she did both at the same time.

He waited until they were back in the car and headed toward the hotel rooms that Collin—the task force's detail person—had reserved for them.

"I read the transcript of what Blitz said to you. That bullshit about your dad. . . I hope you didn't take it seriously."

"Yes and no."

"Meaning?"

"Meaning, I know my father wasn't a traitor, but what Blitz said sent my research in a different direction."

Donovan grunted. "So you didn't exactly rest at Aunt Polly's."

She waved away his concern.

They spent the next three hours in his room, each on their individual laptop, reading and comparing status reports the other teams had submitted. Nothing stood out. No further clues had been discovered from the Kids. They honestly had no idea if the attack would happen the next day or in a year. They didn't know if it would happen at one port or all of them. They didn't know if it would be limited to failure of the ship's equipment and the bad publicity that would entail or if it would actually put the crew and vacationers in harm's way.

Donovan could fill a binder with the things they didn't know.

When the clock ticked past midnight, he reached over and shut Allison's laptop.

"Hey. I was reading that."

"Your eyes were closed."

"For a minute...maybe."

"Go to your room, Allison. Get some rest."

She yawned, nodded, stood, and stretched.

Donovan forced himself to look away. There was an admiring glance, which was usually welcome and then there was staring. He was on the verge of staring, and his momma had taught him better.

"See you at four," Allison said. She stopped at the door and turned back to him—her eyes still tired, but more alert now. "I think this is it. I think it's happening here."

Allison was famous among the Task Force agents for her intuition. She wasn't the best at coding or even understanding the intricate details of an actual attack. She often didn't play well with others. She also had a reputation for ignoring direct orders.

But Allison Quinn's intuition was the stuff of legends. Maybe it was because she'd seen her father murdered when she was only nine years old. Maybe that did something to a person, refined their insights and unconscious knowledge so that they were aware of patterns before they were visible to most people.

She didn't give any reason for her pronouncement, but it was what she added before walking out the door that helped Donovan sleep. "I'm glad you're with me on this one."

And then she was gone.

They were back at the ships by five a.m., going over manifests that detailed the cargo, passengers, and crew. Meeting with Port Authority officials. Meeting with ship security. Watching, constantly, for the one thing that didn't belong.

Donovan's ship sailed on schedule, pulling away from the dock promptly at two p.m. There was no overriding reason to stop it. Donovan stood watching it for one minute, then another. Finally, he turned and jogged onto the *Harmony*, found Allison, and asked what he could do to help.

The situation there was identical to what he'd found on the *Fantasia*.

No one on the crew or the passenger list raised a flag with Port

Authority. Nothing came up in the detailed scans they did of the luggage. All rooms had been checked, then checked again per orders of the ship's captain. Supplies had been uncrated and stored. Absolutely nothing out of the ordinary had been found.

Donovan followed Allison as she walked down the gangway, then along the length of the ship.

"There's something here," she murmured.

"Like what?"

She didn't answer. Simply shook her head.

Captain McKinley called asking for a final status report. Allison put him on speaker since they were the only two people standing outside. Everyone else had boarded the ship.

"Can you give us the all-clear?" he asked.

"We haven't found anything."

"Not the same."

"Yeah. I know."

There was a long pause, long enough that Donovan glanced over at Allison's phone to see if the call had been dropped. It hadn't. McKinley was weighing his options.

"I'm going to give the all clear. Thank you for your attention on this matter." The call abruptly ended.

"Did he hang up on you?"

"He did."

"I guess the conversation was finished."

But Allison was still staring at the ship. She began walking and then jogging the length of the dock, skid to a stop, raised her phone, and snapped several pictures. She was punching buttons on her phone by the time Donovan caught up with her.

"Hold the ship. We're coming aboard." And then she clicked off.

"What? What did you take a picture of?"

"When we're on board." They hurried back to the gangplank that was being lowered and dashed over it and into the ship.

Becca Price trotted around a corner and nearly ran into them. "What is it? What did you find?"

Allison tapped on her screen, pulled up a picture, then used her fingertips to enlarge it. They stood there, the three of them, heads bent and nearly touching as they stared down at her phone. On the side of the ship, just above the waterline and near the bow, were the letters AT.

Donovan couldn't believe what he was seeing. "They tagged the boat? Why would they tag the boat?"

"Looks like it's done with chalk," Price said. "The waves will wash it off before we're out of the harbor. But what's the point?"

"Maybe it was a message to their people. Maybe they didn't decide which ship to focus their attack on until the last minute. Possibly it was a signal to their person..."

"Or persons," Donovan muttered.

"Telling them which ship to board."

"That doesn't make sense." Price stepped back, arms crossed, face set in a scowl. "They couldn't board unless they were on the manifest, and we went through that—you two went through the lists of crew and passengers for both ships."

"So they were on the manifest for both ships." Allison tapped the picture, forwarded it to Kendra Thomas and the Kids. "Donovan, check with the captain of *Fantasia*. Find out if there are any employees or guests that didn't show. Becca, check with your security detail. I want a list of anyone—passenger or crew—who boarded the *Harmony* in the last hour."

The sound of the ship's horn blasted through the afternoon as the *Harmony* pulled away from the dock.

"I'll update the captain," Price said.

"No. I'll do that. Please call ahead for me. Let the bridge know I'm coming."

"He'll want to turn back."

Allison shook her head. "The AT could have people on both ships. If this ship turns around, they'll activate the terrorists on the *Fantasia*—and Donovan and I aren't on that ship. We need this vessel to sail. We need the terrorists to feel safe enough to come out into the open. The important thing is that we know they're here."

And then she said those words that Donovan knew were pure Allison Quinn. They were barely audible. Price had already turned away. No one else was around them. Allison was pocketing her phone, and she hadn't looked up at him, but he heard her whisper as if the AT could hear her, "Game on."

Chapter Four

K ate Jackson looked up from her tablet as John Howard walked into the room. Her supervisor had recently celebrated his fifty-first. He'd previously worked for military intelligence and then the CIA. According to what Kate had been able to find, he'd turned his attention and abilities to the dark side a decade earlier. He was fit, kept his hair cut in a buzzed, military cut, and wore a minimalist wardrobe—always black pants, a black t-shirt, black sports coat, and black shoes.

Color, apparently, wasn't his thing.

"Both task force members are now on the ship," Kate said.

"Great." John rubbed his hands together as if anticipating a tasty dinner. "Put it on the main screen."

The techs in the room kept their heads down, eyes focused on the individual screens directly in front of them. An atmosphere of fear had pervaded the technicians since Stella Gonzalez, the matriarch of their little group, had shot Brett Lindstrom in the head. That happened six months ago, but no one had forgotten. You could replace the shattered monitors and pull out the carpet, but you couldn't erase people's memories.

They remembered.

They understood that any one of them might be next, and

while the money was good—very good—you couldn't spend it if you were dead.

Kate and John had been the only witnesses to Brett's murder, but word traveled quickly enough. One of the techs had packed her bags and left that afternoon. Two of John's security force returned her body to the main house three hours later, lifeless, three bullet holes in her back. After that, no one discussed dropping out of the AT. Maybe eventually they would, but not until things cooled down.

That wasn't happening today.

Instead, everything was heating up.

Hence Kate was dealing with a cruise ship, the two operatives on her screen, and John Howard in her control room. Howard's motives were something of a mystery to her. Sure, he believed his own propaganda. He thought the world needed to be awakened from a tech-induced sleep. But his passion and fury went deeper than that. His commitment came from some tragic, personal wound.

She suspected his personality had always teetered on the edge of stability. When his wife and daughter were killed, he'd stepped over that edge. He resigned from his government post, slipped into the night, and began an aggressive anti-government, anti-tech campaign. He looked unexplainably like the famous director Ron Howard. Somehow that always unsettled Kate more than the deadly glint in his eyes. That he could look like an American icon, one associated with the sitcom *Happy Days* and feel-good movies, and yet be appallingly ruthless was something her mind shied away from.

Who were the monsters?

How could you ever be sure if players from both sides looked the same?

Kate couldn't focus on those things though. Not now. She needed to bring her top game, all the time. She needed to make sure that John, or Stella, had no reason to shoot her in the back.

"We ran a continuous stream of drones over the dock," she explained. "High altitude, of course. No one saw or heard them."

"Walk me through it." John actually sounded delighted.

Kate had learned that he was high energy at the beginning of an op. It was later, as complications set in, that he became paranoid and morose. And when Stella Gonzalez was in residence, the air crackled with the cold friction that existed between the two. Howard needed Stella for the money. Stella needed Howard for the planning. They both needed Kate as well as the techs for their expertise. For better or worse, they were all tied to one another.

"This is from earlier this morning." She swiped another captured feed, sending it from her tablet to the main wall of display screens. "As we suspected, the process for boarding was significantly slower than usual and included more Port Authority personnel."

"Like all the other docks."

"Yes."

"Wonderful. Delays make for disgruntled passengers. It's a good place to start."

Kate located the feed of the two task force agents as someone closed the gangway of the ship. The drones captured images with the very best resolution available on the market, but from the top since their elevation was quite high. What you ended up with was a video that looked down on the heads of people. Not the best process for identifying someone.

"Are we sure it's Quinn and Steele?"

"Both Quinn and Steele checked into a Galveston hotel last night." She tossed up another feed. "We have pictures of them leaving the hotel this morning and parking at the dock."

"Someone enjoys spending his government salary on expensive toys."

"Registered to Donovan Steele. He purchased it on January 12th at a dealership in—"

Howard cut her off with a slight movement of his hand. She'd become quite attuned to his signals and moods since coming to work at the AT lair almost three years ago. That was how she thought of it—a lair, den, dungeon, habitat of monsters. Situated outside the quaint town of Whitefish, Montana, there were enough millionaires per square mile that the massive fortress Stella had built didn't draw attention. They were also close enough to the Canadian border to make a quick escape—as if the Canadians would want them.

"Continue the feed from before they boarded and zoom in."

She did, and they were able to see two figures-almost certainly Quinn and Steele—jog the length of the ship, stop suddenly, snap some pictures, then put in a phone call.

"Play that conversation for me, please."

"We haven't been able to hack her phone yet."

Howard slowly turned to pin Kate with an ice-cold stare. He didn't need to threaten her. The threat was constant and overt. No words were necessary. Instead, he blinked once and motioned for her to continue. She played the drone footage until the two Joint Task Force agents had entered the boat, then paused the recording.

"Great." Howard actually clapped his hands together. "They're on board. Now back up and show me what they took a picture of."

He knew what they took a picture of. He'd ordered it put there the night before, but John Howard liked to have everything confirmed—preferably by his own eyes. Kate tossed up the video of the secondary drone that had stayed back in order to take wide-angle shots. Once she'd manipulated and enlarged the photo, it was plain to everyone in the room that the letters chalked onto the side of the ship were AT.

Kate noticed that even the techs had stopped to stare at the wall of monitors. Sometimes John Howard's boldness was difficult to comprehend. The idea that he would tag a cruise ship in the hopes of luring two agents onto it had sounded ludicrous. But she had to hand it to him—he might be a murderous psychopath, but more often than not the steps he took produced results.

"We have them where I want them, Kate. Excellent work. This is the beginning of our emancipation."

The last word sent a chill down her spine.

John Howard was determined to *free the people*, always spoken with emphasis, from a tech-saturated dystopia. What he would offer in exchange, she had no doubt, would be far worse. And how many people would die in the process? That wasn't John's concern. His loved ones had already died. He had nothing to lose.

And Kate understood that someone with nothing to lose was a very dangerous person.

Chapter Five

Allison and Donovan were given a two-bedroom suite on deck nine that included a balcony.

Allison poked her head into the smaller bedroom and the teacup-sized bathroom. She was supposed to shower in there? Good thing she suffered from acrophobia and not claustrophobia. Finally, she crossed the tiny living area, opened the door to the balcony, and walked out onto it. Being on the ninth deck, looking out at the water, didn't trigger her fear of heights. She might be in a pickle if she had to climb up the side of the ship, but that was somewhat unlikely.

Donovan followed her and sank into one of the deck chairs. "What do you think of our digs?"

"My Aunt Polly's back porch is bigger than that cabin." Allison jerked a thumb back toward their rooms.

"You think that's small? It's twice as big as most cabins."

"And people consider this a dream vacation?"

"You don't cruise to stay in your room. There are lots of things to do on a boat—gamble, dance, attend shows."

"Uh-huh. And how are two JCTF agents going to cover all of that ground?"

"We could ask Thomas to assign more agents, if you're really worried about it."

She shook her head once, definitively. "That would tip our hand if the AT is watching, and I'm sure they're watching."

"True."

Allison wasn't the senior agent here. If anything, Donovan was. She understood that. Donovan had a tad more experience than her. He also went the extra mile, attended optional training, signed up to speak at conferences, sat in on seminars, even wrote up detailed reports of ops that he wasn't involved in because he simply enjoyed the work.

The real difference between Allison and Donovan was that he actually wanted to please his bosses and being promoted was apparently one of his lifelong goals. His experience and his ambition were why he'd been in charge of the attack at the Grand Canyon. On the days she was able to be objective, Allison could admit he'd done a good job there. On the days when she was plagued by memories of the people she'd killed, she cursed him for putting her in such a position, for spreading his people so thin that backup was late arriving, for expecting her to handle things until they arrived.

She had handled things.

It was her job to do that.

What had happened within the walls of that canyon wasn't Donovan Steele's fault.

"At least this time, you're not reporting to me," he said.

"Thank God for small favors." But she made eye contact and smiled. "What do you think should be our first step?"

"Buying you appropriate clothing."

"What's wrong with my clothes?" She glanced down at the black pants and white blouse she'd tossed on at four that morning. It was what she usually wore. Clothes weren't exactly a top priority for her.

Donovan, on the other hand, tended toward top-of-the-line apparel. Designer clothes. Nothing straight off the rack. Being a big guy, maybe that was a necessity. Or maybe, like purchasing a sports car, he enjoyed having the finer things in life.

"You don't exactly look like a tourist, Quinn. If we want to blend in, you need new clothes."

"What about you?"

"Way ahead of you. I stopped in a couple of the shops on the promenade and ordered some things while you were speaking with the captain. Should be delivered to our room any minute."

"You went shopping."

"Yup."

"While I was briefing the captain about an impending cyber-attack."

"Yup, and stop looking at me like I'm some sort of slacker. If we want to catch these people, we need to *not* look like federal agents."

She turned away from him and scowled at the stunning view from their balcony—water and sky. There wasn't much more to see than that. Lots of water. Lots of sky. Finally, she nodded. "I hate it when you're right."

"You're welcome."

Allison rubbed her eyes. Four hours of sleep had not been enough.

"Shopping, lunch, then some shut-eye."

"What about planning our next move?"

"We can do it while we eat."

"If we eat here." She glanced back into their room. "Didn't see much of a kitchen."

"I'll call room service. We'll go shopping. By the time we get back the food will be here, then we take a break. Up before sunset, and we'll plan our next steps."

"I've been thinking of that. I don't see a cyber guy hitting the casino or the bars. Aren't they mostly introverted?"

"The Kids tell us that's the profile, but there's something else." He steepled his fingers and stared at them. "Did you ever see that movie about the MIT students who learned to count cards?"

"Nope."

"The thing about cyberbugs is that they think they're smarter than everyone else."

"Sometimes they are."

"So two of the AT goons get assigned to a cruise ship to do something nefarious."

"Which probably won't happen until we're in the middle of the gulf."

"Agreed, or even in a foreign country...say Mexico."

"Go on."

"They're biding their time in a cabin that is half the size of ours."

"That's not a cabin. It's a closet."

"And they have this skill with numbers."

"Plus, they're arrogant."

Donovan grinned at her, then wiggled his eyebrows. "What are the odds that they'll be able to resist proving their superiority?"

"I'd say none. We start at the casinos."

"Maybe. But first, we shop, eat—"

"And rest. I heard you, Donovan." She softened her words with a smile. One rule of being on an op was you ate when you could and slept when possible. Donovan wasn't wrong, but Allison was ready to jump in, stir things up, force the AT's hand. She wouldn't. But oh, how she wanted to.

Instead, it looked like she was going shopping.

If Allison hadn't been drop-dead exhausted, she never would have agreed to the clothes that Donovan picked out. As it was, she grumbled, "Remind me never to go shopping with you again."

"Are you kidding? I'm going to have to club the guys to keep them away from you."

"From what I've seen, there are college kids, family men, and seniors on board this ship. Attracting anyone from those categories is not my goal."

"And yet, you'll blend in now." He bumped his shoulder against hers, nearly causing her to drop the shoeboxes.

Shoeboxes—as in two new pairs of shoes. She'd lost her mind. She'd lost her mind, and it was Donovan Steele's fault.

"There's no way that Thomas is going to approve these expenses."

"Probably not."

"So I just dropped twelve hundred bucks on four outfits."

"And a swimsuit."

"Tell me again why I need a swimsuit."

"So you can blend."

"Cyberbugs are not going to be sunning on the deck, sipping a frozen Bellini and listening to the Caribbean band."

"They might be."

"And I might send you a bill for these clothes."

Instead of answering, Donovan flashed his keycard at the plate beside their door, turning the light to green. They'd barely dumped the bags on the floor when there was a knock at their cabin door.

Allison pulled her gun and moved into position.

Donovan rolled his eyes and peeked through the keyhole. "It's the lunch we ordered. Are you going to shoot them?"

She holstered her weapon and collapsed onto the couch.

After she'd consumed the club sandwich, potato chips, iced tea, and oatmeal cookie, her eyelids felt as if they had weights on them. She focused on opening her eyes wider, but when she tried one eyelid inevitably drooped shut.

"Which bed do you want?"

"As if you'd fit on the small one." She somehow dragged herself to her feet and trudged to the smaller room. Smaller room. A pretty funny description for a walled-off area in a suite that was just under six hundred square feet. Her college dorm had been twice that size, and she'd considered it barely livable. It wasn't like she needed a lot of space, but she was pretty sure she could hear Donovan snoring on the other side of the wall.

It didn't matter.

None of it mattered.

Not the rocking of the boat. Not the fact that Donovan Steele —a man that she had actively avoided since last September—was in the next room. Not even the fact that terrorists were aboard this ship. If she'd had to stay awake, she would have found a way to do so, but she agreed with Donovan's assessment.

They wouldn't strike this close to the U.S. mainland.

She and Donovan still had plenty of time.

That was her final thought as she slipped into a deep and dreamless slumber.

She woke four hours later to the sound of jazz coming from Donovan's cell phone. Rubbing her hands over her face she happened to look up and catch her reflection in the mirror, which was enough to send her to the tiny bathroom for a shower that was surprisingly refreshing.

When she stepped out into the main room wearing her designer jeans, blinged-up sandals (she'd drawn the line at the two-inch heels Donovan wanted her to purchase), and slinky red top, Donovan looked up and whistled.

"Don't you think the red is a bit over the top?"

"I do not."

"It's loud. And shiny."

"Which means you'll blend in with the other loud and shiny guests. If you showed up in the casino wearing those clothes you boarded in, everyone on this boat would be staring at you and wondering why a federal agent was cruising the Gulf. In your new clothes, you'll simply be one more gorgeous woman." He opened his palms and spread his hands as if additional words weren't necessary.

"Okay. I can do it for the task force, but don't think I like it."

Donovan was wearing shorts that cost more than her last dental visit, sandals, and a golf shirt of some sort. At least it looked like a golf shirt. She had no desire to quiz him on the topic, and she forced herself not to stare.

He always had cleaned up well.

The man's arms looked like he made a hobby out of visiting the gym. No doubt he did. How did he have time for that?

"I'm thinking we should wait a few hours to hit the casino," he said.

"Why not now?"

"Casinos on ships are always busy, but the serious crowd shows up later in the evening. I was thinking we'd go to the main dining room first."

"Because?"

"Our friends might be hungry. I asked for a late seating. I figured the AT would opt for fewer people in the room."

"A late seating?"

"Cruises have two dinner seatings—6:00 and 8:00."

"How do you know these things?"

"Dated a girl who liked to cruise. Years ago, but the basics have remained the same."

"Didn't we just eat?"

"And yet we're about to do so again."

They walked to the elevators, which were glass and looked out over the yawning empty space that ended in the promenade below. She didn't like it.

Didn't like the crowds.

Didn't like the glass elevators.

Didn't like the fact that she could literally see a terrorist pushing someone over the guardrails to splatter on the floor below. This wasn't a safe place. There were too many families. Too many distractions. Too many ways it could all go wrong.

As they stepped onto the elevator, Donovan bumped her shoulder and slipped an arm around her waist. She glowered at him, but that had absolutely no effect on his smile or his blatant invasion of her personal space.

He murmured in her ear, "Smile, sweetheart." Then he

nodded slightly to their right, where a younger couple was studying them.

"First time he's cruised," Allison confided to the couple. "He doesn't want to admit it, but he has terrible vertigo."

"My mom wears a patch behind her ear for that," the young woman said. "You might check and see if they have some in the stores on the promenade."

"I'll do that. Thank you." Donovan pulled Allison closer and kissed her on top of the head. "That's my woman. Always looking out for me."

It was all she could do not to bring her foot, clad in her new sparkly sandals, down on his instep.

The elevator jerked to a stop and all thoughts of sparring with Donovan fled. They were midway down between floors five and six. Looking out over the open-aired space, Allison could see that all of the other elevators facing the promenade had stopped at the same time. There was a stunned silence in their elevator, and then everyone began talking at once. Just as the older gent standing next to the doors reached for the emergency button, the elevator started moving again. Nervous laughter and expressions of relief filled the small space.

It seemed that everyone was headed to the main dining room, but as they entered the lights began to flicker.

"Are you thinking what I'm thinking?" Donovan murmured.

"Yup." And then the radio that Price had issued Allison buzzed.

"Quinn," she answered.

"Is Steele with you?"

"He is."

"Meet me in engineering."

Instead of the elevator, they opted for the stairs. Allison worried they'd have to flash their badges, but Price had cleared the way. With a "they're waiting on you" from security, she and Donovan hurried down the hall and into the main engineering room.

Head engineer Brock Ferguson had apparently been waiting on their arrival. Captain McKinley gave them a nod, and Price motioned for the engineer to begin.

"It's all been pretty minor. First, the internet winked out a few times, then the elevators malfunctioned, and finally, the lights throughout the ship tapped on and off."

"Any damage?" McKinley asked.

"No. Not that we've been able to tell."

"But this isn't random?"

"One of the three, and I might have thought so," Ferguson said. "But not internet, elevators, and lights."

Allison crossed her arms and stared at the monitors in front of her. "They're testing their code."

"What code?" Price asked.

"Could be any of a number of things," Donovan said. "Malware, DoS, code injection, IoT..."

"Stop." McKinley's voice did not broker any argument. "I'm alerting the Coast Guard. I will not have this ship put in danger. I will not place our guests at the mercy of a few punks with computer skills."

"These aren't punks, sir. They're far more proficient than that." Donovan was staring at something on the main monitor. He walked over to it and pointed to a graph that indicated power usage. "See this? The spikes here? They're doing far more than messing with your elevators and lights. They're sinking their teeth into your system."

"And I have no doubt they're already into your comms." Allison shook her head. "Anything we say needs to be said in person. If you have to use the radios, simply refer to your location, and we'll meet you there. But make no mistake, if you call the Coast Guard now, the AT will launch whatever attack they have at the ready."

"And you have a better idea?" McKinley pinched his lips together.

"I do. Donovan and I believe our best bet is to draw them out, make them feel comfortable. Let them think that they're superior and we're clueless. They'll make a mistake. They always make a mistake."

McKinley didn't look convinced.

"My boss is monitoring this, Captain." Donovan crossed his arms. "You need to trust Kendra Thomas."

"I don't even know her."

"She will have the Coast Guard on standby. She will make sure they remain out of sight but within striking distance. She is monitoring this situation."

McKinley blew out a breath. "Okay. We do it your way—for now." Then he turned and strode from the room.

"He's under a lot of pressure," Price explained.

"We all are." Ferguson wiped sweat from the sides of his face. "I'm the head engineer. I can keep this boat running through just about any scenario. But I'm not a coder. I'm not a systems analyst."

"Who is?"

Instead of answering, Ferguson raised his radio and told someone named Lilith to report to engineering.

Lilith Maguire was a red-headed, freckle-skinned twenty-something. No piercings at all, but her arms were sleeved with tattoos. Her shoulder-length hair sported random skinny braids in places, with the rest left wild. She looked as if she'd come in from a storm. Her green eyes sparkled. She wore torn jeans and a Grateful Dead t-shirt.

She tossed a look at Allison and Donovan, then another over at Price. Finally, she sank into a chair and asked Ferguson, "What's up, boss?"

"We're apparently being attacked by cyberterrorists."

Price said, "This is Allison Quinn and Donovan Steele."

"I work for Homeland Security," Allison explained. "Donovan's with the FBI. We are both assigned to a Joint Cyber Task Force, and that assignment has brought us here."

Lilith didn't respond in any way. She simply waited.

"You don't seem surprised," Donovan said.

"I've been telling them since the day they hired me—"

"Which was only three months ago," Ferguson interjected.

"That we're vulnerable to an attack. No one listens." She leaned back in her chair and studied them. She didn't offer opinions or suggest possible scenarios.

Allison gave her points for her professionalism.

On the other hand, the fact that she'd only been employed with the cruise lines for three months meant she could be an AT plant. Allison glanced at Donovan, who immediately began tapping a message into his phone—no doubt asking for a closer background look at one Lilith Maguire.

"Give us five minutes," Donovan said, and he walked into the hall, still thumbing in messages.

Allison followed him out. Once the door to the engineering room had closed, she leaned against the wall, shut her eyes, and let her first impression of Lilith Maguire rattle around. When Donovan put his phone in his pocket and mirrored her pose, she asked, "How do we know what side she's on?"

He shrugged.

They waited for what seemed like an hour but was actually only three minutes, according to her watch.

His phone dinged.

"Already getting some data back from the Kids." He moved closer so she could read what was coming across his phone.

> Lilith Maguire received her degree from MIT at nineteen. Graduate work at USC. Doctorate in computer science awarded six months ago. Turned down job offers from four big tech companies. Six months hiking in Europe. Joined the cruise lines three months ago. The Harmony is her first posting.

"If she's a plant, someone did a very good job of creating her background."

"She's not a plant," Donovan said. "Read this."

The next message was from Thomas, and it simply read,

She's clean.

"Huh."

"Yeah. How would Kendra Thomas have any information on a computer geek hired by a cruise line?"

"I don't know, but if Kendra says she's clean..."

"Then we proceed as if she's clean."

Back in the engineering room, Donovan sat down next to Lilith. "Do you know how to look for anomalies in systems?"

"Of course."

"What are your normal tasks?"

"Pretty simple, really—repair and maintain the ship's servers."

"Why did you say that the ship is vulnerable to an attack?"

Lilith rolled her eyes. "Dude, the whole planet is vulnerable."

"Did your coursework include cyber defense?"

"Not specifically, though learning to build and maintain a system does include learning to protect that system from attack."

Listening to this conversation, Allison didn't think Lilith was lying or covering up. Allison had met a lot of cyberbugs. They were edgy, dissatisfied, and tightly coiled with anger. Lilith was the opposite of all those things. She looked as if she'd just come in from a beach party. She probably had... only a cruise ship's version of a beach and a pool.

"Lilith." She waited for the young woman to meet her gaze. "Why did you take this job?"

"Easy." She held up her right hand, emphasizing each point with a raised finger. "Free food, a nearly unlimited supply of alcohol, days off in the Caribbean, a new batch of eligible men every week, and…" She stared at her thumb, wiggling it back and forth. "I had a fifth reason when my mum asked me the same question, but now I've forgotten it."

Allison didn't respond to the barb that she was acting like Lilith's mother. She glanced at Donovan who nodded once. It was settled then. They'd work with what they had, which apparently included one redhead with a lot of attitude. "Donovan will give you a crash course in cyber defense."

"I'll order dinner sent up," Price said.

"And in the meantime, I'd like to meet with your security crew." Allison ran a hand through her hair. It seemed to be expanding. She'd forgotten that sea air could do that to her mess of brown curls. "We go to wherever they're stationed. I don't want us all together at once. It would look too obvious if they're watching, and we should assume they are watching."

"Are you up for a lot of walking?" Price gave Allison's blingy sandals a skeptical look.

Allison sighed. "Yeah. I'm up for it."

She just hoped she didn't have to chase a terrorist in her stupid sandals. If it came to that, she'd jerk them off and run barefoot. That thought—the image of her racing barefoot down the corridor in order to tackle a cyberbug—somehow improved her mood.

It was time to catch a terrorist.

Chapter Six

Allison and Donovan ended up eating late that evening in a pub. Long buffet tables held platters of pizza, cold shrimp, something that was supposed to resemble chicken nuggets, and a variety of side dishes. The dessert bar was seeing a lot of activity as well—soft serve ice cream, pies, cakes, and cookies.

"I'm used to eating alone when I eat this late," she grumbled.

"Welcome to the real world, Quinn. These people all slept until noon, and they'll do the same tomorrow. They're just hitting their stride at..." He glanced at his watch. "Twenty minutes past eleven."

"Stride, huh?"

"Yup. That's why they're smiling. And drinking."

It was true. Nearly everyone held a frozen drink or a cold beer or a mixed drink. Of course, it was a pub, so that was to be expected.

Allison and Donovan filled their plates, then found a corner circular booth at the back of the pub. They sat next to each other, facing the mass of partiers—trying to spot a proverbial needle in a haystack.

"Stop frowning at that pizza," he said. "It isn't half bad."

Donovan had stacked enough food on his plate to be worthy of a man his size.

"I don't usually have time to eat on active ops."

"Understandable, though as our training taught us... " He paused to finish the piece of supreme pizza in his hand. "It's critical for an agent in the field to eat whenever possible. Got to give fuel to the engine."

"Now you're sounding like my Aunt Polly."

Donovan nodded and reached for another piece of pizza. "Lilith did everything but accuse you of mothering her."

Allison shrugged. She didn't care what Lilith thought of her as long as she was on board with helping them. "How did her training go?"

"She's smarter than I am, that's for certain."

Allison stopped with her glass of tea half raised to her mouth, placed it carefully on the table, and grinned. "Did you just admit someone's smarter than you?"

"Come on. I'm not that arrogant."

"No, but you can be a bit—"

"She's smarter than me in regard to understanding the ins and outs of coding. I can get there, but it takes time. Lilith took to what I told her like a—"

"Don't say fish to water. We're surrounded by water. I don't want to think about it."

"Are you seasick?"

"No. I'm not seasick. We're a bit isolated, is all. In spite of what you said about Thomas having our backs."

He nodded. They both knew it was true.

Kendra Thomas did, or would, maintain backup if it was at all possible. Sometimes it wasn't possible. Donovan hadn't mentioned that part, but they both knew it. They had both been in such situations before. They had both been in exactly that situation together.

"So Lilith is watching for intrusions."

"And following them, not stopping them."

"Good. That's good."

Someone not trained in cybersecurity was tempted to slam the door shut when noticing a system intrusion. It's what you'd do should a burglar come into your front yard and threaten you. Retreat into the house. Slam and lock the door. Locate your firearm. Call and wait for the police.

Cybersecurity was different. If you tried to lock the door on a system, they'd find another way in. It was more important to find out where the intrusion was originating, to trace it back to its source. That was the only effective way to deal with cyberpunks. Even then, sometimes you were forced to use your weapon.

"Where'd you go, Quinn?"

She shook her head. She had a tendency to overthink things given any amount of down time. She was doing that now, and it only served to sap her energy.

"How did your briefings with the security teams go?"

"Good, though I couldn't really tell them what to look for."

"Nerds. They should look for nerds."

"Not always true, and you know it."

"I'll give you that. Terrorists come in all shapes and sizes."

"The security team is to report any anomalies they see with the infrastructure of the ship directly to Price, who will coordinate and send the reports to us."

"Any suspicious characters so far?"

"A couple drunk and disorderly situations—which they are accustomed to handling. If they see anyone who is suspiciously lucky, more interested in something behind the scenes than they should be, or carrying any type of technical gadget that they aren't familiar with...any of those things and they're to back off and call Price, who will contact us."

"Excellent." Donovan finished the last bite of food on his plate, then asked, "You going to eat that cookie?"

She picked up the cookie and waved it at him. "How do you consume so many calories?"

"How do you not?"

She handed it to him without answering. She didn't want to talk about anything personal with Donovan Steele. She certainly didn't want to be on this boat with him, let alone sharing a suite with him. How had she ended up in this mess?

For a moment, those memories that she kept locked away burst free. She closed her eyes, and her mind filled with the memory of him leaning over her, pouring clotting powder on the bullet wound, the searing pain, and his voice whispering, "Don't pass out on me, Quinn." The concern on his face had been startling.

It had been more than professional. And then later, in the Range Rover, as they'd waited out the storm—

"Are you falling asleep on me? Don't fall asleep on me. We need to play some roulette, try a hand or two of poker."

She opened her eyes and scowled at him.

"It won't work, giving me your mad dog look. You know I'm right. We need to be out there, watching for them. Now let's go show off that red, blingy top."

Fifteen minutes later, they were spending the task force's money at the blackjack tables in the main casino. At least Allison hoped it was the task force's money. If it was hers, she needed to get better at gambling.

She was doubling down on a six and two with the dealer showing fourteen when Donovan—who was standing behind her chair cheering her on—leaned down and whispered, "Roulette table. Two o'clock. Guy keeps increasing his bet and winning."

Allison won the poker hand, accepted the payout, and pocketed the casino chips. "I'll take the west..." Damn. Which way was west? If they were traveling south and she was facing the back of the boat . . .

"I'll go right. You go left."

"Got it."

He reached down and brushed his lips against hers. "Never know who's watching," he murmured, which probably saved him from getting a black eye.

Instead of punching him, she tapped his cheek and said, "Think I'll go order an old-fashioned, honey."

He laughed, then slipped to the right. For a big guy, he was surprisingly agile.

She took her time at the bar, pretending to check her texts but actually taking pictures of the man and woman at the roulette table. The girl fit the cyberbug profile perfectly—pale skin, acne, bad haircut, slim but dressed in bulky clothes to conceal it. The guy was a surprise. He possessed an athletic build, was fair-headed, obviously paid attention to his clothing and hair style, and he wore designer glasses.

Designer glasses.

He fidgeted with them each time the roulette wheel took a spin. He was using the glasses to record and analyze the wheel's action. Nice. Who needed mathematical genius when you could simply depend on your high-tech toys?

The question was whether she should approach.

They were right there.

Donovan was in place.

She could slip up behind them, have their arms behind their backs and their wrists in zip ties before they knew what was happening.

Allison replayed the conversation she'd had at dinner with Donovan.

So she's watching for intrusions.

And following them, not stopping them.

Yes, they could arrest these two right now. But the AT wouldn't have made it that easy. They'd have two more. Hell, maybe ten more. As soon as these two were apprehended, their unresponsiveness to any communication would alert the others, and the AT would accelerate their plan. They'd do the thing they'd come here to do. She still didn't quite know what that was.

Why would anyone target a cruise ship for a cyberattack?

She dropped her phone into her purse, paid for and picked up the old-fashioned she'd ordered, then walked toward the exit, being sure she passed close to the two cyberbugs. Donovan would follow. They had what they needed. They had two faces. Put them through the on-board passenger profile program, and they'd have two names.

From there, they could follow the thread right back to the door of the AT.

———————

Donovan had always been able to conserve his energy. He thought it was one of the chief reasons he made a good agent. He could relax and recharge when the situation called for it. He could also change into high gear almost instantly.

When he spotted the cyberpunk at the roulette table, he'd gone instantly into high gear. Zero to sixty in 2.6 seconds—just like his vehicle.

"I got pictures," Quinn was saying.

They were again avoiding the elevators and opting for the stairs. The last thing they needed was to get caught in an elevator, and Donovan had no doubt that disabling all twenty-six of the elevators on board *the Harmony* would eventually be one of the AT's plays.

Once he and Allison were back in their suite, they got to work.

Allison uploaded the pictures she'd taken via her secure phone. At least Donovan hoped it was secure. If the AT had hacked the FBI's and HS's communication, he didn't think they'd settle for attacking cruise ships.

Donovan sent a description of the glasses the guy was wearing to the Kids. He had an answer back from them before Allison had returned from the bathroom, this time wearing black pants and a black t-shirt. Over that she pulled on a black hooded sweatshirt. He tossed his phone at her, then changed his clothes while she read what the Kids had sent.

"It's worse than I thought," she said.

"How so?"

"They must be well-funded."

"I'll say. Those glasses aren't even on the market yet. They paid a lot for them."

"They're more advanced than what we give to our military personnel." Allison frowned down at the text. "Ability to see around corners. How is that possible?"

"No idea. But if the Kids say it is, it is."

"Night vision. Complete computer integration."

"Basically, they can see anything."

"Therefore, shoot anything."

"And they have the power of their devices without ever picking anything up—full Alexa integration, built-in camera." Donovan pulled his weapon, checked it, and slipped it back into his shoulder holster. Then he donned a black jacket over the entire thing. They were in the middle of the Gulf headed south, but the nights were still cool.

"You know what they don't have, Donovan?" Allison checked her weapon and re-holstered it. "Courage."

He laughed. "Possibly lacking a brain too."

"Don't forget no heart."

It struck him as funny that they didn't talk about what they were going to do next. One look and they understood each other. It was time—past time—that they take the offensive.

"You're sure they didn't see you put the tracker on them?"

"I'm better than that, Steele."

"Right. So you put it..."

"In his jacket pocket. He was too busy playing with his glasses to notice me brush up against him."

"And the girl?"

"Staring morosely into her drink."

"Perfect."

Her phone vibrated, and she stared down at it, then looked up and smiled. "We have movement."

They huddled over her phone screen and watched as the dot

moved. The Kids had managed to overlay the tracking program with a blueprint of the ship. What was amazing was that it worked vertically as well as horizontally.

"These guys aren't worried about using the elevator," she muttered.

"Why would they be? They're the ones controlling the playing field."

"Not for long, Donovan." She tapped the screen.

The dot had stopped at a cabin two floors down from theirs on the other side of the ship. Room 784 which had a balcony, but wasn't a suite. It would be like putting two terrorists in a sardine can.

"They won't be controlling the scene for long." Allison sounded determined—almost eager.

Donovan dug in his backpack and pulled out a surveillance package. They both put communication pieces in their ears. "Ready?"

"More than you can imagine."

He almost laughed. Quinn reminded him of a bird dog that had caught a fresh scent. She was practically quivering. He recognized that his own adrenaline was pumping, that he was feeling the rush of a turn in the op. He wasn't immune to any of that and didn't think he ever would be, no matter how long he was a field agent.

But what he was feeling, in this moment, was more than that. He was honest enough to admit it to himself if not to the beautiful woman standing in front of him.

He accepted that he had feelings for Allison. She wasn't ready to hear about them, but the fact remained. He admired her, cared about her, wanted to know her better. He wanted to know her personally, not just working beside her on an op. Those feelings had been growing for a long time—since her injury in Washington, during the Grand Canyon op, and throughout the time that stretched between then and now. He'd quit fighting his feelings for her somewhere around the time she'd started avoiding his calls.

Too many nights, he woke expecting to see her blood on his hands. Remembering the paleness of her complexion and the steadiness of her gaze as she lay in the snow, about to bleed out on the side of a mountain in Washington State. He couldn't forget the feel of her body next to his as he attempted to keep her body temperature stable. As the storm raged around them. As they waited.

He didn't want to forget the fear or the tenderness. They'd been irrevocably bonded together in that moment.

Allison jerked a head toward the patio.

They stepped out into darkness. There were plenty of lights on a cruise ship as it made its way down the gulf, but each cabin or suite's individual lights were operated from inside. Luckily for them, few of those lights were on. People were either asleep or gambling. Allison and Donovan climbed carefully and easily from their balcony to the one next door, making their way down the length of the ship.

Yes, they could have gone down the hallway, but what if they'd been seen? An op could turn the wrong way based on one variable they hadn't accounted for, one person who saw something and raised a ruckus. Better to do it this way, silently making their way through the darkness.

He was only marginally aware of the ship's motion.

The sound of the waves, though, was unmistakable. The rhythmic swooshing sound filled the night. The motion of the ship rocking was minimal. He watched Allison as closely as he watched where he put his hands before climbing onto the next balcony. He didn't notice any sign that she was struggling with her acrophobia. He knew that about her. Knew what she'd been through at the Grand Canyon and had some idea of the toll it had taken on her.

As they rounded the front of the ship, she swung up onto the pool deck but remained in the shadows.

"At least the band is still playing." He spoke in a low voice though it probably wasn't necessary. He could feel the thump thump thump of the drums through the soles of his feet.

"'The music will cover the sound of our footsteps, but we're going to attract attention, given our clothing."

"Yeah." He looked toward the bow of the ship, saw a sign that said, Harmony's Kid Camp, and nodded that way. Price had given them complete access to the ship, meaning their keycard would work on any door. They gained entrance to the area, then hurried past darkened rooms filled with small, brightly colored, plastic slides, art stations, even miniature kitchens. Donovan's mind wanted to go there, wanted to think about the number of people who were at risk—the children and adults.

He didn't.

It wouldn't help.

Instead, he focused on keeping up with Quinn who could move faster than a black cat down a dark alley.

She popped out the other side of the Pirate Cove Playland, looked both ways, then darted across the deck and over the balcony. He followed without question. He didn't have time to question, plus Quinn was one of the best trackers on the task-force. Why would he question her? Also, she had the phone that was displaying the tracking device.

They climbed down, which was trickier than going sideways. It involved hanging on to one darkened balcony and dropping down to the next. They purposely came out one floor below the perps' suite.

Allison paused when she came to a balcony with a sleeping guest on it. The woman must have purchased the drink package, as she was snoring loud enough to be heard over the waves and the engine. She'd pulled two of the deck chairs together and was splayed across them. Someone had tucked a pillow under her head and covered her with a sheet.

They tiptoed across unnoticed.

The adjacent balcony was across a three-foot gap, which meant they were now at a place on the ship where a cross-ship hall intersected with a main one. Allison looked back at him, and he thought he could see her grin in the darkness. Then she lunged for the balcony. She again glanced back at Donovan and gave him a thumbs up. Easy for her to say. She probably weighed under a buck thirty.

There were no valid excuses on an op though. He bent his knees and sprung forward. He had no trouble bridging the gap, though he landed with a loud thud.

She shook her head and frowned at him.

Like he could make his lunges quieter.

She passed her cell phone to him, pointed up, and began to climb. The device she intended to plant would appear to be a round sticker to anyone who happened to notice it. It wasn't quite as flat as that, though. It was the size of a coaster with a weird sticky compound on the back side. Donovan had seen similar devices attached to glass, steel, bark, even a dog once. The device provided sound and video, allowing them to hear what was being said and see any movement. It was seriously cool technology and had to be the world's smallest video transmitter.

They might not have the next-gen eyeglasses that their perps did, but the Kids managed to give them some pretty cool stuff. They had a practically unlimited budget and enjoyed playing with the devices before they passed them on.

Allison tapped her comm unit, and Donovan checked the screen of her phone.

They had video, surprisingly clear given that it was looking through the drapes. Fortunately, the camera was able to filter that out. He could see the two perps from the roulette table as plainly as he'd seen them in the casino. He tapped the sound icon, which sent the feed directly to his communication piece. The two were discussing whether to go back out for food or order room service.

Donovan again tapped his comm unit, signaling Allison that the device was working. She climbed back down and stood beside him.

They were lurking on the balcony of a cabin that had been

dark, when suddenly the door from the hall opened, and the lights came on. They could clearly hear two female voices arguing. Apparently one was a slut because she'd flirted with "every man she saw," and the other was in danger of being "an old maid."

Allison took the phone, tapped a few buttons, and brought up the blueprint of the cruise ship. Two cabins over was an empty room. She pushed the phone towards Donovan, he nodded, and she led the way.

Their key card would open any cabin's door, but balcony doors could only be opened from the inside. So they stood there, in the dark, the waves swishing against the ship, the night growing even more still. They listened and watched and finally judged that the cabin was, in fact, empty. Allison and Donovan settled onto the two deck chairs.

Allison propped the phone on the deck's table, and they both keyed in their comm units. Between the black clothes they were wearing and the precision of the comm units, they were effectively invisible. Someone could have hung over the balcony above them, could have been looking directly down at them, and still not seen or heard them.

They listened for five minutes, then five minutes more. Finally, Allison reached out and tapped his arm. Donovan nodded, and then sent the comm feed to the Kids. The time on Donovan's watch now read one-thirty in the morning. "Let's head back inside," he whispered.

He was a little surprised when she readily agreed.

They made their way back to the pool deck, retraced their steps through the Pirate Cove Playland, then stepped into the long hallway they'd avoided earlier. They were counting on the fact that most people would be in their cabin by now.

Only one person saw them—an older woman who was sitting in the library area on their floor. If she thought there was anything odd about the way they were dressed, she didn't show it. Probably, she wasn't even aware of them.

When they were back in their suite, Allison held up a hand to high-five him. Donovan wanted to pull her into his arms. He wanted to put his hands through that mass of curls she wore like a crown.

Instead, he slapped her hand. "Good work, Quinn."

"Not so bad yourself, Steele. Though that landing on the balcony was rather clumsy."

"I'll work on my lunges."

He thought she'd go straight to bed.

Or maybe stare at the feed on her phone, though there was no reason to. The Kids would have fresh eyes on it. They'd send an alert if there were any actionable intelligence.

But Allison didn't do either of those things. She surprised him. She always surprised him.

Pulling off her sweatshirt, she dropped it onto their couch, then opened the door to the balcony, walked outside, and sank into one of the chairs.

Did she want to be alone?

Did she want company?

"Come look at these stars," she said, which was all the answer he needed.

Donovan sank into the chair next to her, waiting for his heart rate to slow and his adrenaline levels to drop. They must have sat there for twenty minutes. His eyes were growing heavy, and he was trying to decide between sleeping on the balcony or moving inside to the bed when she spoke again.

"I remember the stars being like this when I camped with my dad."

"Funny how the memories from our childhood stay with us." He knew her memories of that time were both precious and tragic. But it was still good to have them, right?

It's what made them human.

What made Allison the way she was.

What motivated her to be the best agent she could be.

Donovan had different memories and different reasons to excel at his job. Some of those things Allison knew. Most she didn't. It didn't matter. What mattered was that they were a team —a good team. And they would stop the two perps now sleeping in cabin 784.

He and Allison would either apprehend or neutralize them. It wasn't overconfidence. It was more the fact that this was what they were trained to do. This was what they had been born to do —or at least it seemed that way.

One thing he was sure of.

They would not allow two people with a big tech budget and malevolent intent to jeopardize the people on this ship. They would not allow this cruise to become another tragic story in the twenty-four-hour news cycle. It sounded rather goofy to his sleep-deprived brain, but failure was not an option.

Chapter Seven

Kate Jackson was awakened by an alert on her phone. Since all communication from outside middle-earth was blocked, she guessed it was about the current operation.

> You. Me. Stella. 0800. My office.

She did not want to start the day meeting with John Howard and Stella Gonzalez. Most of the time, she found the stress of this job to be manageable. *Most of the time.* Private meetings with those two were the exception.

For some reason Stella unnerved her more than John did. It wasn't simply that she'd watched the woman pull a small handgun from the pocket of her designer pants and murder Brett Lindstrom in cold blood. That was disturbing. What made it worse was the complete lack of emotion from Stella when she'd killed the man. She'd simply pocketed the pistol and walked out of the room.

She showed no more remorse, no more emotion, than if she'd stepped on a bug. Stella's entire demeanor was one of unlimited power and resources coupled with a disturbing psychopathic nature.

Kate didn't have a photographic memory. Professionals now thought there was no such thing, though that was what her sister had called it—always with a teasing smile. No, what Kate possessed was an eidetic memory. She possessed the ability to vividly recall an image.

As she showered and dressed, Kate thought of her psychology classes, the textbooks, and the case studies. Stella Gonzalez ticked all of the boxes for a clinical diagnosis of antisocial personality disorder. She was, in Kate's opinion, a psychopath.

Persistent antisocial behavior—check.

Impaired empathy and remorse. She hadn't so much as blinked when she'd killed Brett Lindstrom. Hadn't shown any reaction at all—so check.

Impulsivity—uh, yeah.

Narcissism—without a doubt.

John Howard was a person whose personality had been warped by terrible loss. His wife and daughter had been killed in an automobile accident. Hit and run. John firmly believed that the government had put a contract out on Lillian and Penelope. They had taken away his family to ensure his silence about several black ops programs.

Kate didn't believe that. She'd thoroughly investigated his past before arriving at middle-earth. By all accounts, a drunk driver had hit them, driven away, and abandoned his own vehicle. The case was technically still open, since the driver had never been found. Kate suspected John might have had something to do with that.

The loss he had endured was tragic. It didn't excuse the things he did, but it certainly explained them.

Stella, on the other hand, was dangerous at a biological level—a cellular level. Kate realized some of her profs would scoff at that assessment, but she firmly believed it. With Stella, there was no hope of rehabilitation, no chance she would see the light. With someone like Stella, the most you could hope for was to stay out of her line of sight.

And now Kate had a meeting with her.

An 0800. Damn John and his military time.

She was at the door to her boss's office three minutes early. He nodded once and pointed toward a chair, which only upped Kate's anxiety. She'd rather not be told to sit. That indicated a long meeting, which she had no interest in being a part of. Since she was in charge of the technical side of things at middle-earth, she was expected to put in an appearance whenever Stella twitched a finger.

Middle-earth.

John had picked that name. To Kate's mind, it conjured images of Tolkien and hobbits and lost rings. But there was nothing noble in John Howard's use of the term. It was simply another indication that he was on the brink of losing whatever sanity he possessed.

Stella walked in eight minutes past the hour.

Kate had noticed that Stella enjoyed irritating John. More specifically, she enjoyed hammering home the point that this was her kingdom, and she ultimately set the rules.

As usual, the CEO of their little organization was overdressed —black Saint Laurent pants and jacket, gray cashmere sweater, and her ever-present head wrap that was a startling red and gold. The woman reminded Kate of a bird. Probably a hawk or vulture. She was thin to the point of emaciated, bordering on elderly, and more than once, Kate had caught the woman staring at her. Once she'd reached out a bony finger and ran a long red nail along the length of Kate's arm.

Which was very creepy.

Was the woman jealous of her skin?

Kate couldn't help that her skin was still smooth and elastic, while Stella's looked like crepe paper.

Stella Gonzalez had no plans to *go gently into that good night*. She'd go kicking and screaming, wearing designer clothes, and taking as many people with her as possible.

"John has informed me that we're a go for Operation Jetsam." She walked to the drink cart, poured herself a scotch for breakfast, then sat, legs crossed, eyes pinned on Kate. "Can't say I care for that name. Kate, how do you feel about it?"

"I have no feelings about the name."

"Ah." She sipped from her drink and smiled over the rim of the glass at John. "She has no feelings."

"Let's get on with this, Stella. It looks to be a busy day."

"Right you are." She turned back to Kate. "We have two operatives on the *Harmony*."

"Correct."

"Have you been in communication?"

"No. Per our plans, they are in a communication blackout until they reach Costa Luna."

"All right. And they are not aware Quinn is on the ship?"

John took that one. "They've been told two task force agents are aboard. Per your instructions, that's all they've been told. Frankly, I find that decision unfathomable. If they knew who to watch out for . . ."

"Then they would act differently around them, John. We've been over this. Your people are not undercover spies. They wouldn't have the slightest idea how to keep a low profile should they happen to bump into Allison and her cohort. No. I want them in the dark for now. We'll tell them when they need to know."

Kate noticed a slight twitch below John's right eye, but he didn't argue with Stella. He simply waited.

Stella rattled the ice cubes in her glass. "What about the weather forecasts?"

"Long-range forecasts indicate that the approaching storm will hit twelve hours after the ship leaves Cozumel." Kate had to work to keep any emotion out of her voice or her expression. She wouldn't want to be shot in the head for questioning Stella's commands.

"Excellent." Stella finished her drink and set it carefully on the coaster. "Current estimate of casualties?"

"Slightly below what we had anticipated since the ship isn't quite full."

"The number, Kate."

"Four hundred and twenty-six. If the storm continues on its current path, and if we can completely isolate the *Harmony*."

Stella sighed, stood, and walked over to John's video screens. They showed the current position of the *Harmony* in relation to the U.S. mainland and Costa Luna, as well as its position in regard to all other ships in the Gulf—both military and commercial.

Still staring at the screens, Stella said, "And you're certain that Allison Quinn is on that boat?"

"Current data says *yes* with a ninety-two percent certainty."

Stella tsked and finally turned to stare at Kate. "Ninety-two percent? That's the best you can do?"

"Stop badgering her." John allowed a bit of his displeasure to color his tone. "I don't know what your fascination with Quinn is, but the larger picture is that we have joint task force agents on thirty-seven ships. We have them scattered far and wide. We have them running blind. We have them right where we want them."

Stella shrugged, then put her hand to her scarf as if to pat down her hair.

Kate didn't think this woman could do a single thing that would shock her. She could pull a Walther PPK from her turban and start firing. Kate wouldn't be surprised. She might be dead, but at least she would have seen it coming.

"Notify me the minute the ship has docked at Costa Luna." And with those words, Stella Gonzalez—queen of the realm—sailed from the room.

Kate remained, waiting for John to dismiss her.

"She's out of control," John muttered.

Since Brett Lindstrom had been killed, John confided in her on a semi-regular basis. She didn't have to respond very often. Mostly, she was a sounding board. But any information was useful, and information straight from John Howard was the most important kind.

"Our stated purpose is to wake up the American populace to their subjugation at the hands of the duly-elected government and the Tech Giants—the five largest American tech corporations." He stood and began pacing in front of the live feeds. "Last September, we proved that we can manipulate the task force—both the FBI and so-called Homeland Security. Did we lose operatives to the cause? We did. Well, in a war, there are casualties, Kate."

He turned abruptly and studied her. "How do you feel about that?"

"How do I feel about it?"

The barest hint of a twitch tugged at the corner of his lips. "Repeating my question doesn't suffice for an answer."

"I feel that there is a cost for any endeavor. The higher the endeavor, the higher the cost."

He didn't answer immediately. Then the twitch blossomed into what, for John Howard, passed as a smile. He clasped his hands behind his back and walked over to his window. Wilderness, mountains, and beyond that, Canada.

Kate had no idea why he thought Canada would be better than the U.S. The problems he perceived in society existed everywhere. The over-reliance on technology was a global issue. The lack of privacy rights existed in all nations. The intrusion by big tech companies reached the far corners of the Earth.

Still, John looked longingly out the window, as if he would like to hasten the day he had to make his dash for freedom. Grasmere, Canada was the closest border crossing at only sixty-seven miles away. But Kate suspected John would cross via back roads through Glacier National Park. The sheer size of that area would make it a satisfactory hiding place—more than one million acres, one hundred and thirty named lakes, and two mountain ranges. She wouldn't be surprised to learn that he had a cabin stocked with supplies somewhere in that wilderness. Though she'd found no evidence of that when hacking into his phone, computer, or online services.

His voice became more business-like as he sat at his desk. "It's plain to me that you're terrified of Stella. Don't be. I understand and appreciate that you're the brightest hacker this organization has ever seen. I'll protect you."

"Like you protected Brett?" She hadn't realized she was going to say it, but now that she had, she raised her chin, met his gaze, and waited.

"That was... unfortunate. I've taken precautions to ensure it won't happen again." He waved her away. "Go. Watch over our staff. We need to continuously monitor all government communication, and I want access to Allison Quinn's phone. Make that a priority."

"Yes, sir."

She fled the room much as one would flee a tornado bearing down on her current location. Kate wasn't really afraid of John Howard. She wasn't even afraid of Stella Gonzalez. They were no better or worse than any other malcontent she'd worked for. But they were well supplied, and that worried her. Technology wasn't the answer to every problem, but in matters of cyberwars, it could tip the balance in the direction of the person with the latest and best devices. Those devices as well as their applications were changing every day.

John and Stella hadn't yet realized the unlimited potential of artificial intelligence in regard to cyberattacks, but they would. She'd seen his search history, and he was already sniffing around for a black-market developer who would sell him a system with private AI capability. A system that didn't have any of the usual safeguards around it.

John wanted an intelligent machine that would implement his plans and not ask any questions.

He hadn't purchased it yet, but he would.

Kate intended to be prepared for the arrival of that day.

Chapter Eight

The next day was a full day at sea. Allison expected the AT to continue exploiting any virtual doors into the ship's systems—which meant the first thing on her and Donovan's itinerary was a meeting with Lilith.

"They were at it all night," Lilith said. She shrugged, guzzled an energy drink, then turned her attention back to the server display.

"Were you watching them all night, or did you..." Allison waved toward the three monitors surrounding the girl. "Write a program or something?"

"Nah. I'm hot on their trail. I couldn't sleep."

She looked disturbingly chipper. What was it with twenty-somethings? No bags under her eyes. Hair still looked messy in a way that made Allison think of glamour photo shoots. Sometime during the night, she'd swapped out the Grateful Dead t-shirt for a Pink Floyd one.

Donovan took the seat on Lilith's left, but Allison opted to stand.

"Tell us what you think is happening," Donovan said.

"It's actually a pretty sweet piece of code."

"The AT hire only the best." Allison meant it as humor to

lighten the mood in the room, but Lilith and Donovan nodded solemnly as if she'd spoken sacred words.

"So it's an intrusion program, for sure. But it operates on a rotating basis." Her fingers flew over the keyboard, and the three monitors came to life with different graphs, charts, and lines of code. "As you can see, each intrusion lasts only milliseconds, then rotates to a different access point. The somewhat dated watchdog program the cruise line uses—"

"How dated?" Donovan sat forward as if to better see the intrusions.

"Three months. Can you believe that?" Lilith stared at Donovan and then Allison with wide-eyed wonder. "Three months is like... an eternity in cyber time."

"You were explaining about the intrusions." Allison nodded at the charts and graphs. "What do those lines mean?"

"I wrote a new program that stacked the intrusions according to the access points." What had been random dots on a screen now coalesced into lines that might as well have had an arrow with a ballistic missile on the end of them. "They're halfway through our firewall. Based on the timeline we're seeing here, they'll break through tomorrow morning."

"What time tomorrow?" Donovan asked.

Lilith stared up at the ceiling, doing the calculations in her head. "I'd say eleven a.m., but I could be off by ten minutes either direction."

"Close enough." Allison crossed her arms. "They're timing it to break through at the moment that we dock."

"Why?" Lilith's hands stilled over the computer keys.

It occurred to Allison that this young woman was very smart and extremely well-educated. But that didn't help her conceive the motivation, intensity, and end-game of what a terrorist would and could do.

"Docking is a pretty busy procedure," Allison said. "People getting off. People getting on. Tour groups assembling."

"Yeah, but there's, like, guys with machine guns on the dock.

You've seen them before, right? They wear camo and bullet proof vests. Have the words *Policía* on one side, *Marina* on the other. About half of them cover their face with a bandana so the cartel can't identify who they are and retaliate by killing their families. And they're the good guys."

"Yup. We're aware." Donovan wiggled his eyebrows at Allison as if to say, *she's pretty bright, right*? "Keep at it, Lilith. You're a valuable member of this team, and we need your help if we're going to stop these people."

Allison thought the pep talk was a bit over the top, so she added, "What he meant to say is get some shut-eye. Think long game. We don't need you falling asleep when the action happens."

Brock Ferguson caught up with Allison and Donovan as they made their way down the hall. "Could we talk?"

"Not here," Allison said.

He nodded and lead them a few doors down, swiped his keycard, and opened a door to a very small suite. In Allison's mind, the word *suite* only applied because there were technically two rooms—a bedroom and a sitting area. In reality, they were standing in one room with a half-wall erected in the middle. There was also a small porthole window near the top of the wall. Other than that small glimpse of sky, it must have been like sleeping in a closet.

"I would have thought they'd give the lead engineer a nicer suite," she said.

"It's not about the quality of the room. It's about the location."

Which did make sense. The captain and crew were on the top deck, next to the bridge. The engineers and mechanics were in the bowels of the ship, close to the computers and engines.

"You don't look so good," Donovan said. "Are you okay?"

"No."

Allison stood by the door. Donovan stood with his back to the wall. Brock sank into the single chair. He stared at the floor, massaging the area between his neck and his shoulders. The guy was tense.

"I've never been in this situation," he finally admitted. "It's my job to keep this ship going. To ensure the safety of the guests. I'm not sure I can do that if the computers stop. That's what we're talking about, right? All systems down? And the fact that we have redundancy in all systems won't matter either. Because everything will be down."

Donovan glanced at Allison, who nodded once.

There were things they could share, and there were things they couldn't. It was time to tell Brock Ferguson everything that wasn't classified.

"We've had eyes on the AT group for several years." Donovan crossed his arms, splitting his attention between the porthole and Ferguson. "The agencies we work for have probably been watching them since they first thought of stepping off the grid. I suspect the AT started like most of these groups—with a few guys in a basement or sitting around a bar grumbling about the state of the world."

"This is a completely unique situation for you," Allison added. "But it's not for us. This is what we do."

"You chase computer nerds, trying to stop them from bringing down the grid?"

"In a nutshell, sure. Let's say that's what we do. The important thing, Brock. . ." Donovan waited until the man met his gaze. "The important thing is that you're not in this alone. You have myself and Allison. She's one of the task force's top agents, and I'm pretty good too. You have the resources of the FBI and DHS. We're not going to let anything happen to you or your crew."

Brock nodded once and swiped at the sweat beading across his forehead. "Okay. Right. You've done this before. But, like... to this extent?"

Allison followed procedure until it didn't make sense to her anymore. Most of their work was not for public consumption. But Brock needed to have confidence in them.

"That thing in the Grand Canyon? Last fall? That was us."

"Grand Canyon?" He shook his head. "I remember something about the national power grid and terrorists and a national park, but they never said where. In fact, the news didn't provide many details at all, and soon after it happened, something else took the limelight—a shooting or a bridge collapse or some political pundit getting canned."

"The event you're referring to was us," Donovan confirmed. "If we can catch a terrorist in the Grand Canyon, we can catch one here."

"You did that?"

"Yup. Well, we did. Allison was actually the agent on the ground. Trust us. We can find, stop, and apprehend a terrorist on a cruise ship. You don't have to worry about that."

Brock stared at Allison in a way that might have offended her if she wasn't completely immune to it. For some reason, people saw a five-foot, six-inch, one-hundred-and-thirty-pound woman and concluded she was no match for a terrorist. Most cybercriminals were caught by outsmarting them or outshooting them. It rarely required a large size or brawny muscles.

"Just do your job, Brock." Allison's mind was already moving on to the next thing. They could only hold this guy's hand for so long. "You do your job. We'll do ours."

"What does that even mean?"

"Keep the engines running. Be alert. Be vigil. And contact Price or us the minute you notice any small shift in the status of your domain. Got it?"

"Yeah. Yeah, I got it."

They were back on their deck when Allison received a message notification. Their rooms were currently being cleaned by housekeeping, so they opted for the open library area. The same woman they'd seen the night before was again sitting in front of the open area that dropped to the promenade. She again didn't make eye contact, which Allison was beginning to think was a little suspect. She didn't have time to worry about octogenarian tourists, though. Donovan led the way through the room to the farthest grouping of chairs.

They sat, pulled out their phones, and read the message from the Kids.

> Male. Facial match with 98% accuracy. Dustin Cradduck. Misdemeanors for possession less than 1 ounce. Graduate of Phillips Exeter Academy, full ride to Harvard, math scholarship.

> Female. Eloise Grant. Facial match with 92% accuracy. No priors. No educational records. No recent social media. No employment data point.

Allison glanced at Donovan. He was staring at something across the room. Thinking.

"There's a Cradduck that is a VP at one of the big five," she said.

He snapped his fingers. "That's what I was trying to remember. Tall guy, athletic looking, light hair."

"Sounds like Dustin's dad all right. Guess he didn't want to march along in his dad's shadow."

"What about the girl, though? No social media at all? No educational records? That's kind of...impossible."

"Not really." Allison had actually come across a similar situation a month earlier in Boston. "The program the Kids wrote to look backwards in the national database found Cradduck's history because he had priors. Our girl Eloise, she's too young to have even been on the national database yet."

"She embraced the dark side before college."

"Certainly while she was still a minor. I'll bet you a lobster dinner that she had a social media page when she was much younger. That explains the 92% accuracy. She dumped social media while she was still a pre-pubescent."

Donovan sat back, nodded, tapped his fingertips together.

"Then, when these two joined the AT, someone hacked into the system and erased their files. That's why the Kids had to use the program."

"Not hard for someone with the AT's skill level to do."

Their phones binged again. Both looked down.

> Surveillance indicates they are aware two JTF agents are on board, but they do not have your identity. Thomas advises extreme caution. We'll keep you updated.

Allison was about to stick her phone in her pocket when it binged once more. This time the message was from Price. It was short and to the point.

> Kitchen. Stat.

"Kitchen? Don't they have several of those?"

But then another text came through.

> Ice cream.

"Ice cream?" Donovan cocked his head, then looked at Allison. "Freezers?"

"Yeah, which probably means—"

"We have our first body."

Donovan wasn't exactly surprised. Dustin and Eloise had managed to gain access to the ship somehow. The most likely scenario, which he and Allison had batted around the night before, was that they had each taken one of the employee's identities.

"Explain to me how this could happen," Price said. "And why. Why would this happen?"

Allison, Donovan, and Price stood in the freezer, staring down at two bodies that had been hidden behind the pallets of ice cream. One was male, European, dark-haired, average height and build. The other was female, a bit on the heavy side, with a tattoo on the inside of her right arm. They looked nothing like Dustin and Eloise, though they were close in age. The ship's doctor was kneeling beside them, examining the bodies and tapping notes into a tablet.

Donovan nodded toward the door of the freezer. The place was stinking cold, but he didn't want to move merely for comfort. He wasn't sure about the doctor yet. They'd need to send his name and photo to the Kids. When they were out of the woman's earshot, he turned to Price. "Our two cyberbugs needed a keycard."

"They could have stolen one," Price said. Her demeanor was moving past shock and straight into anger.

Donovan took that as a good sign.

"No. That wouldn't work." Allison looked down at the two pictures she'd taken with her phone and immediately forwarded them to the Kids for identification, though she suspected they wouldn't be on any watch list. They were just two people in the wrong place at exactly the wrong moment. "You told us that the cruise line makes it a priority to count and recount the number of people on the ship."

"Comes in handy when someone is reported to have fallen overboard," Price said. "We're able to confirm that they've actually fallen into a drunken stupor in a deck lounge chair."

"So your program monitors the key cards as well as the specific times and locations that they're used per day. Correct?"

"Yes. So in the instance of the person who had too much to drink, which happens every few cruises, we can trace the I.D. back to their last liquor purchase. Every single time, we've located the person within twenty feet of their last I.D. scan."

"So the system you have in place is good at monitoring the movement of your employees and your guests."

"Correct."

"Our perps needed two key cards. They couldn't be stolen. If they were, they'd be reported stolen, deactivated, and the crew member would be given a new card. Do I have that right?"

"Yes..." This time the word was drawn out.

Donovan noticed Price begin to fidget. Well, who wouldn't be a bit nervous with two dead bodies in the ice cream freezer? "Instead of stealing a card, our perps followed these two on board and killed them."

Allison picked up the scenario. "They took the key card and stored the bodies back here."

"They probably hoped you wouldn't see them until you were back in the States, restocking your freezer." Donovan could practically see it happening as if it were a scene from a prime-time television show.

"After they disposed of the bodies, they would have hacked into your system." Allison continued. "They reassigned these two keycards to guests and gave themselves a cabin—which won't be the cabin they're actually staying in. That would have taken a handy piece of coding to work around, but these people are nothing if not innovative."

"Wouldn't we miss two employees?"

"I'm sure they would've used the employee's email to send in a request for time off—sickness, death in the family, you name it."

"We went through that list looking specifically for someone who was a no-show. There wasn't a single name."

Donovan shook his head. "Once the initial accounting was

done, they erased it. Erased all record of it. There would be nothing to see. Nothing to find."

"And you have what?" Allison stared up at the ceiling. "Didn't you say something like twelve hundred crew members?"

"From sixty different nations. It takes a lot of people to run a ship this size." Price crossed her arms. She was shaking. Visibly upset.

Donovan didn't think she was on the verge of losing her composure, but she was having to come up to speed quickly. Donovan didn't envy her. No doubt she'd had a nice, predictable job before they'd set sail.

Price glanced back toward the bodies. "How do we figure out who those two are?"

"We'll have a fingerprint match," Captain McKinley strode up to the freezer as if he were taking the helm. "Something we couldn't have done if they hadn't been stored in this freezer since a body that has undergone any degree of decomposition is harder to match."

"Oh." Price literally shook her head.

McKinley turned to Donovan and Allison. "This situation is deteriorating, and it's unacceptable. Were it not for a call I received from the Commandant of the Coast Guard, I would put you two off this ship when we dock at Costa Luna. As things stand, I've been ordered to cooperate in every way in your investigation."

Donovan knew they didn't necessarily require McKinley's cooperation. They'd worked with uncooperative civilians before —an op in Kansas City came to mind. Cooperation from all relevant authorities on site would make things happen more smoothly, though, and every detail in an op could be the detail that things turned on. So Donovan smiled and said, "Thank you, Captain."

"Don't thank me." His voice was a hiss as the man stepped forward into Donovan's personal space. "I do not approve of the way this situation has been handled, and while I can't directly blame you for the death of these two..."

His steely gaze took in the young man and woman.

When he turned his eyes back to Donovan, they held more than a little contempt and a lot of hostility. "Assuming you weren't yet on board when this happened. However, should anyone else die on this vessel, you will be held responsible, Agent Steele."

He flicked his gaze to Allison. "You both will."

And then he stormed away from the freezer.

So much for having the cooperation of the captain.

Allison shrugged, the beginnings of a smile tugging at her lips. Allison loved sparring with local authorities. Her dust-ups were practically legendary. Donovan had the random thought that it was good to be on this op with her, that there was nowhere else he'd rather be except maybe a white sands beach, holding a cold beer, and enjoying the sight of Allison in a two-piece bathing suit.

"I've finished my preliminary examination," the doctor said.

"This is Dr. Patience Mbachu," Price explained. "She's been with the cruise line for five years."

"Six, actually. Time flies when you're cruising."

The doctor was somewhere north of middle-aged, from one of the African countries if Donovan were to guess, and obviously a fitness buff. She was tall, toned, and seemed surprisingly unphased by what she was seeing. Mbachu stripped off her gloves, pushed them into her pants pocket, and held out her hand. Donovan and Allison both shook with her, introducing themselves.

Allison glanced around, then asked in a low voice, "Do you have any clue what the cause of death was?"

They were alone, standing in the doorway of a giant walk-in freezer bigger than their suite, and still, she was worried someone might overhear. Donovan thought if their perps could bug a freezer, there wasn't anywhere else safer to go, so he added, "Tell us what you know, doc."

"This is preliminary, of course. I don't have a proper forensic suite here on the ship."

"Preliminary is better than nothing," Donovan assured her.

"Death by asphyxiation."

"They were strangled?"

"Smothered, more likely, since there are no ligature marks around their necks."

"And you can tell that because of—" Allison let the question hang there.

Mbachu smiled as if she were used to her pronouncements being questioned. "Bloodshot eyes, more extensive than you'd find from a night's partying. I suspect bloodwork will show an increase in their carbon dioxide levels."

"Smothered, in a freezer, on a cruise ship." Price looked like she needed a place to sit down. She began to chew on her thumbnail, then clasped her hands around her middle.

"Any ideas how that could have happened?" Donovan didn't doubt what the doctor said. He was trying to envision how it had gone down.

"Easiest way would've been chloroform on a rag, which doesn't incapacitate as quickly as you see on television. Actually can take between four and five minutes depending on size, body weight, etc. It will do the trick if held long enough with enough force."

"Did you find evidence of that?" Allison asked.

Mbachu cocked her head, then said, "Come and see."

When they were kneeling beside the bodies, she held up the right hand of the female victim. "See the fingernails? They were torn fairly recently. I was able to pull a few fibers from under the nails. I suspect the killer was wearing industrial grade Kevlar gloves."

"You could tell that from the fibers without a microscope?"

It was Mbachu's turn to shrug. "It's a guess, but one based on experience. I've seen a similar MO before. I also found a similar situation with the male, along with bruising on the side and back of his left ankle. . . as if he were trying to kick at someone who was holding him from behind."

"Okay." The doctor's scenario made sense to Donovan. It didn't make her right, but at least it posited one way this could have happened. "Our perps come up behind these two employees —assuming they are employees. Maybe it happened while they were on the dock. The perps used chloroform on a cloth to knock them out, which would've taken four to five minutes."

"How does that go unnoticed?" Allison was shaking her head.

Price hadn't knelt with them, opting to stand three feet away. She cleared her throat and said, "There are places on the dock that aren't in the direct view of the cameras. If you knew where they were, you could avoid them."

"Then it's just a matter of slipping your arm around the person, using their keycard to access the ship, and bringing them to the freezer."

Allison was shaking her head before he finished speaking. "Whoa. Hang on. There's no way that would have gone unnoticed."

"Actually it could. We have twenty-six elevators, and approximately twenty percent of our employees report very early in a staggered rotation." The color was returning to Price's complexion as she worked through the possible scenarios. "We don't schedule a guard for those boarding between three and five a.m. If you have the keycard to gain access, you board the ship."

"Drag them to the freezer and use a life preserver or pillow or even plastic wrap to smother them while they're still unconscious." Mbachu waited as if anticipating additional questions.

No one said anything for the space of a minute.

Finally, Allison asked, "Do you have a morgue on board?"

"We do, though there's only space for two. Let's hope we don't have any additional bodies to store."

Which Donovan thought was well said. The last thing they needed was bodies stacking up in the ice cream freezer.

They were leaving the area when Allison turned back. "For a

doctor on a cruise ship, you seem to have a solid grasp of forensics."

"I had a medical practice for twenty years in Chicago. For most of that time, I picked up extra shifts with the Medical Examiner's office." Then, as if she needed to explain further, "It helped with student loans."

"And so you, what? Chucked it all for a cruise ship gig?"

"Spend twenty years in Chicago. You'll understand." Mbachu glanced back at the two bodies. "I'd seen enough murders and overdoses in the Windy City to last me a lifetime."

That was something Donovan understood, and he could tell Allison did, too. She nodded, said, "Right," and started out of the freezer. Turning back one more time, she added, "Thanks for your help."

They left Price at the elevators after she'd shared the identity of the person who had found the two bodies. Fortunately, it had been one of the guards who was doing a routine check of every cubbyhole in his area. Perhaps not so routine. Allison and Donovan had requested detailed checks be done on every shift.

At least they didn't have to explain to a waiter or cook why there were bodies in the freezer. The guards were up to date and aware of the onboard situation. Their assistance was one more piece of the puzzle that might bring this operation to a quicker conclusion.

Donovan and Allison made their way back upstairs, still avoiding the elevators. Donovan said, "Nice to have a capable forensics person on board."

"Yeah. What would be even better is to catch these assholes before any more bodies pile up."

Donovan couldn't have agreed more. But something told him they hadn't seen the worst of it yet.

Chapter Nine

Allison spent the rest of the day spinning her wheels. Compulsively pulling out her phone, hoping she'd missed an update from the Kids. She hadn't. Three times she made her way to the bottom of the boat and checked on Lilith, who seemed irritated by the monitoring.

"I know to call if anything changes."

"And your program?"

"Confirms they're still on target for eleven tomorrow. I've come up with a couple of roadblocks to throw in their way once you tell me I can."

"Not yet," Allison cautioned.

"Aye, aye." Lilith offered her a mock salute, then turned her attention back to her screens.

She met again with Price, who had nothing new to add.

And she considered meeting with the captain, but Donovan talked her out of that. "He's former military. He understands command structure. Trust me on this. He won't go against the Commandant's orders."

"But who is briefing the Commandant?"

"Thomas. Or maybe Langston?"

Kenneth Langston was the head of the DHS side of things,

though Allison reported directly to Reid Clark. Clark was someone that Allison trusted implicitly. Like Donovan, she'd heard rumors that he was considering retirement. But that hadn't happened yet.

Or had it?

Did it matter? Because she did trust Kenneth Langston and Kendra Thomas. She'd simply rather work for Clark. It was a point of contention between her and Donovan. She preferred to work solely and directly with DHS personnel. He insisted the FBI was equally capable.

Maybe.

There had been rumors of an AT plant within one of the organizations. If that was the case, it would be on the FBI's side because there was no way in hell there was an informant on her side of the equation. She would bet her life on that. She had bet her life on that.

Conversely, there had also been rumors that the task force had someone inside the AT. She didn't know whether to believe that or not. It sounded too good to be true.

Beneath all of her restless energy and ceaseless worrying ran the memory of her father. Each op was supposed to take her one step closer to apprehending her father's killer. Of course, she understood that was something of a lofty goal. On the other hand, she'd made little progress since the Grand Canyon op, when Brent Watkins—aka Blitz—had claimed her father was a traitor.

Story is he was one of us, and he got cold feet—so they killed him. Left a kid all alone in the woods of northern California. Left you.

She'd nearly killed the man then. The only thing that had stopped her was Donovan Steele and his group arriving on the scene. Steele had saved her, or he'd kept her from doing what needed to be done. She saw it both ways, depending on her mood.

She'd gone home.

Gone to her Aunt Polly's ranch in Texas.

She'd been required to take time to heal physically from her injuries and emotionally from the knowledge that she'd killed four of Blitz's team. It always made sense to her, in the moment. She didn't doubt. She didn't hesitate.

But in the wee hours of the morning, when she couldn't sleep and couldn't bear tossing any longer, she had her doubts. She'd get up, make some hot tea, stare out a darkened window, and wonder.

What if she hadn't killed them?

Maybe they could have been rehabilitated.

Maybe they would have turned and worked for the right side.

Dr. Michie, her department-appointed therapist had assured her it was normal to have doubts. That didn't mean what she'd done was wrong or not fully justified.

It wasn't wrong.

It was fully justified.

But the fact that she wondered, that she struggled with taking a life—those things made her different from the people she sought to stop. It made her a good agent, and it made her a good person.

Allison wasn't so sure about the last part.

"What are you scowling about over there?" Donovan walked out onto the balcony and sank into the chair next to her.

"Everything."

"Ah."

He didn't push, and she appreciated that about him. It gave her space to breathe and gather her thoughts. With anyone else, she would have left it at that. But this was Donovan Steele. The man who had saved her life—probably more than once.

She didn't meet his eyes. Just kept staring out at the blue water that stretched to the horizon. "I can't wrap my head around the purpose of an attack on this ship. The Grand Canyon op had a certain type of sense to it."

"Acquiring the kill codes."

"Exactly. The AT wanted money or wanted to prove what they could do."

She glanced at him and knew she had his complete attention.

He sat back. Cocked his head. Did that thing rubbing the thumb of his right hand against his palm—a tell she'd noticed before. It usually meant he was concentrating. "Probably both."

"They created a terrible scenario, wrote and inserted the code that could pull it off, then sold codes that could stop the attack to the highest bidder." Allison shook her head. "That entire operation was about hubris and greed."

"Succinct evaluation of a complicated op, but I agree. Go on."

"Even the recent event in Dallas makes some sense."

"Hacking into the electric cars?"

"Right." Allison closed her eyes, pictured the gridlock at the juncture of Dallas's biggest highways. "Maybe it was a warning to the elite, to the upper class, to the haves versus the have-nots."

"What kind of warning?"

"That they're vulnerable, too. Maybe more vulnerable."

"Maybe."

"But this? What is the point? What does the AT hope to achieve?"

Donovan sighed, then crossed his arms. "It's hard to climb inside the mind of an anti-government group when you work for the government. Hard to understand the perspective of people actively working to shove the world toward anarchy when you've spent your career trying to maintain law and order."

"Yup."

"Hacking the infrastructure of every manufacturer of electrical cars across the U.S. could be flexing their muscle."

"Only they didn't."

"Didn't what?"

She popped out of her chair and paced the seven feet across the balcony. "They didn't hack the infrastructure of electrical cars across the U.S. They hacked every electrical vehicle in the Dallas area."

Donovan shifted, but he didn't interrupt her.

"We had no other reports, right?"

"None that I heard of."

"Why Dallas?"

He steepled his fingers together.

"Where were you when you received Thomas's call?"

"I was actually visiting family who live on the north side of Houston."

"So your being a part of this could just be coincidence. You drew the short straw."

"It's not that bad."

"But I had been assigned to the Dallas office for the entire week." She repositioned the chair so that she was facing Donovan, then perched on the edge of it. "Do you think that's a coincidence?"

"I'm not following."

"Maybe the AT wanted me on this ship."

Something flicked across his face too quickly for her to name. He plastered on his customary smile. "Um. Paranoid much?"

"I'm serious."

"So am I, Allison. What makes you think that this is targeted against you?"

"Because it feels like it could be." When he still didn't look convinced, she sat back, pressed her fingers to her lips, then finally voiced what had been circling in her mind all day. "Nina knew my name."

"Nina?"

"The Grand Canyon op. Nina Brooks. When I confronted her and after she'd already slashed Zack's stomach open. I stepped into the clearing, and she addressed me by name. Not *hey you*. Not *bitch*. Allison. She called me Allison."

"Okay."

"Then a few minutes later, when I was trying to bait her, she said Gollum would be pleased to hear me call him by that name."

"I read that in your report. We still don't know for certain who Gollum is."

"But the point is that they know me." She let her mind slip back to the op, to the Colorado River winding amidst the towering walls of the canyon—walls that had appeared red in the dying light. She could practically taste the exhaustion and fear and desperation of that evening. "There's something else. Earlier in the day, when I realized Zack was following me, I confronted him, and he swore he didn't have a phone. He did, and they tracked it. There was a drone. The drone, it was close enough to photograph us. To ID us."

"Okay. What are you getting at?"

"Blitz admitted that he'd heard of my father. And he said..." She reached for his words. They were there on the edge of her memory. "*You're her. You're his kid.*"

Her throat went suddenly dry, but she pushed the next words out. "*You're the legend. Not him.*"

Donovan sat forward in his chair and reached for her hands, which were suddenly ice cold. "And that's when he said your dad had been a traitor."

She nodded. Glanced up at Donovan. "He wasn't," she whispered.

"I know that."

Allison jerked her hands away from his, stood, strode to the balcony, and gripped the railing. "All of that was in the reports, but afterwards, I went to my Aunt Polly's. There was an old computer of my dad's there. I hacked into it. All of the files had been erased, but I was able to reconstruct pieces of his records. I found references to an organization that I am sure morphed into the AT. I found references to a woman who was the head of it."

She turned and faced Donovan, who was watching her closely. "This woman was intent—even then—on exploiting the cracks in the technological infrastructure we were building across the country. I think... I think my dad had worked his way into their organization."

"A cyber spy?"

"Yeah. And then he betrayed her, and that's why they killed him. That's why they killed him, and now they're after me."

He popped out of the chair at her last three words. Joined her at the railing, but he didn't look out at the water. He stood beside her—studying her and waiting. His presence was large and solid and reassuring.

It took every ounce of Allison's strength and courage to drag her focus away from the horizon and meet his gaze.

When she finally did, he said, "None of this is your fault."

"Except maybe it is." She felt the anger warring with despair inside her.

This battle that she was locked in, she feared it would never end. Some moments—like this one—it seemed as if the struggle she'd been pulled into would continue, drawing the very life from her bones, until she or Gollum won.

"Maybe those two people in the freezer are dead because of me. And maybe..." She forced herself to swallow, to voice her biggest fear. "Maybe this attack they're planning isn't technological at all."

Donovan was working to catch up with Allison's thought process. Part of what she was saying made sense. But part of it reeked of exhaustion, stress, and maybe even burn-out. "Why would you think that?"

"Which part?"

"Let's start with the first part. The main part. That they're after you."

"Okay. As I said. The cyberattack on Thursday that affected all brands of autonomous vehicles could have happened nationwide. It didn't. Only cars in Dallas were affected, while I was there."

"Simply because two things happen at the same time..."

"Correlation doesn't necessarily imply causation."

"Right. Though you could be correct that someone in the organization has a beef to settle with you."

She let out a breath in relief. "I sounded sort of crazy, even to myself."

"Not crazy." He reached forward and tucked a strand of curly hair out of her eyes, pushed it behind her ear, considered kissing her.

She batted his hand away, and he grinned at her. This was the Allison Quinn, senior agent, that he knew. She was back. She'd stepped away from the edge of despair.

"They couldn't have known that you'd be deployed to this ship."

"Our agents are spread pretty thin, and I was in Dallas."

"You're suggesting this wouldn't have happened if you hadn't been assigned here."

"We found nothing the first day. Remember? And then the next morning, as the ships were pulling out—"

"You saw the chalked symbol on the hull of the boat."

"We showed up Thursday. The signal was placed on the boat sometime Thursday night. The two *Harmony* employees were killed sometime in the early morning hours of the next day."

"And we boarded at the last minute. How would they know that unless—"

"They had drone surveillance—same as they did at the Grand Canyon. You and I both know the JCTF can't monitor every drone in the sky."

"True enough."

"When they were sure I was here, the operation was given a green light." She paused and turned an imploring look on him. "Do you believe me now?"

"I believe it's possible. Truthfully, I'm not sure it matters. They're on board. We're here, and we're going to stop them."

"Right."

"I am going to write this up and send it to Thomas and the Kids."

"You're going to write it up?"

"I think I can be more objective than you. I think..." He held

91

his hands up, palms out in the universal *I surrender* gesture—or in this case, *don't kill the messenger*. "I think it will sound more objective coming from me."

"Probably."

"We'll document our suspicions, then focus on stopping the two—"

"Or more."

"Two or more AT people on board."

"I need a shower." She pivoted toward their suite, but before she went into the closet-sized bathroom, she turned toward him and said, "Thank you."

"For?"

"Listening."

Donovan wasn't an emotional guy. He didn't view life through that lens. But the sheer vulnerability in Allison's expression brought a lump to his throat.

"That's what partners do," he said lightly.

As she showered, he typed up the report. When he finished, he sat there and wondered what that must be like. To suspect that someone was after you personally. To know that there was a history you were involved in that would have to one day be resolved. To worry that the battle would continue on and on circling ever closer to you until one way or another—it ended.

By the time she came out of the shower, drying her hair with a Dream Sail Cruises towel, she resembled the agent he'd worked with for the last five years. She was wearing her designer jeans and a *Harmony* t-shirt.

"You can't wear that."

"I can't wear what?"

"That shirt."

"You picked it out."

"True, but it's 70s night. I left you a new shirt on your bed."

She glowered at him, walked the short distance to her room, and returned with the sleeveless tie-dyed tee. "Tell me you're kidding."

"I never kid about the 70s."

"Why would I wear this?"

"So you'll fit in."

"And you're wearing?"

He arched his eyebrows in a suggestive way, or what he hoped was a suggestive way. It was good to see her aggravated again. It had to be a sign that she'd found her footing.

She was probably about to argue with him, but both of their phones dinged at the same time.

The message read:

Occupants of 784 are on the move.

Five minutes later, they were hurrying down the hall, wearing their 70s clothes, their firearms strapped into ankle holsters.

As they neared the library, the music pulsed from below. They stopped to peer over the balcony and were met by the image of a sea of people swaying to the sound of George Harrison's "My Sweet Lord." The promenade was packed. It looked as if all four thousand, two hundred people aboard the *Harmony* were crammed into one place.

Donovan glanced at Allison—eyes narrowed, jaw clenched, hands gripping the rail. She was thinking what he was. This would be the perfect time for the AT peeps to do what they'd come here to do.

They turned toward the stairs but stopped abruptly when the woman in the chair, the same woman Donovan had noticed at least three other times, said, "Be careful down there."

As one, they turned to study her.

She was probably in her 80s. Her walker was within reach, and a mixed drink sat on the table beside her. It was her eyes that gave Donovan pause—sharp, aware, missing nothing.

She nodded toward the promenade and said, "It wasn't all

rock and roll in the 70s, you know. There was a lot of chaos, too —coups, civil wars, domestic conflicts... Watergate, the Vietnam War, Tricky Dick. Watch yourselves."

And with that final warning, she pushed herself to a standing position, reached for the walker, and moved off in the opposite direction.

Donovan turned to Allison. "You don't think..."

"No. I mean. How? And..."

"Why?"

"Yeah."

They trotted to the stairs and down toward the promenade.

Surely the AT wasn't recruiting octogenarians. Plus, what grudge could someone of that age have against the current leaders in business or government? Or, seen from a different perspective, maybe they'd be the perfect recruits. Society had basically left them behind. Modern culture had turned from a people that respected its elders to one that stored them away in nursing homes or hospice centers or senior cruises. Out of sight, out of mind.

Did he think the woman was a terrorist?

No. He didn't.

But it was a reminder that no one was above suspicion. And as Allison had pointed out, there could be more than two terrorists on board. They only had a bead on two. One way or another, those two needed to lead them to what was about to happen. That was how they'd stop it.

Follow the trail. Stay focused. Do what had to be done.

As they pressed into the crush of 70s revelers, he felt himself smile. Donovan thought he could almost enjoy it, if it weren't for the two bodies in the freezer.

Chapter Ten

K ate stood to the side of the main screen that dominated the display wall. All eyes in the room were on her.

"You have your assignments. You know how to do this. The trick is going to be responding in real time, which we're not accustomed to doing. We usually set our bugs to tunnel their way through and flee the scene—metaphorically speaking."

Laughter sprinkled through the room.

She shouldn't like these people, but she kind of did. In general, they were smarter than the average Joe. All they lacked was an environment where they could use their intelligence. Society had deemed them unemployable for many reasons.

Socially awkward.

On the spectrum.

Arrogant.

Incapable of following directions.

They were socially awkward. They might be on the spectrum. Each man and woman in front of her was confident, largely due to their near-genius IQ's. But arrogant? Kate took issue with that. Was it arrogance to know you could do a thing and express that in a matter-of-fact way? The men and women watching her were certain of their skills. Some had come from the country's top universities. Others were self-taught. Each had earned the right to be confident.

And incapable of following directions? They followed her directions because they respected her. They followed John's directions because they were afraid of him. Under Stella's gaze, they usually froze.

These programmers and computer specialists were definitely employable. The problem lay in the fact that they saw right and wrong differently. Maybe they saw it as zeroes and ones. Regardless, they were capable and willing to follow any directions—if the pay was right and the directions made sense.

The pay was right.

And given their mission, the directions made sense.

"George, you're on the casino's gaming server."

"Yup."

"Make sure no one wins."

"Aye, aye." George offered a quick salute followed by a knowing smile.

"Jocelyn..."

"Housekeeping. Got it. Half the rooms will be hot. The other half will have people wishing they'd packed sweaters instead of swimsuits. Also, I have the lights set to go on and off in a seemingly random rotation. Oh, and I've hacked into their supply system, so none of the food or drink items requested will be delivered from the storerooms."

Julio high-fived Jocelyn, then added, "I was able to solidify the code we've placed in the elevator system. If they push up, it'll go down, etc. Also, the elevators will randomly stop and start."

"All the elevators?" Kate asked.

"All twenty-six."

A murmuring wave of appreciation flowed through the room. Jocelyn and Julio were both very good hackers—among the best of this group, which was saying something.

"Who took the entertainment sector?"

Their newest recruit, a nineteen-year-old Wisconsin farm boy with a patchy beard and a shaved head, raised his hand.

"What's your plan, Mike?"

"Let's see. I'm going to wait until they're jiving to YMCA to interrupt with a nice, slow Willie Nelson piece. Lights out in the ice rink one-third through the show."

"Ouch," Julio said. "Wouldn't want to be ice skating in the dark."

"Piano guy is going to lose access to his iPad, which should render him useless, and I upped the temperature in the swimming pools and lowered it in the hot tubs—so anyone missing the action inside the ship should be equally unhappy with the entertainment options on the party deck."

Kate nodded appreciatively. "I want the rest of you working to block all communication. No texts out as of this moment. Email down. Satellite television off. We want our cruise guests to begin to question their vacation choice."

"I was thinking about that." Chloe was the oldest hacker in their group. Forty-five years old, she had spent the first twenty years of her career working for one of the mega tech companies, only to be down-sized when she turned forty. Her eyes still blazed with the need to get even, and though she'd worked for John Howard longer than Kate had, that fire was not dimming. Hell hath no fury like a woman spurned, Kate thought.

Only that wasn't the line. Not exactly.

> Heav'n has no Rage, like Love to Hatred turn'd,
> Nor Hell a Fury, like a Woman scorn'd.

That was it. Kate had come across it in her junior-level literature class. She'd been surprised that it wasn't a line from Shakespeare. Rather, it was penned by an English playwright and poet. William something. Connor? Conroe? Congreve. That was it. William Congreve.

Chloe was waiting for Kate's nod.

"What did you have in mind?"

"How about we let our avid texters get through? The ones we know will be quick to post their complaints to social media. The ones with a large following. That way, we won't simply be messing with the people on board the *Harmony*. We'll also be antagonizing the people back home."

"Which is the type of innovative thinking we need." John Howard strode to the front of the room. "Yes. Do it."

How long had he been standing at the back of the room?

Everyone's eyes quickly averted to their monitors.

Kate had created a nice work environment for her band of merry men and women. They worked well together. Looked out for one another. In general, it was a pleasant place to spend their eight-or-twelve-hour shift. That is, it was until the amiable environment dissipated like so much fairy dust when John forced his way into their midst.

He cleared his throat to command their attention, straightened his jacket, and walked to the front of the room.

She should have known he wouldn't be able to stay away.

"Remember our goal is maximum anxiety. We want disgruntled guests, not dead ones. Not yet, anyway."

Dead ones.

The thought made Kate nauseous.

She understood her job. Knew she needed to stay and see this through. But at what point did she pull out? How did she decide what was an acceptable loss of life? How was any loss of life acceptable?

She pushed the questions away.

Unless John had been misleading her, and she didn't think he had, tonight wasn't about casualties. Tonight was about prepping the stage for the larger event.

She didn't like facilitating such things, but—for now—she could live with it.

Chapter Eleven

Allison didn't like anything about their current situation. The promenade was literally packed with people looking to get their groove on. What surprised her was the age range—everything from the white-haired guy in an Elvis suit to the teens wearing headbands. Had every passenger on the entire ship gone footloose and fancy free? Allison thought they'd all had too much to drink. They were certainly acting like every inebriated fool she'd ever come across.

Donovan pointed to a restaurant that was raised a few feet above the promenade's floor. They trudged up the stairs and pushed their way through. Allison turned to look back at the masses one more time, and that was when she caught sight of Dustin Cradduck. She turned her back to the man, jerked Donovan close, and said, "Look across the promenade to the person selling glow bands."

"Okay."

"Same side of the room, ten yards farther..."

"Got him."

"Do you see Eloise?"

"No, but since those two are a pair, I'd be willing to wager she's probably close." He continued to scan the crowd. "Got her."

"Yeah?" Allison smiled up at him, resisting the urge to turn and stare at their two perps.

For all she knew, Dustin was filming with his super smart glasses that very moment. The last thing she needed was to be dropped into whatever computer algorithm he was using. She kept her back to the action, grateful she didn't have to watch the hoard of people dancing to *American Woman*. And then, looking toward the back of the restaurant, her gaze locked onto a familiar face.

"Did you have the Kids take a closer look at Dr. Mbachu?"

"I did. She apparently is who she claims to be."

The good doctor had noticed them as well and started walking toward them, but Allison stopped her with one quick shake of her head. Better that they go to her. Better that they move farther into this restaurant where Dustin was less likely to key in on them.

When they reached Mbachu's side, Allison said, "Doctor."

"Agent Quinn. Steele." Mbachu smiled politely and waited.

"I didn't take you for the 70s disco type." Donovan stepped closer to Allison so that they formed a kind of shield between the doctor and Dustin.

"Actually, I enjoy seeing people cut loose. Just look at the men and women out there. They're dropping their inhibitions faster than you or I could shed our vocational skin."

"Okay," Allison said. "Strange way to put it, but I guess I see what you mean."

Allison wasn't quick to confide in anyone while on an active op, but if the Kids said they could trust Dr. Mbachu, then they could. And right now, they needed an ally. "How would you feel about helping us out?"

"Helping you?"

"Do you see the man on the other side of the arboretum floor? Blond, tall, athletic."

Her eyes scanned the crowd.

"He's wearing what looks like a golf t-shirt."

"Ahh. Got him. Maybe he didn't get the tie-dyed memo."

"I'd like you to make your way across the floor until you're standing behind him. Five feet is close enough. See if you can tell what he's doing."

"Looks as if he's simply watching the crowd."

"He isn't. He's one of the persons who put those two bodies in the ship's freezer."

Mbachu didn't look shocked exactly, but her expression became suddenly serious. "All right."

"Also, keep an eye out for this woman." Steele reached for his phone and brought up the picture of Eloise. "That's his cohort. She'll be in the crowd somewhere."

"If we know who they are, why don't you just—"

"We can't arrest them. Not yet. We think there could be someone else. If we arrest those two, whoever else is working with them will run."

Donovan added, "Or, an even worse scenario, intervening now could accelerate their plans."

"Very well." The doctor pushed through them and sailed out onto the floor.

Feeling less vulnerable since they were so far into the restaurant, Allison turned to watch her go. Mbachu cut quite the figure in the midst of the crowd. Tall. Athletic. Almost regal. If she was worried about what she was walking toward, she didn't show it.

As they watched, Dustin remained where they'd first spotted him. He was definitely monitoring something, and it wasn't the tremendously long line of people now shuffling to *The Love Train*.

A waiter approached asking if they'd like a table. One scowl from Donovan and the man apologized and left.

Mbachu was now directly behind Dustin. She appeared to lean in, squint through the crowd, then raise her arm and waved at...

"Who is she waving at?"

"No one. This gal's a natural."

Ten minutes later, she was back at their side. By this point, the back of the restaurant was basically deserted. Everyone was either on the floor jiving and jamming or pressed in close to watch and laugh with their fellow shipmates. Allison, Donovan and Mbachu moved into a circular booth along the back wall. From there, Allison could still keep her eyes on Dustin...just barely.

Mbachu placed her hands on the table, one over the other, and said calmly, "He's positioned directly across from the video monitors."

"Video monitors?"

"They're mounted along the top of this wall. They show what folks are doing around the ship. It's a continuous feed from the swimming deck, the various entertainment shows, even the casino floor. The idea is for you to think the entire ship is having a grand old time."

Donovan leaned in closer. "Did you see Eloise?"

"Sitting at a table outside the Starbucks. She seems to be staring very intently at a tablet."

The song changed to *In the Navy*, and the crowd of revelers went absolutely bonkers. The ship's cruise director appeared on the catwalk above the crowd. Tina was ultra-thin, thirty-something and possessed enough energy to fuel a jet-ski. The stairs to the crosswalk had been closed off, but suddenly the crosswalk itself was filled with *Harmony* crew members. One was dressed like a cowboy. Another like a construction worker. An Indian in full headdress, a cop, and a sailor. It was all so politically incorrect that Allison flinched.

The men danced in a burlesque fashion, and the women below began throwing beads at them. Allison only hoped they would keep their clothes on. The last thing she needed at this point was a half-naked, music-crazed crowd.

"He's watching the monitors," she said, glancing at Mbachu for confirmation.

"Yes. He seemed quite intent on them."

"He's waiting for something to happen. He wants to confirm it—"

"And report back," Donovan was tapping a message into his phone.

"So whatever is about to happen is not confined to this area of the ship."

"And the girl?" Mbachu cocked her head, apparently more curious than frightened. "What is the girl doing? She can't see the monitors from where she's sitting. I checked."

"Eloise is reporting back what he sees," Donovan explained. "They're communicating via an earpiece."

The song moved on to *YMCA*, and Allison felt the beginnings of a pounding headache. She, Donovan, and Mbachu instinctively rose to their feet. To anyone else they might have looked like a trio of friends watching a fun-filled night.

"It's going to happen all over the ship," Allison said. "It's going to happen now."

And in that moment, the music screeched to a stop and was replaced by a Willie Nelson ballad. The crowd froze, then began heckling the cruise director.

Donovan's phone binged. "It's Lilith. She says it's happened. She wants to know..."

"Yes. Tell her yes."

But it was too late. Whatever Lilith had been watching wasn't the actual intrusion. The intrusion had already happened. The crowd was growing more restless, wanting their 70s back, wanting their jive back.

Their phones binged again. This time from Price.

Casino. Now.

Chief engineer Brock Ferguson's cryptic text came through next.

I've lost control of all systems.

And then, as if things couldn't get worse on a ship ferrying over four thousand people in the middle of the Gulf of Mexico, the lights went out.

Sometimes Donovan experienced a stab of guilt for the adrenaline rush he experienced when an op switched to all systems go. That's the way he thought of it. Nothing held back. Use everything at your disposal. No waiting or analyzing.

His job was simple. Do what he'd been trained to do.

It was what his sister referred to as being in the flow. Shay was a meditation counselor and was always trying to get him to *breathe in and out* or *observe his thoughts* or *be present*. He honestly didn't know what any of those things meant.

"I don't know how to do those things. And it's frustrating to try."

"Stop telling me what you're feeling, Donovan. Just be aware of your thoughts."

Whatever that meant.

But he understood flow.

He welcomed that moment in an op when the next step was the natural next step. When there was no other direction to turn. When actions were a result of training and instinct.

"Stay here," Allison said to Mbachu. "There's likely to be injuries if people panic."

But these seventies lunatics weren't panicking. Not yet. They'd pulled out their cell phones, hit the flashlight buttons, and resumed boogying... this time without any music. Or there was music of a kind. The crowd had begun singing *The Night the*

Lights Went Out in Georgia, which was a 70s song though not of the disco variety they'd been enjoying earlier.

"Casino or engineering?" Allison asked.

Donovan shook his head. "Neither. I'm going for Dustin."

"I'll take the girl."

"If they're already in the wind, meet me at the front of the casino."

It was easy enough to make out what direction he needed to go, what with all the cell phone light, but more difficult to make out specific faces. He wasn't exactly surprised when he made it to where Dustin had been sitting and found a couple in their sixties arguing about whether Tanya Tucker or Reba McEntire had done the better version of the dark ballad being belted by hundreds around them. For his money, Donovan thought the original by Vicki Lawrence was by and far the best. He didn't stop to argue the point.

He arrived at the entrance to the casino at the same moment that Allison did. "Gone," she said.

"Same."

"Can you tell me why these fools aren't even worried that the lights are out?"

Donovan pulled her out of the path of a group of women dancing in a conga line, hips swaying to "That's the night they hung an innocent man."

Donovan turned and peeked into the casino. "Any guess as to why Price would tell us to go in there?"

"Not really." Allison stood there, hands on hips, staring at the promenade crowd that hadn't thinned at all.

No one was headed back to their room. A little darkness apparently didn't bother them at all. They probably thought it was part of the evening's entertainment. Donovan turned back toward the casino floor.

The slot machines continued making their clarion call, but once he blocked that out...

"Something's wrong."

"I'll say. Dustin and Eloise just shot out the lights and slunk into the darkness. The question is why."

"Something else is wrong."

He turned her toward the casino floor at the same moment that one of the slot players pulled back a fist and slammed it into a pit boss.

The lights in the piano bar, which was past the casino, were on. The lights near the poker tables were off so those people had apparently drifted to the slot machine side of the room. The crowd was tremendous and seemed to be growing.

Donovan and Allison pushed their way into the mass of people and arrived at the center of the fray in time to hear a burly guy with a paunch belly shout, "I haven't won a hand in the last half hour."

"I'm sorry, sir."

"Don't tell me you're sorry. Tell me you'll give me that money back and fix this damn machine."

"I'm afraid that's not possible."

"I've put seven hundred dollars into this machine without a single winning hand. Care to explain to me how that could happen?"

Donovan wanted to tell him to stop playing dollar video poker, but he kept silent, still trying to assess what was actually happening here.

The casino worker looked as if she were in over her head. "Sir, I'm sorry, but the payout on the machines is posted . . ."

"Say *payout* to me one more time, and I'll coldcock you like someone just punched your friend over there."

Security personnel had surrounded the man who punched the pit boss. The presence of additional security wasn't calming the people down though. If anything, the gamblers were growing more mob-like. Half a dozen other players had added to the growing voice of discontent and were shouting their complaints.

"These games are rigged," one man shouted.

"But they were working." This from a woman wearing a

World's Best Grandma tee. "They worked fine until a few minutes before the lights went out. It's like you all just sucked us to this side of the room and then stole all our money."

"It's robbery."

Donovan pushed his way through the remainder of the crowd. He was about to suggest in no uncertain terms that they close the machines down, but by the time he reached the impending altercation, the lights blinked back on. A cheer went up as the fans of the table games raced back over to resume tossing their money toward the dealers to play poker, roulette, or craps.

Another cheer broke out from one of the slot machines when an elderly woman cried, "I won. I won the whole thing."

Donovan motioned for the pit boss to join them by the payout cages. "FBI." He flashed his badge.

The woman, whose name tag said Perez, blanched.

"We're here in an unrelated matter," Donovan explained.

"Probably unrelated," Allison added.

"Can you tell us what happened?"

"Total chaos, that's what happened." She shoved a trembling hand through her short, black hair. Glancing at her watch, she added, "Lights went out. . . fourteen minutes ago. They went out across the entire floor. We have emergency backups, but for some reason those didn't work. Before the dealers could figure out what to do, the people playing table games pocketed their remaining chips and wandered over to the slot side of the room."

Donovan frowned at the machines. "The slots were still working even though the lights were out."

"Only they weren't." Allison shook her head. "Not if what those people were saying is true. Machines are designed to pay out just enough to keep you playing. Sounds like that didn't happen."

Allison crossed her arms and frowned at the mass of patrons now flooding the casino floor. Donovan glanced back toward the promenade and confirmed the lights were back on there as well.

"Yeah. It's all kinda strange, I guess." Perez's gaze jerked to the left, then to the right. "I don't understand what happened."

Donovan turned to study her. No way she was in on this. Just another civilian caught in the crossfire. "What about the guy saying he hadn't won in the last half hour?"

"Not winning a single hand? I doubt it. He probably drank too much and forgot. Like your partner said. The games are designed to give fairly frequent wins."

"We actually studied the gaming models in statistics." Allison shook her head in mock disgust, or maybe it was real. "Preying on the weak, wouldn't you say?"

"Weak?" Perez had begun to recover from the near riot quickly. She ran a hand through her dark hair and stood straighter. She looked like a woman who had once again claimed solid ground. "Half of these people cruise specifically so they can spend the majority of each day and night throwing away their money. It's a rush of sorts. And occasionally, they even win."

"Do me a solid." Donovan pulled a business card from his pocket. "Check the poker machine the big guy was complaining about. See if there was a malfunction of some sort. Let me know what you find."

"Okay."

"And Perez..." He waited until she raised her eyes to his. "Let's keep this between us."

As they walked through the casino to the piano bar, Allison said, "She's probably texting her bestie right now about the FBI guy in her casino."

"Probably."

"So much for keeping a low profile."

"Yeah. I think we're past that point."

Donovan had been through the piano bar several times on his circuits around the ship. You had to walk through it if you were going from the casino to the back theater or the bank of elevators on that end of the ship. Whoever designed the common areas floor plan knew what they were doing. It was all about moving people to where you wanted them to be, to where they'd spend the most money. And as far as he could see, no one was complaining about that. As Perez had said, that's what they booked passage on a cruise ship to do.

Donovan easily spotted the guy who was supposed to be at the piano, but he wasn't tickling the ivories. Instead, he was relaxed in a back booth, nursing a drink and watching the thinning crowd of people.

"Can we join you?"

The piano man looked up in surprise, but he motioned for them to take a seat. He was probably in his thirties, had a dark head of hair that looked like it had been designed for a photo shoot, and a ready smile. Donovan had heard him the night before. The man was pretty good on the piano—easily able to transition from rock and roll to jazz to country.

"My name's Donovan. This is Allison."

"Nice to meet you. I'm Jeremy."

"Taking a break?"

"Yup. I have been since the lights went out." He raised his glass of what might have been whiskey.

Donovan exchanged a quick glance with Allison, who was trying to tamp down her impatience. Allison preferred chasing bad guys at top speed to knocking down leads. It was the way she rolled. Sitting in a bar wasn't her idea of actively pursuing a cyberbug.

"Lights are on now," Allison pointed out.

"Right. But my iPad is still down. And it shouldn't be. I have plenty of power."

"You need an iPad to play the piano?"

"I don't." He sipped the whiskey, then gently placed the glass on the table, turning it in his hands. "Piano bars aren't like normal music venues. The crowd wants to interact. They like to determine the sets. I could play that piano for hours without looking at a sheet of music, but if I'm going to play one of the two hundred songs on that laminated sheet . . ."

He slid one across the table to her.

Donovan peered down at the list of songs. They included

nearly every genre of music, and there were at least two hundred listed there.

"Some I have memorized. Maybe a third. For the rest, I need my iPad. Chord charts. That sort of thing."

"Got it," Donovan said. "Did you notice anything odd before the lights went out?"

"Odd?"

"Unusual. Which I realize for a cruise ship would have to be pretty far out there."

Jeremy laughed. "You're right about that. Okay. Let's see. My iPad went out about fifteen minutes before the lights did."

"You're sure about that?" Allison leaned forward. "Timing is kind of important."

"Important because—"

"Better you don't know," Allison hedged.

"We're investigating the anomalies on the ship." Donovan tapped the table. "This ship seems to be experiencing quite a few."

"I'll say." Jeremy began ticking items off his fingers. "The iPad went out first. Then people's drink orders got messed up. I was already sitting here at that point, so I had a good view of the entire thing. Raquel was working the bar, and let me tell you, she had her hands full. The credit cards wouldn't charge. People couldn't charge things to their rooms. It was a real mess. Then the temperature dropped."

"Dropped?" Allison's attention was now completely focused on Jeremy.

Donovan was seeing the random pattern of events coming together.

Jeremy had been ticking items off on his fingers, but he paused to take another sip of the whiskey. "Where was I?"

"Temperature dropped."

"Right. I'm talking freezing. I didn't know any a/c, let alone one on a cruise ship, could go that low. After that, the lights went out. And then we heard the fight break out in the casino, and some girl dashed through here from the theater saying they needed a medic."

"Anything else?" Donovan asked.

"Hm. Let me think. Oh yeah, the elevators went on the blink."

"How so? Like they weren't working?"

"Oh, they were working, just not correctly. If you look that way..." Jeremy jerked a thumb over his shoulder. "You can see the elevators on this end of the ship. I could hear people complaining when they started acting up. Some were so upset by the entire thing that they came in here asking for a drink. Apparently, if you pushed the sixth-floor button, it might take you down to the basement. A few stuck between floors. Some made it to the top, and the doors wouldn't open."

Allison was already standing, giving Donovan the *we need to go* look.

He stood too. Fetched another of his handy business cards that only listed his name and phone number, handed it to Jeremy, and shook the man's hand. "Call me if you see anything else that doesn't jive?"

"I'll do it."

"Thanks, man."

At that moment, the iPad that had been sitting on the table came to life.

Donovan dropped a twenty-dollar bill into the tip jar as Jeremy settled behind the piano. The opening chords of *American Pie* followed them out into the main corridor.

"I'll check out the theater," Allison said.

"I'll go to the front desk and talk to the manager on shift. Try to determine how many systems were affected. Meet up in engineering?"

"Yup."

And then she was gone. Donovan almost pitied the terrorist that Allison had her sights on. The man—or woman—didn't stand a chance. His mind flashed back again to the Washington

State op they'd worked together. It had gone bad from the beginning. The blizzard. The threat to take out the entire northwestern sector.

The kid that Allison had shot and killed on top of the mountain.

Only he wasn't a kid. He turned out to be one of the bureau's most wanted cybercriminals. Allison had done that *after* she'd been shot. The woman did not back down.

And the Grand Canyon op? The banks of the Rio Grande had been littered with the bodies of cybercriminals. Donovan had been terrified that he'd arrive to find her body among those.

And he'd pushed.

Because of that fear.

He'd confronted her even though her face was bruised and swelling. He demanded to know why she didn't wait for backup. And Allison had looked at him with such exhaustion, such utter devastation, that he'd wanted to pull her into his arms.

He hadn't, which was a good thing because a split-second later, she'd lit into him.

Do you think I wanted to go through the last twelve hours? Are you suggesting I wanted my face to look like this or that maybe I was looking forward to killing four—count them, Donovan—four people?

She'd stalked away then. Pulled herself up into the saddle of the exhausted horse she'd ridden through the canyon. She didn't look back. Simply rode away like she was in a damned western.

Gone home to Aunt Polly's.

Ignored his phone calls.

He'd known they would be assigned to the same op eventually. He'd bided his time. And now, here they were. Allison plunging headfirst into the storm as she was prone to do. Maybe that was how it should be. Maybe that was how they'd solve this. It didn't bother him as much as maybe it should have. In fact, he couldn't think of anywhere he'd rather be than right by her side as they faced whatever lay ahead—together.

Chapter Twelve

When Allison arrived in the engineering room, Donovan was deep in a discussion with Lilith, who appeared to have lost some of her spunky confidence.

"They shouldn't have been able to do any of these things," she said it as if she were repeating a mathematical principle. "I've been watching their code burrow into our system. They weren't far enough in to do any of the things we've seen in the last few hours."

"It's happened to cyber analysts with years of experience," Donovan said. "You thought you were watching them. In fact, you were seeing what they wanted you to see. You're going to have to go deeper into the code to find the actual, real-time intrusions."

"Okay." She blew out a breath, ruffling her red bangs. "Okay." Narrowing her eyes, she placed her fingertips on the keyboard and took up the battle.

Allison nodded toward the hall, and Donovan followed her out. "Ferguson and Price are waiting for us in her office."

"Should be interesting."

The first time Allison had stepped into Price's office, she'd been so struck by the smallness of it she hadn't paid attention to much else. It was small. No mistake there. But now that she'd spent some time on a cruise ship, she understood that all spaces could fall under the heading "efficiency." Price had nicely decked out her little portion of the ship. Soft lighting, a bookcase lined with ivy plants across the top, an uncluttered desktop holding a computer, a captain's chair behind the desk, three comfortable arm chairs in front of it.

Ferguson was sitting in one, rubbing his temples with the pads of his fingers. He looked spent.

Price, on the other hand, acted as if it was normal to hold meetings close to midnight.

"I thought it would be best if we debriefed here."

"And Captain McKinley?" Donovan asked.

"Sleeping. He has early shift on the bridge." Price steepled her fingers together. "Ferguson, why don't you bring Agents Steele and Quinn up to speed?"

"Okay." He attempted to sit up straighter.

The guy honestly looked as if he were carrying the weight of the world on his shoulders. In some regards, he was carrying the weight of the ship. Of its passengers. Allison had been on enough ops to know that some civilians rose to the occasion, some didn't. She wasn't yet sure which Ferguson would be.

"When I texted that I'd lost control of all systems, I meant all." He reached for the bottle of water on the desk in front of him. Hands shaking, he unscrewed the cap, guzzled half of it, then continued. "We lost the ability to communicate with the power generation system, which includes anything electrical. Lighting, elevators, computers. If it was powered by electricity, our controls were unresponsive."

"Propulsion?" Donovan asked.

"It continued to work, though in an unresponsive manner."

"You lost me," Allison said.

"We couldn't find evidence that the propulsion system was actually tampered with. Think of a ship as operating on auto-pilot. It's a pretty direct path across the Gulf. The captain has the ability to take the nav system off auto, but he would only do that in the case of bad weather or because of a specific request from the Coast Guard."

"But this boat continued on its preassigned path."

"Correct. In fact, there are lanes across the gulf. Cruise ships stay in one. Freighters in another. That sort of thing. The propulsion and navigation programs continued to run, but when we tried to tweak one of the settings, we weren't able to do so."

Allison didn't like it. Whoever was running this show was either gearing up for the big event or trying to get their attention. If the latter, mission accomplished. If the former, what exactly was the AT planning to do? She no longer had any doubt this was the AT. Everything about the op fit their previous patterns.

"Just as disturbing as that was the fact that the communication systems went down."

"How were you able to text us?" Allison asked.

"I have no idea. I shouldn't have been able to."

She nodded. It made a sort of sense viewed from the AT's perspective. They would want people to be able to text each other —it would increase the feelings of chaos and panic. She motioned for him to continue.

"Water and sewage systems were unresponsive, but since the actual outage was less than thirty minutes, there were no problems there."

"HVAC?" Allison was thinking of what the piano guy said about the room turning so cold.

"Crazy." Ferguson seemed to be recovering from the shock of having sustained a cyber-attack. As he reviewed what had happened, his mind was slipping into analytical mode. "The HVAC system for a cruise ship is quite sophisticated. We're talking temperature control, sure. But also ventilation and air quality management. This system didn't simply become unresponsive. It went to extremes in different parts of the ship. We had rooms that dropped to fifty degrees and rooms where the temperature hit eighty-seven. That shouldn't have been possible."

"Because..."

"Because those settings don't exist within the HVAC controls. Think about it. Do you ever set a room's thermostat to fifty? No. And the same for eighty-seven. Too hot. Too cold. There's no need to include it in the options.

"What else?" Donovan asked.

"Fire detection went offline. Thankfully there were no fires. And get this. The system that saw the most activity during the time our controls were offline was passenger services. We're talking elevators, entertainment systems, public address system, etc."

Allison thought of the music going suddenly from disco seventies to old-school country. Why? What was the AT trying to do here? What was the point?

"Maximum discomfort," Donovan said, as if he'd heard her unasked question. "They're trying to make everyone uncomfortable. Trying to put the passengers and crew on edge. That explains the slot machines that didn't work and the mixed-up drink orders."

Allison gave a brief summary of what they'd learned.

Price took this all in with a relatively calm demeanor. Allison had to hand it to the woman. She knew how to stay cool during a crisis.

"Is it possible that what we saw tonight is their endgame?" Price sat back in her chair, eyes focused on the far wall. "Maybe it's no more than a few hackers hoping to send a ransom note to the *Dream Line Cruise* headquarters."

Allison was shaking her head before Price finished her question.

Donovan asked, "What type of message?"

Price drummed her fingers against her desk. "Something along the lines of *Look what we did on the* Harmony. *It could be all of your ships next.* Don't they..." And now she turned her gaze directly on Allison. "Don't they demand to be paid in Bitcoin? It seems like I read a news story about that."

"Your everyday hackers, yes. Not the Anarchists for Tomorrow. They don't want or need the money."

"How's that possible?" Ferguson asked. "Who is funding these people? And why?"

"Whoever they are, their resources seem unlimited." Donovan sat forward, elbows on his knees. "As for the why, it's in the name. Anarchy."

Price adjusted the watch on her arm. "We dock in five hours at Costa Luna. Captain McKinley is adamant that he wants to allow guests off the ship. The excursions have already been booked and paid for."

"We have no problem with that," Allison said. "Whatever is going to happen will happen on board this ship. If people want off, let them off."

Donovan sat back in his chair, crossed his arms, and leveled his gaze on Price. "Dustin Cradduck and Eloise Grant are the key to this. According to our surveillance, they haven't returned to their room."

"And our facial recognition systems haven't spotted them yet. Which, frankly, puzzles me. If they're on board, they have to pass by a mounted camera or, at the very least, an employee wearing a body cam. How have they avoided being detected?"

"They've hacked into your system," Allison said. "Well, we already knew that, but what I mean is they've hacked deeper into the biometric software. Somehow they're erasing their steps as they make them. Erasing their footprint... or faces. Whatever."

Price sighed, then stood. "We all need some sleep. Please update me if there are any changes. Otherwise, I suggest we meet here again in twenty-four hours."

Donovan and Allison left the office, walked down the hall, and were on the stairs, headed to their room, when Donovan weighed in. "Twenty-four hours before our next meeting? If she thinks the AT is going to wait twenty-four hours to make their next move, she's a fool."

"I don't think Becca Price is a fool. She didn't get the job she has from being reckless. She is out of her depth, though. Like most civilians."

The first thing they did on entering their suite was to clear all rooms. It was perfunctory. Allison didn't expect the AT to be waiting for them. Even if they knew she and Donovan were on the ship, she didn't think they would be aware of what suite they were in. They'd made sure to keep their names off the passenger manifest.

It didn't look as if anyone had been in the rooms. They didn't find any surveillance devices in the usual places—lamp shades, television, sliding glass doors.

Allison sank onto the couch, slipped off her shoes, and rested her feet on the coffee table. Donovan sprawled across the armchair.

They sat there for a few minutes in blessed silence, then Donovan tossed a decorative pillow at her. "Why are you frowning?"

"Seems wrong to be..." She waved at the suite. "Resting while the AT is out there planning their next move."

"Agents have to sleep."

"I guess."

"Terrorists sleep, too."

"Right."

She was beginning to nod off. Conscious enough to think she should get up and move to her bed, but too relaxed to actually take that action.

"Hear those waves?" Donovan's voice sounded as if it were coming from the other side of the suite, not right next to her.

"Yup." And she could hear them because it was impossible not to on a ship. They crashed into the hull of the *Harmony* and dispersed, only to be replaced by others. A ceaseless parade of waves and water and life.

"They look and sound as if they're getting closer, but then the one approaching you disappears, and another takes its place."

Allison opened one eye. Donovan was in that place—that

zone—that you entered on an op. He was seeing the details, and he was seeing the big picture. You couldn't work your way to that place, but if you were very fortunate it came... eventually.

"An op's like that. One wave of trouble after another. But then the moment comes. The big one. And you know it." His eyes met hers.

She was awake now.

Remembering.

Trying not to remember.

"The decisive moment." Memories surfaced of killing Justin Knox. Anthony Cooper. Nina Brooks. Jayron Neal. David Johnstone. She hadn't forgotten their names. Most of the time, she didn't want to. Allison thought she should remember the names of the people she had killed—the criminals she had battled in the effort to keep the moms and dads and kids safe. She thought those memories—as painful as they were—would keep her sharp. Maybe they could even act as a talisman against danger to come.

She swallowed, pushed past the memories and the guilt. "You're talking about the watershed moment."

Donovan nodded, still studying her. "You know when it's here. And it separates all that came before from all that happens after."

"But you can't predict it."

"No more than you can predict the waves."

Allison wasn't usually forthright about her feelings. She didn't see much point in examining them or discussing them, despite what her DSH counselor said. But as she stretched out on the couch, knowing she wouldn't move to her bed, wanting nothing more than to rest for a few minutes, she heard herself confessing. "I'm glad you're here, Donovan. Glad you've got my back."

"I'll always have your back, Alli."

She drifted away to the sound of the name that only her father called her... her father and Donovan.

"Dustin will pick up the package at this location in Costa Luna." Kate sent the map from her tablet to the far-right monitor on John's wall.

For someone who was seeking to rid the world of technology, he enjoyed his toys. The wall held a grid of twenty high-definition monitors—five rows, four monitors each row. They could be used individually or together as one giant screen. This morning Kate would need to use all of the individual monitors in order to report on every aspect of the active op.

Next to the map she'd displayed on the top, left monitor, she put a live feed of the far side of the island.

"Looks like a rather poor area." Stella sniffed and pressed a hand to the red scarf wrapped around her head.

As usual, their boss had arrived at the meeting overdressed. It was an outfit that Kate had seen at least twice before. Loro Piana linen pants—one thousand dollars. Gray Michael Kors split neck silk top—one thousand and fifty dollars. Red signature cashmere scarf by Saint Laurent—one thousand, two hundred and ninety dollars. Sparkly Balenciaga pumps retailing at twenty-four hundred.

It was a game they played late at night in the tech center. Finding Stella's clothes at the Nordstrom store—Stella preferred Nordstrom to other retailers—and estimating the total cost of her outfit kept them awake when they were waiting for confirmation that a worm they'd coded and sent out had managed to crawl its way into the targeted system. They even placed bets on the total cost. Whoever was closest won fifteen minutes of uninterrupted video game play. Kate thought it was the little things that made a group cohesive.

Stella was in her late seventies or early eighties—as close as they could tell though they'd never found an exact birthday. Actually they'd found several and calculated the average. Her wild extravagance made some of the hackers more comfortable in an otherwise hostile work environment. Anyone who could spend five thousand, seven hundred and forty dollars on an outfit surely had the resources to pay them what she'd promised.

Kate didn't share that perspective.

She made certain the woman's vast resources were not overstated. She'd seen the proof when hacking into Stella's accounts one evening. The woman had gross assets in excess of one billion dollars. Stella would have hired other hackers to make sure her current hackers didn't rob her blind. Kate had retraced her digital steps, erasing any evidence of them, and silently backed out of the banks and financial institutions.

So, Stella Gonzalez was rich.

She wasn't the first one-percenter to feel the need to subvert the American government.

Based on what Kate had seen and in spite of her net worth, Stella had an intrinsic need to flaunt her money. That might be a weakness Kate could exploit, should she ever need to.

"We couldn't have found a better place to purchase what we need?"

"Costa Luna is one of the newer ports," Kate explained. "It was a small fishing town only a few years ago, but now it's a common stop for cruise ships. As you can see from the map, it's situated approximately halfway between Cozumel to the north and Belize City to the south."

"And why is that important?" Stella's tone had changed from disdain to challenging.

"Both of those ports are more modernized—which for our purposes translates to a far greater number of surveillance cameras and a larger law enforcement presence."

"Surely we could buy those people."

"You might be surprised," John said. He stood, straightening the cuffs on his black sports coat. "People born and raised in a particular area have a strange attachment to their little villages and small towns. Belize or Cozumel might not be willing to risk their newfound economic freedom. Some see the cruise ships and the resulting tourist dollars as the savior of their pitiful economies. Those people would not be interested in bringing the cruise industry to its knees."

"Surely with enough money in the right palms—"

"Not everyone can be bought, Stella. That's precisely why we picked Costa Luna. A struggling economy translates into people who are easier to manipulate."

Stella waved a well-manicured hand, complete with shiny red polish to match her scarf. "Continue."

"There will be three other ships docked with ours. This is useful as it will pull attention away from our operation." Kate threw up the next picture, a close-up of the docking area. "The pier dumps passengers out into a large port area. That area is filled with drinking establishments, entertainment such as performances by indigenous people, as well as lots and lots of shops. It's quite crowded, even at eight a.m. on a Sunday."

"Cradduck will procure transportation here and meet our contact on the far side of the island." John nodded toward Kate.

Kate swiped her tablet's screen and an enlarged picture of the compound where their contact lived appeared on the display wall. It looked like a scene from a movie, set in the midst of thick jungle foliage and surrounded by a concrete wall complete with broken glass embedded along the top. The guard house at the front of the property was manned by two guards, each holding a machine gun. She added a half dozen pictures of the area in between the dock and the compound, then threw up a few views of the *Harmony*'s current position in relation to the island.

"There's no other way into the compound?" Stella asked.

Kate shook her head. "Not unless you want to climb over that wall, which would be difficult and dangerous."

John sat in the chair next to the couch.

Kate had noticed he always picked the spot farthest from Stella. She didn't think John was afraid of their boss. She didn't think John was afraid of anyone or anything. Like Icarus who had flown too close to the sun, John's arrogance could most certainly bring about his demise. But he acted cautiously around Stella. As if she were a poisonous snake and though he had the antivenom, he'd rather not endure the bite.

"Even if our task force agents managed to follow Cradduck to the compound, which is doubtful, they'll be met by those guards at the gate. Both men are well-armed."

"And why did we have to do this?" Stella stood, walked to the drink cart, and poured herself a scotch.

So much for breakfast, Kate thought.

"We have to do this because the item Cradduck is picking up can't be bought anywhere. It's actually difficult to procure, and we didn't want to risk taking it through onboard security."

"Won't there be security when this Cradduck fellow reboards the ship?

John was evidently tired of arguing with Stella. He waved a hand at Kate as if to say, *you explain it to her.*

"There will be security as they reboard," Kate agreed. "But it's much less invasive. The most commonly smuggled items are cigarettes, liquor, and weed. Cradduck will pass through security with no problem."

"And this guy, the one in this compound, he has what we need?" Stella's tone and expression were incredulous.

"He does." John stared at the screen. "Trust me he does."

They hadn't told Kate exactly what Cradduck was picking up. She had a long list of possibilities—ranging from invasive software to AI technology to handheld EMP devices.

"I suppose I have no choice but to trust you." Stella settled back onto the couch, crossing her long legs. The woman had to be older than Kate's granny, but she dressed and acted as if she were a cougar intent on grabbing all of the attention in the room.

And she did.

You never completely took your eyes off Stella Gonzalez.

That would be a very foolish thing to do.

Stella's voice took on a cold, brittle tone. "I want reassurance that you have not forgotten the main objectives of this mission."

John made eye contact with Kate and jerked his head toward the door. She didn't have to be told twice. She swiped the images off John's monitors and hightailed it to the hall, but she paused long enough outside the door to catch the beginning of an argument between her two bosses.

"Our main objective is to catch that woman," Stella said.

"No. We both agreed that is secondary. Our main objective is to upend a worldwide, nineteen-billion-dollar industry."

"I want both, John."

"And we will deliver both. On that, you have my word."

Stella asked for a refill. John reminded her it wasn't yet eight in the morning. Kate slipped away. She had some hacking to do. She needed to know what exactly Cradduck was picking up in that compound.

She needed to know just how deadly this plan of attack could be.

Chapter Thirteen

"I don't like it," Donovan said.

"You're better on a computer." Allison checked her weapon, pushed it into her ankle holster, and adjusted the leg of her jeans. "Can you see that?"

"No."

"Good." She checked the contents of the blingy fanny pack Donovan had purchased, then clipped it around her waist. "I'd prefer a flak jacket."

"You can't wear a flak jacket."

"Fanny packs look stupid."

"At least you'll have your gear." But Donovan was frowning. "I don't like it."

"You already said that." Allison walked over and stopped directly in front of Donovan. She reached up and patted his cheek. "I'll be home in time for dinner, dear."

He glowered at her, then shook his head and laughed. "Letting you loose in a Mexican port without supervision sounds like a bad idea."

"Uh-huh."

"Keep your phone on."

"10-4."

They'd received a text from the Kids alerting them to the fact that Cradduck had left the suite and Eloise had stayed. They couldn't take their eyes off either one, which meant they had to separate. In addition, Lilith had been at it all night and needed someone to spell her while she caught some sleep.

Donovan would stay on board, take over Lilith's system-monitoring duties, and keep an eye on Eloise.

Allison would follow Cradduck.

Movement suited her better than surveillance, so it was an arrangement that felt good to her.

As they prepared to leave the room, Donovan said, "Hang on a minute." He went to the far side of his bed, pawed through the shopping bags and pulled out a *Dream Line Cruise* ball cap— white logo on a blue background and an extra helping of bling.

"Please, no."

He snugged it on her head, then stepped back to study his handiwork. "Perfect. You'll blend right in and protect your pretty little head from the island sun."

"Great."

They walked down the hall, side by side, neither speaking.

"Be careful," he said when they parted at the staircase.

"You know I will be."

"I don't know that." He leaned closer, lowered his voice. "But I know how good you are. If I were Dustin Cradduck, and I knew you were coming after me, I'd cut and run."

She rewarded him with a smile, then headed toward the disembarking station. Each passenger leaving the ship had to pass through security. She stood back, checking her watch and tapping her foot impatiently. Occasionally saying things into her phone. Things like "You need to hurry" and "We're losing daylight" and "I'm about to leave without you." The phone wasn't connected to anyone at the moment, but she hoped the imaginary conversation would help her to blend in. The cap was actually a pretty good idea, too, as she saw quite a few people sporting them.

Should Dustin Craddock walk past her, he'd see one more tourist intent on dropping cash in Costa Luna.

Each passenger had to scan their HarmonyPass. When they did, a picture popped up, confirming the passenger was who they claimed to be. The system then recorded that the passenger had left the ship. It was a good system. One more way that the *Dream Line Cruise* people were able to keep up with the large number of passengers.

Allison thought that Cradduck might try to duck around the security tables, but he didn't even hesitate. Instead, he entered the long queue, dressed in jeans, a plain t-shirt, and wearing a ball cap. A small backpack hung over his shoulders. He moved forward in the line, apparently unperturbed by the slowness of the process, his eyes on his phone's screen. In other words, he looked like nearly every other person in line. At this point, most of *Harmony's* passengers were on Island Time, Cruise Time, Bloody Mary for Breakfast Time.

They were one chill group.

Even the terrorist among them.

Allison could picture Eloise sitting at her laptop, her tentacles deep within the ship's software, erasing Craddock's record as soon as he passed through the scanner. Allison waited until he'd cleared security and exited the ship, then she walked to the front of the line. Price stood behind the scanner operator, as they'd pre-arranged, and waved Allison around the device without a word.

Dustin Craddock walked down the long pier as if he'd done so a dozen times. And maybe he had. Maybe he was a frequent cruiser when he wasn't creating havoc. The immediate area around the four docked ships was crowded with people, but Allison was able to keep an eye on him without being overly obvious as they walked down what appeared to be a quarter-mile-long dock.

The air was thick with the smell of sargassum, and when Allison looked into the water, she wondered that anyone would swim there. Perhaps they cleared the brown mess out of the beach areas. She wasn't here to visit a beach or take a swim, unless Cradduck planned to meet his contact underwater.

The crowds didn't thin out as she stepped onto land. If anything, the immediate area was even more crowded as all four cruise ships dumped shoppers and tourists into the small hub. Quite a few of the passengers from the *Harmony* diverted to a covered area with a big sign that read, "Excursions meet here." The other half continued toward the shops and restaurants.

Lively mariachi music came from three guitarists.

Vendors called out, shopping their wares.

Cigars. Tequila. Locally made jewelry.

The shops bordered a large central area that contained a saltwater swimming pool, swim-up bars, and hanging bridges sporting exotic birds. Tourists stopped to take pictures of a group of pink flamingos.

Allison's first problem was when a group of college students nearly swarmed her in their mad dash for the Sunday morning open bar and breakfast. She suspected they wouldn't get any farther from the shadow of the ship than the bar. In fact, they seemed to have started their drinking on board, as their mood was festive and raucous.

She extracted herself from the group in time to see Cradduck head toward a row of shops. Which was when her second problem hit—a group of women trotting toward the *farmacia*. They took up the entire sidewalk area, chatting and comparing lists of items they hoped to purchase. Allison thought about shooting one of them to get the rest out of her way. She'd have to fill out at least a dozen forms if she did, and it simply wasn't worth it. At least, that was the joke agents shared when complaining about civilians.

She pushed her way through the crowd in time to see Cradduck disappear behind a building labeled *baños*. Suddenly, the crowd evaporated. There were very few people in this part of the port area. She jogged to catch up with him. When she dashed out on the sidewalk that bordered the far side of the building, she saw

Cradduck climbing onto a motorcycle and pulling out into traffic.

Traffic.

The street was teeming with activity—cabs, buses, bicycles, pedestrians, tourists, workers, and dogs.

Lots of unaccompanied dogs.

Lots of people.

Cradduck in their midst.

A line of very old, very questionable jeeps were parked at the curb to her right. Their engines were idling, windows rolled up, and she suspected the a/c units were blasting cold air. Why else would they be idling at the curb? Allison dashed over, pulled out a wad of cash, and pushed it into the hands of the man standing beside the jeeps.

"Ma'am. These are not for rent. These are for passengers who have reserved—"

She hopped into the jeep, slammed the door, pushed the clutch all the way to the floor, heard the gears grind, and threw the standard transmission into first. The jeep jerked forward. She merged into traffic, checked her rearview mirror, and let out an explosive curse.

"Who are you?" she demanded.

"Who are you?" The woman who stared back at her looked to be retirement-aged, and she was dolled up for a day in Mexico, wearing a brightly embroidered Mexican shirt, matching sun visor, knock-off sunglasses, and bright pink lipstick.

"And what are you doing in our jeep?" The second woman asked. She'd opted for a *Don't Mess With Texas* t-shirt and a Houston Astros ball cap. "You left two of our friends back there in the dust. They're going to be pretty pissed."

"Sorry. My mistake. I thought this one was empty."

"Not empty," the first woman said.

"Nope," the second confirmed.

Between their jeep and Cradduck was a thrumming mass of humanity—tourists on bicycles, tourists on mopeds, and local people trying to get to work. Out of the corner of her eyes, Allison saw the occasional man or woman wearing camo and a flak jacket with the word *Policía* printed boldly across the front. As if holding a machine gun at full ready wasn't a solid enough clue that they were police.

"I'll let you out at the next light."

"Let us out?" The pink-lipped woman shook her head. "Huh-uh. No, thanks. I'm not walking back there. It's hot and humid, and I didn't wear walking shoes."

"Plus, we could get mugged."

It was a moot point. They'd popped through the bottleneck and come out on the far side of a roundabout. Cradduck was pulling away from her, gunning the motorcycle and accelerating quickly. Allison couldn't pull over and let these two out. It was their misfortune to be in the jeep she'd nabbed. They were going to have to hang on for the ride.

"My name's Allison."

"I'm Pat," the woman representing Texas said. "That's Charlotte."

At least she hadn't nabbed a jeep with a family. The only thing worse than her current situation would be risking children being caught in the crossfire. Two women could at least follow directions. She hoped.

Charlotte wore the Mexican-flavored clothes. Pat was one hundred percent Texas. Allison was willing to bet the woman was sporting deer skin boots.

"Are you a thief?" Charlotte asked.

"Or are you a Mexican gangster?"

"We didn't really want to go on that excursion anyway."

"Plus, we can probably get our money back now."

"This could be way better."

Allison didn't think this ride was going to be better than an excursion, but she also couldn't dump them on the side of the road. On a more positive note, she had managed to catch up with Cradduck, though she held back so he wouldn't see her. When he took a left onto a dirt road, she slowed down even more. She worried he might see her through the cloud of dust he was kicking up. Best to give him a little lead time. The area he'd turned into looked fairly undeveloped.

Pulling into what might have been a center lane, she attempted to put on her blinker only to find it didn't work.

"The excursion included a beach. Do you think we'll see a beach?"

Allison completed the turn, accelerated because now Cradduck was pretty far in the distance, and then she had to swerve to miss a pothole the size of the jeep. She swerved again to miss the next hole in the road, but caught the jeep's left rear wheel in another nearly bigger than either of the first two. She punched the accelerator, determined not to end up stuck in a pothole as Cradduck raced toward his meet and greet.

All three occupants grunted as the jeep went airborne, then settled back on all four tires—probably bald tires, she was guessing.

Pat leaned forward. "The website said it would be a bumpy ride."

"So maybe we're in the right place," Charlotte muttered.

"Is that our tour guide you're chasing?"

Another bump. This time they bounced so hard that Pat hit her head on the ceiling of the jeep and Charlotte let out a squeal. Allison jerked the wheel to the left in time to miss what looked like a boulder in the middle of the road.

"I'm coming up there to sit beside you," Pat said. "You need a lookout."

"I do not need—" Allison stopped midsentence as she swerved to miss a hole and nearly high-centered the jeep over an area where the road had been built up. A scraping sound indicated she'd done some damage to the bottom of the vehicle, and then the right windows scraped against jungle foliage. The road was disturbingly narrow in places.

Pat somehow managed to climb into the front passenger seat. "Huh. No safety belt. That's rather dangerous."

If she only knew who they were really chasing, the missing seatbelt would be the least of her worries.

Allison lost the left front tire in a hole that was wider than half the road. The only way to miss it would have been to hit the trees on the right side of the road. No wonder Cradduck had opted for a motorcycle. She punched the accelerator and the jeep lurched forward with more scraping sounds.

"I wouldn't worry about any damage to this vehicle," Charlotte said. "That guy who put us in this jeep said they were tough and could handle the terrain. That was the word he used—terrain. Like we weren't even going to be on a road."

"They also said don't worry about the engine light, brake light, or fuel gauge." Pat smiled at her as if she'd just delivered the morning weather report and it guaranteed comfortable temperatures and sunny skies.

With a sinking feeling in the pit of her stomach, Allison took her eyes off the road and Cradduck's dust cloud in order to inspect the dashboard.

Mileage—297,431.

Engine light—on.

Brake light—flashing.

Fuel gauge—empty.

"He said none of those gauges work. Because of the heat and all." Charlotte had unbuckled and was leaning forward between the two front seats.

"You might want to stay buckled," Allison said. "Since you have a buckle."

"Don't worry about me," Charlotte said. "I'm tough. Like the jeep."

"She had two shots of tequila before leaving the shopping mecca," Pat explained. "I only had one."

"One and a Mexican beer."

"At least I didn't take one of those pills from the *farmacia*. That bottle wasn't even sealed shut."

Allison thought she needed to do something to distract these women. Otherwise, they'd rehash events all the way back to the moment they'd left Galveston. "What ship are you two traveling on?"

"The *Harmony*," they answered in unison.

"We were the first ones in line to disembark. Didn't want to miss anything."

Which explained how they'd managed to drink and shop before finding their excursion. They must have been the first ones off the ship.

"Steer left!" Pat shouted, followed by a wonder-filled whisper. "Was that a monkey in the trees?"

Allison couldn't spare a look at the trees. It was all she could do to keep her eyes on Cradduck and the quagmire of holes. The last thing she needed was a busted axle out here. No way these two ladies were walking back. And she didn't have time for a tourist rescue mission. She needed to see where Cradduck was going. She needed to ascertain what he was picking up. It must be something dangerous. Why else would he be here? Why else would he be traveling down this neglected dirt path which was supposedly a road?

The jungle pulled back, revealing a cluster of six buildings— four on one side of the road, two on the other. Three men sat at an old kitchen table between the building and the road. Dangerously close to the road, in Allison's opinion. They looked to be in their nineties. Glanced up in surprise. Nodded in greeting.

"Watch out for the dog."

Allison swerved right and nearly took out an abandoned and rusted-out pick-up truck. Glancing back, she saw two small children standing behind the dog, each holding up trinkets as if Allison might turn around, stop, and shop awhile.

"Who are we following?" Charlotte asked. "Are you with the

CIA? I read a book about that once. The CIA can run operations in foreign countries. Is that what this is? An operation?"

Pat was shaking her head before Charlotte finished speaking. "I think it's a drug bust. Didn't they say there were drugs everywhere down here? Maybe she's with the *federales*. Allison, do you work for the Mexican government?"

"Or the CIA?"

"Don't you have to tell us if you do?"

Maybe she *could* leave them on the side of the road. What's the worst that might happen?

Suddenly, they began passing homes.

Big homes. Tropical foliage peeking above the walls hinted at manicured gardens. Cameras on the corners of the residences. Concrete walls surrounding the property topped with conch shells and glass and wire.

Allison felt herself slip into full operational mode. They were in the thick of things now. A cruise ship took on the personality of the country it originated from. Being on the *Harmony* had been no different than being at any tourist location in America.

But this was very different. Barbed wire on top of a wall. Glass cemented into the concrete.

A cruise ship was like the country of its home berth.

The *Harmony* was like America.

This wasn't like that.

They weren't in America anymore, and they couldn't expect to call 9-1-1 if they found themselves in trouble. Allison wasn't even sure her SAT phone would work, though she thought that it should. Unless the person Cradduck was meeting put out a blocking signal. Could someone with that degree of technological proficiency live on this road? And even if they did, even if her SAT phone failed to work, what difference did it make? There was nothing that Donovan or Thomas or Price could do. They couldn't send in reinforcements.

They couldn't respond fast enough.

Cradduck would be long gone by then.

One way or another, she was going to have to handle this on her own. And she was going to have to take Charlotte and Pat with her. She was still driving well back from Cradduck who suddenly made a hard left. She could just make out his vehicle in the distance.

"Where did he go?" Pat peered through the dirty windshield. "Did we lose him?"

"Can't you make this jeep go any faster?"

Allison slowed as they approached the corner of a larger property with a tall concrete wall. It, too, was covered in glass and wire and shells. Cradduck's left must have taken him to the front of the property. She inched the vehicle into a left-hand turn but stopped well shy of the property's entrance. Pulling a miniature pair of binoculars out of her fanny pack, she studied the scene.

"I think I see iron gates," Pat said.

"And a guard house. Is that a guard house? Are those men holding machine guns?" Charlotte was now practically in the front seat with them.

Allison could clearly see what was happening through the binoculars. The men were studying something that Cradduck had thrust at them—identification or a note of some sort. One man stepped into the guard house. The other waited at the barrier, still holding his machine gun at the ready. Finally the one in the guard house waved a hand and the second person opened the gate.

Cradduck disappeared down a circular drive.

The gate closed.

Allison backed the jeep up as slowly and quietly as possible. She continued in reverse until they were back at the point where the private road met the ill-maintained one. She backed out onto the original road. When she had the jeep facing toward town, toward the direction they'd come from, she stopped. But she didn't cut the engine of the vehicle. She wasn't that sure it would start again. The last thing she needed was to be stranded out here with Pat and Charlotte, parked at the hacienda of some mercenary or drug lord or arms dealer.

Speaking of the two women, they were staring at her now—eyes wide, mouths slightly ajar, suddenly mute.

"Who can drive a standard?"

"I can." Pat raised her hand as if she were answering a question in class. "But it's been a while."

Allison was already out of the jeep, opening Pat's door for her, motioning her toward the driver's seat. Charlotte remained in the back seat—frozen with indecision or fear or both.

"Keep the jeep idling. Don't move it. Wait here." She started after Cradduck, then turned back and hissed, "Don't leave me."

Chapter Fourteen

Donovan's morning had gone well. According to the Kids, who were monitoring the camera Allison had affixed to the balcony door, Eloise was still in cabin 784, sitting at the table, working on her laptop. They hadn't been able to isolate and hack into the laptop yet. But they would. The Kids were that good.

Lilith was getting some much-needed sleep.

One of the assistant engineers had replaced Ferguson, who looked dead on his feet.

Donovan opened another window to the electronic infrastructure of the ship and began coding a program that would search for and report back on micro intrusions. Micro intrusions were so small that most programs never recognized them. They lasted approximately one-tenth of a second. Something impossible to conceive in human terms but well known in the cyber world. The cyber world moved fast—much faster than most people realized.

Donovan was deep into that place that only coding could take him, completely focused like a cellist playing Brahms' *Sonata No. 1*. His fingers flew over the keys. His mind envisioned the code as he was writing it. His instinct anticipated and solved problems before they presented themselves.

And then Becca Price walked into the room.

"Sorry to bother you, Agent Steele."

"It's fine." It wasn't fine. He was nearly there. He needed ten more minutes at the most.

He put the screen into sleep mode and turned to face her. She looked worried. No, more than that. She looked almost frightened.

"What's happened?"

"Nothing. Probably. Or something. I'm just not sure."

"Show me."

She led him down the corridor, but didn't explain why until they were once again seated in her office. Pulling up two different video feeds on her two monitors, she sat back as if waiting for him to say something.

"What am I looking at?"

"Oh. Right." She closed her hand over the computer mouse and set the first screen to play.

Donovan leaned forward. He recognized the pool deck, the music stage, and beyond that—the viewing area that peered down into the bridge. It was an odd set-up that reminded Donovan of a fish bowl. The bridge was set high on the ship, but the pool deck was even higher. That's what made it possible to peer down into the bridge. Donovan had checked this out at the beginning of the cruise. He'd been assured that there was no access to the bridge from that deck and that the glass was bulletproof.

As the video moved forward, a passenger wearing only a pair of swim trunks peered into the windows surrounding the bridge, cupping his hands to block any reflection. He turned, spoke to someone, then took something out of his pocket and stuck it on the glass. Next, it looked like he took out. . .

"Is that a box of matches?"

"Looked that way to me too. Hard to be certain since his body blocks most of the view."

The man approached the window, paused, then stepped back and covered his ears, his body still blocking the view of whatever he had stuck to the window.

Seconds passed.

Nothing happened.

Shaking his head, he slowly dropped his hands and moved forward, peering another few seconds into the bridge. Finally, he pulled whatever he'd stuck to the window back off. He stared at it, again spoke to someone that the camera didn't show, then stuffed the item in his pocket and walked away.

"Play it again."

Price did, not speaking, giving him time to process what he was seeing.

Finally, Donovan said, "And the other feed?"

"Same guy. We caught him walking off the deck."

She clicked and zoomed and clicked again.

Definitely the same guy—twenties, white, muscular. He didn't look like any cyberbug Donovan had ever met, but then again, they were coming in all shapes and sizes these days. Most importantly, the image that Price had enlarged was the man's HarmonyPass.

The man's name was Gordon Jones.

From what Donovan could see, and the video was actually fairly clear, the photo on the ID matched the man who was wearing it, the same man they'd watched peering into the bridge.

"I assume you have his cabin number?"

"I do, and he swiped the door lock a few minutes ago."

"Could you contact Dr. Mbachu and ask her to meet us there?"

"Absolutely." She tapped on her phone, thumbed in a message, then shoved it back in her pants pocket. "Done."

"Let's go, then."

As he followed Price down the long hall and up the stairs, Donovan considered what he'd seen. This guy was more than likely not with the AT. But this was the sort of lead that you also didn't ignore. You couldn't afford to ignore it. Because the AT's mode of operation was constantly evolving. It would have been a bold, arrogant, and foolhardy move to try and break through the glass to the bridge in broad daylight. Then again, terrorists weren't always the genius-type persons that urban myths made them out to be.

Mbachu was waiting in the hall outside the room, holding an old-fashioned doctor's bag. She nodded in greeting. Price knocked on the cabin door, waited, then knocked again. Finally, she held her keycard up to the lock mechanism, and the light flashed green.

They stepped inside.

The cabin resembled a disaster zone. Food trays, clothes, bottles, and trash were everywhere. To Donovan the place looked like a college dorm room for someone who was more intent on partying than actually attending class.

Gordon was passed out on one of the unmade beds.

Two of his buddies were sitting on the balcony, drinking Crown Royal straight from the bottle. They hadn't heard Price's knock on the door and seemed only mildly surprised to glance into the room and find strangers in the cabin. In fact, they didn't get up and come inside, choosing to remain in the lounge chairs.

"See if you can wake him up," Donovan said to Mbachu, then stepped out onto the balcony with Price.

The roommates' eyes registered mild alarm at the sight of Donovan. So maybe they weren't so drunk that they didn't know what was happening. Maybe this was all an act. To cover what?

"Jeffrey Baker and Roberto Acosta," Price said.

Jeffrey and Roberto attempted to stand, but they couldn't quite make it. So more drunk than they at first appeared.

"Did we, like, do something wrong?" Jeffrey's gaze flicked from the bottle to Price, then to Donovan—once, twice, a third time.

Watching him was making Donovan dizzy.

Roberto was shaking his head. "Nah, man. You can't just...like...come in our room."

"Actually, we can," Price assured him.

"There's privacy laws and shit." Roberto took another swig from the bottle and passed it to Jeffrey, who tried to wave it away.

"You agreed to random room searches when you signed the user agreement."

"What user agreement?" Roberto asked, just not willing to let it go. "I didn't sign nothing."

"You did. Digitally. When you purchased your ticket."

Price took the four steps to the table, picked up the bottle, and wiggled it back and forth. "The same user agreement which states that if a member of this crew determines you to be a danger to yourself or others, any alcoholic beverages may be confiscated, and you can be placed in the brig."

Roberto and Jeffrey shared a look, then turned and stared into the cabin where Dr. Mbachu was still working on Gordon Jones.

"You got a boat?" Jeffrey asked.

"Ship," Price corrected.

"Whatever. You wouldn't, like, incar . . . incarn . . . cars . . ."

"I would definitely be in my rights to incarcerate you," Price said. "I've used the brig before. I won't hesitate to use it again."

"Let's back up a minute," Donovan said. "These two seem cooperative. Maybe you can just take that bottle and secure them in their cabin until they've slept it off."

"I could..."

"Of course, by *cooperative*, I mean they have some explaining to do."

Roberto and Jeffrey capitulated pretty quickly though their speech remained slurred and several times they lost track of the story they were telling.

They'd been partying since breakfast.

Could be they'd forgotten to eat any food or drink any water.

Price accessed the video of Gordon at the bridge windows and showed it to them.

When they'd watched the entire thing, Roberto put his head

in his hands, muttering, "I stold . . . old . . . *told* that fool he was get us in trouble."

"Gordonzos the . . . thing . . . you know . . . comedy guy of us," Jeffrey explained. "Said he'd seen that, that, that trick in uh uh action flick."

"Seen what trick?" Donovan asked.

"So, you like, like take, like chew up a glob of gum . . ."

"Chewing gum?"

"Uh-huh. Chew it good. Put it in some liquor." He reached for the bottle his buddy was holding, nearly fell out of the chair, and giggled.

"Then what?" Donovan gave the kid his most somber glare.

"Uh uh uh, put this string, thing of string on the gum. Smash the gum around it. Stick it onto the thingy."

"The window?"

"Yup. And . . ." Jeffrey made the motion of flicking a lighter. "Light the string thing."

"Didn't work," Roberto pointed out. "Told him it would, wouldn't and then . . . It didn't."

"Why would Gordon want to blow the glass on the bridge?"

"Some babe he saw, assistant capitan lady office or something. Gordon's lively. Nope. Lonely. That's it. Lonely." Now Jeffrey did stand, knocking over his chair in the process. "Lemme at him. I'm gonna, gonna kick his, his, his ass.

"Gordonzo is like a . . . like a high school, you know, kid." Roberto shook his head with all the disgust he could muster in his drunken state.

"Always gets us in trouble. Lemme at him." Jeffrey made as if he were going to storm past Donovan.

That wasn't happening.

"Hang on, bud."

"Not your bud."

"And you're not in the brig—yet. Why don't we keep it that way?"

Jeffrey glowered at him but backed away.

Price watched over the two while Donovan consulted with Dr. Mbachu. Gordon Jones was "moderately impaired," according to the good doctor. She'd managed to rouse him, and though his speech was less than clear and his balance a bit off, he produced the offending piece of gum, which reeked of Crown Royal. It even had a little string hanging from it that had been singed on one end.

"Didn't work," he slurred. "She still won't go *up*, I mean *on*, no *out* with... with me."

At that point, Roberto and Jeffrey stumbled into the room, heads bowed as if they'd been appropriately chastised.

Price informed them they were in violation of at least three maritime laws and could be thrown in the brig for the duration of the trip, then turned over to Port Authority when they docked back in Galveston. That sobered everyone up faster than any cup of coffee.

After the three men agreed to stay in the cabin and sleep off their inebriation, Price ordered some food and coffee for them. Then she suggested they clean up the room since no steward would be allowed in the place while they were confined to their cabin. "I'll know if you go out that door before tomorrow—so don't."

Three stupid, naïve young men nodded solemnly.

Donovan, Mbachu and Price stepped out into the hall. Price apologized for the false alarm, then hurried off to deal with a supply emergency.

Donovan turned to Dr. Mbachu. "You're sure none of them have alcohol poisoning?"

"No vomiting, no loss of consciousness. In my opinion . . ."

"Your professional opinion," Donovan teased.

"Yes." She smiled broadly. It softened her features and took a good five years off her looks. "In my professional opinion, they were overserved, but they'll recover."

"Excellent." Donovan realized he was suddenly starving. "Are you hungry? I haven't eaten."

"Actually, I had a yogurt before Price's call came in."

"Yikes. That was your lunch?"

"When you live on a cruise ship, it's best to avoid the buffet lines."

"I suppose."

Dr. Mbachu bustled away. Donovan checked his phone—no messages, no texts—and went in search of food.

He was enticed by the Starbucks sign, so he made a left on the promenade and hustled toward the café. While he was waiting on his iced latte, he noticed the piano guy waving at him. Walking over, he shook the man's hand.

"Jeremy Knight, right?"

"Right, and you're Donovan Steele."

"I am."

"Where's your partner?"

"Away."

His manner must have become stiff, cautious even, because Jeremy held up his hands, palms out. "You can't tell me. That's fine."

"Actually, I was just on my way to find the buffet line."

"There's food here. It's all free. Which is to say, it's included in the price of the cruise ticket. The Starbucks you have to pay for, but the food is no charge. It's not bad. Just tell the guy at the counter what you want."

Donovan did, then he rejoined Jeremy, who seemed in no hurry to leave.

"Must be strange, living on a cruise ship."

"I don't live here all year. I have a sweet place near Sedona, Arizona."

"What's your schedule?"

"Ten weeks on, ten weeks off. And they move us between ships, which is nice. You get a chance to see more of the world."

"Favorite cruise?"

"Greece."

"I've never been."

A waiter brought his food and asked if he needed anything else. Donovan was beginning to understand how the cruise life could be pretty alluring. People seemed to be eager to wait on you. Who wouldn't love that? He ate his salad and sandwich as Jeremy regaled him with stories of the sea. The guy was entertaining, whether he was sitting in front of a piano or in the corner booth of a café. And if Donovan's instincts were correct—his instincts were nearly always correct—Jeremy was a straight-up kind of guy.

He decided to push a little and see what kind of reaction he received. After all, he and Allison had been too busy to learn anything about the dynamics between personnel and guests on the ship.

"Let me tell you a completely random story and get your take on it."

"Sure."

So, he did. He told Jeremy about a certain crew member who had seen something on the monitors, become alarmed, and decided to confront the tourists. He described what had happened on the pool deck but put it in a hypothetical context.

Jeremy was shaking his head before he'd even reached the part about the guests being confined to their cabins.

"What?"

"Sounds off."

"How so?"

Jeremy pushed his plate and cup aside and put his elbows on the table, intertwining his fingers, staring down at them as if they held secrets. "First off, guests being overly interested in the bridge is fairly common."

"It is?"

"Have you seen the windows that look down on the bridge?"

"Yeah."

"There's a sign that says *Please Don't Tap on the Glass*. You'd think the captain and crew were monkeys in a cage, the way people act."

"Okay."

"So bothering the crew is common enough that they had to put up a sign. Plus, the guy you're describing sounds fairly inebriated."

"He was."

"Someone drinking too much and acting like an idiot happens at least once a day on any cruise ship. Lots of guests buy the drink package. Do you know what that entails?"

"Not really."

"Put it this way. You'd need to consume at least eight drinks a day to break even." He put the last two words in imaginary quotation marks. "Most people see it as something of a challenge, to come out ahead, to put a dent in the ship's liquor supply."

"That happens a lot?"

"Happens all the time. I once saw a woman when we docked in Cozumel who had to be brought back on the ship in a wheelchair. Her head was lolling this way and that. She couldn't have been twenty-five. It was pretty pathetic."

"You're not against drinking, though."

"Hell, no. I like to have a drink while playing my four-hour stretch."

"You had an entire bottle on the table last night."

Instead of being offended, Jeremy laughed. "Raquel and I have a system. I purchase an entire bottle down in the promenade, and she keeps it behind the bar for me."

There was something about the way Jeremy said the name *Raquel* that spoke of more than a cruise friendship.

Donovan smiled, looked left and right.

Jeremy laughed.

Donovan met his gaze. "You and Raquel?"

"Yeah."

"How long?"

"Couple years now. When this ten-week stint ends, she's going back with me to Sedona."

"Congratulations."

"Thanks."

"She seemed nice. Seemed a little out of your class," Donovan teased.

"Don't I know it."

Donovan leaned back and looked around the small café. There was still a line of customers waiting for their drink order. He'd never seen a Starbucks where there wasn't a line. Caffeine was the drug of choice for most people—including himself. From where he sat, he could see out on the promenade, could watch the crowd of people moving this way and that.

Finally, he turned his attention back to the man sitting across from him. "How's your iPad?"

"Working fine now." Jeremy shook his head. "Something isn't right on this ship, though."

"Because..."

"Because of last night. Also, that completely random story you just shared? It lines up with everything else that doesn't fit. The head of security shouldn't have overreacted to what you described."

"I didn't mention head of security."

"You didn't have to. And for the record, I've seen far worse happen at the bridge windows. Honestly, I don't know why they have them."

"What should the head of security have done?"

"Nothing. Usually, that would have been handled by one of the security guards. Basically, it would have been a no harm, no foul situation."

"Huh." Donovan knew that Price had a reason to be on edge, and that could explain her overreaction to Gordon Jones. "You still have my cell number?"

"I do."

"Call me if you see anything, anything at all, that doesn't jive."

"I'll do it."

Donovan checked his phone as he walked back to the engineering room. Still nothing from Allison. That worried him, but then she wasn't the best at updating her team when she was in the midst of an op. He'd experienced that firsthand in the Grand Canyon. And there were valid reasons that she'd gone dark then.

Were there valid reasons now?

Was she in trouble?

He walked into the engineering room and found Lilith in his seat. Well, her seat, but where he'd been coding the anti-intrusion program when Price had interrupted him.

"Mind letting me on that terminal a minute?"

"Have at it."

She logged out. He logged in.

He looked at the screen, but shook his head. What he was seeing couldn't be right. He logged off and back on again. Still nothing. Nothing in the history. Nothing in the activity log. It was as if he'd never been on this terminal, but he had.

Something isn't right on this ship.

Something's off.

He quizzed Lilith, who said no one else had been at the terminal since she'd shown up twenty minutes ago. Then he spoke to Ferguson, who had once again replaced the assistant engineer.

Neither Lilith nor Ferguson had seen a thing.

But somehow, the program that Donovan had been writing was missing, gone, erased—as if it had never existed.

Chapter Fifteen

Allison had no trouble scaling up the concrete wall. Even the glass embedded along the top didn't stop her. She'd been trained on worse. She perched on top of the wall, hoping that she was hidden by the branches and leaves of the tree growing close enough to the wall that she could have swung over onto a branch and down the trunk as quickly as one of the iguanas that darted from sun to shade.

The back of the house had been exquisitely landscaped—flower beds bursting with color, at least three fountains, and a large swimming pool.

Her camera phone had been adapted to contain a very powerful zoom lens, so she perched there, hidden, watching and filming.

The back wall of the hacienda was floor-to-ceiling glass.

As she perched on top of the wall, recording what she was seeing, she thought that those glass walls were a sign of the naiveté of the person within. The homeowner thought that the remote location and concrete walls protected them from prying eyes.

Wrong.

The two Dobermans lying at the owner's feet seemed uninterested in the exchange going on between Cradduck and his supplier.

Cradduck handed the man a fat envelope he pulled from his jacket pocket. Money, no doubt. In America, most deals were done via electronic transfers, bitcoins, etc. She supposed it was possible that in Latin America, cash was still king. Or perhaps Cradduck was being especially careful. Cash was harder to trace than an electronic transfer.

The seller was older, rounder, and bald. He was definitely someone she didn't recognize, but she'd send the video to the Kids. Perhaps they could identify him.

This older man opened the envelope as if to ascertain that it was the agreed-upon amount. Then he tossed it on top of a long, narrow table that flanked the south wall. He casually walked over to what looked like an original Frida Kahlo painting. Like so much of Kahlo's work, this painting appeared to be a self-portrait in bold colors with her signature steadfast gaze.

If it was an original, this man had serious money.

If he was that wealthy, why would he be doing business with the likes of Cradduck?

It looked as if the painting was mounted on the wall via a hook or wire on the back. He reached behind the framed canvas and lifted the painting off the hook, nudging it up just slightly. Behind the right side of the painting was a sort of hinge, and when the owner of the house pulled on the left side, it opened like a kitchen cabinet.

Behind the picture was a safe.

He spun the dial, opened the safe, and removed a brown envelope. It was much smaller than the one Cradduck had given him, the one stuffed with money. Allison guessed it to be three inches wide and maybe five inches in height.

And that was when things got strange.

Cradduck stepped back and started waving his arms.

The man shrugged as if Cradduck's protests made no difference to him. He tossed the envelope of money into the safe, then placed the smaller envelope on top of it. He reached for the safe's door as if to slam it shut.

Cradduck caved.

Pulling a pair of latex gloves out of his pocket, he snapped them on, then accepted the small envelope. But instead of putting it in his jacket pocket, which would have been the easiest thing to do, he zipped it into the small backpack he was wearing. Then he stripped off the gloves and stuffed them into his pants pocket.

The two men walked to the front door, which Allison could see from her perch. The living area extended from the back glass wall to the home's front entry. She could even see as far as the guard house, but there was no activity there. Apparently, once someone was allowed on the property, they left for other duties. Maybe to walk the perimeter.

When Cradduck and the homeowner stepped through the door, Cradduck walked straight to his motorcycle and slung his leg over. He even popped the helmet on, but he didn't turn the key to start the engine.

The dogs began to whine, staring at their master. Finally, the homeowner turned and looked in Allison's direction. He probably couldn't see her. But he would recognize that the dogs were alerting on something. Allison got a very bad feeling in the pit of her stomach. She slipped to the ground, ran to the waiting jeep, which was still running, and threw herself in the passenger side seat. She could hear the dogs barking. They were probably already sprinting her direction.

"Go. Go, go, go."

Pat floored the accelerator, causing the jeep to lurch forward. Charlotte had turned around and was trying to see out the back window, but honestly, the back seat of that jeep was barely big enough for a child. An adult shouldn't have even been sitting back there.

"What is it? What's happening?" Charlotte's head swiveled to the left and right. "Do I hear dogs?"

Allison pulled her firearm from her ankle holster. Thumbed

off the safety and pulled back the slide on the Glock. They should be able to outrun the dogs, but if the guards joined the pursuit, all bets were off.

Charlotte yelled, "She has a gun."

Pat drove them into and out of one of the large potholes.

"Sorry. Sorry."

Allison rolled down the jeep's side window, wedged her body in it so that she was facing back toward the hacienda, braced herself against the frame, and took aim.

"You're not going to shoot the dogs, are you?" Pat's foot came off the accelerator, her eyes on the rearview mirror.

"I won't if you can get us out of here."

Which, in hindsight, might have been the wrong thing to say. Pat drove as if she were being pursued by hounds from hell.

Charlotte no longer looked as if she might faint. She bowed her head, pressed the palms of her hands together, and began to pray.

Allison maintained her position, but there was no sign of Cradduck or the guards or the homeowner. Perhaps Cradduck had hung back, sensing that she was out there. Maybe he'd heard the jeep's engine. Or possibly he'd planned all along to return via a different route. Was there another road out here? She didn't see how there could be. She stayed in position, half in and half out of the vehicle, her firearm aimed in the direction Cradduck should come.

The dogs had given up the chase.

No Cradduck in sight.

No guards.

By the time she'd settled back into the seat, Pat had made a turn onto the main, paved road that rocked the jeep onto its two left tires. The right side of the jeep hit the pavement like an anchor dropped from on high.

Charlotte had stopped praying and was demanding to know what had happened. Pat was worried about the dogs. And Allison was trying to envision what might be in a small brown envelope, what Cradduck's reaction meant, and why he'd felt the need to put on gloves before touching it.

She didn't have any answers.

But she did know, without any doubt, that the answers would point them to something darker and more dangerous than what they'd imagined.

Pat parked the jeep where Allison had first found it. No one was waiting there. No one seemed to care that she'd parked in an "excursion only" zone. Perhaps tourists came back to the port early all the time, having had enough of the Costa Luna experience. Allison wanted to stay and watch for Cradduck, but the ship's security could tag him when and if he reboarded. She suspected he would.

She needed to get back to Donovan.

She needed to tell him what she'd seen, and they needed to contact the Kids.

Charlotte and Pat tumbled out of the jeep.

"You can't tell anyone about this," Allison said. Perhaps the fact that she was holstering her weapon added to her persuasiveness because both Pat and Charlotte nodded their heads in the affirmative.

"Right."

"We won't tell anyone."

"We won't even tell Debbie and Robin, but they're going to wonder where we were all day."

"They're going to wonder why we left them."

"Tell them that someone took the jeep, someone who was mistaken and was supposed to be in a different jeep. Say you drove around the port, then came back and did some shopping." She pulled out a wad of money, counted out two hundred dollars, and put it in Charlotte's hands. "Lunch is on me."

She didn't hand them a business card. She couldn't think of a single reason that these two ladies would have any further involvement in this op. But she did caution them to act as if they'd never met. "You see me on the ship, you keep going."

"Got it," Pat said.

"Will roger," Charlotte said.

Allison left them at the tiki bar and hurried on to the ship.

The ship pulled away from the Costa Luna dock at six p.m. sharp, exactly as scheduled. Cradduck had boarded the ship, per Price, but neither he nor Eloise were currently in Cabin 784.

Donovan and Allison were back in their cabin, briefing their boss.

"They're on the ship, but we can't find them." Kendra Thomas sounded more tired than disappointed. She'd begun the conference call by saying that she was coordinating six different possible cyberattacks on cruise ships, but theirs was by far the most worrisome. "It's imperative that we figure out what they're doing, stop them, and apprehend them."

"We will find them," Allison said. "They can run and hide, but this ship isn't infinitely large. We'll find them."

"Run, rabbit, run," Donovan mouthed.

Allison had noticed that Donovan had a fascination with hunting rabbits. Must have been a childhood trauma that he was trying to overcome.

"As for what Cradduck might have picked up . . ." Thomas paused.

Allison could hear her clicking her mouse and typing on her keyboard. "Here it is. The list provided by the Kids is long. Items that would have fit in the envelope you describe include the following. Zip drive. Pictures. Passcodes. Information on how to reach a contact. Micro drone. Poisonous substances not limited to but possibly including nano chemical agents, toxins or biological agents. Also radio frequency jammers, malware, and DEWs."

Donovan had been leaning his head against the back of the couch, but at the last word, he popped to attention. "DEWs? As in Directed Energy Weapons?"

"Well, I'm certainly not talking about moisture you find on the grass in the morning."

"I didn't realize they were that portable."

"Advancements are made in technology every day, Agent Steele. Best not to rule anything out."

"Why the gloves?" Allison asked. She was pacing the width of their small living room. "I keep going back to that, as well as his reaction. Cradduck looked as if the seller had pointed a gun at him. He looked afraid."

"Speaking of your seller, we believe his name is Emmanuel Ortiz. He's wanted in at least three countries, though there are no active warrants for him in the United States. He appears to be a procurer of weapons and technology, the deadlier, the better."

Allison's eyes locked with Donovan.

None of this sounded good.

"As for the gloves, I wouldn't put too much effort into figuring that out. Cradduck might be a germaphobe. He might be extremely cautious regarding his fingerprints appearing on something. I could come up with a dozen reasons for Dustin Cradduck to behave in such a manner, each worse than the last. Just be careful."

"You got it, boss." Donovan stood and stretched.

"By the way, there's a storm in the Gulf. Looks like you'll be in its path on your return to Galveston. It might get hairy. Keep me updated and stay safe." Thomas signed off without another word.

Allison's gaze darted to the balcony. "Did she say storm?"

"Yup."

"Should we be worried?"

Donovan shook his head. "This ship clocks in at over two hundred thousand gross tonnage."

"I don't know what that means."

"It means that you don't have to worry we'll tip over in a strong wind or a heavy rain. The amazing thing is that something this heavy floats."

"And now I'm going to worry about sinking!"

Donovan grinned. "You need food. We both do. Let's eat."

"You're kidding."

"I don't kid about food."

"Didn't you already eat several times today? You told me about the coffee shop thing with the piano man. You ate then."

"But you didn't. Let's go."

"You're not my mother, you know."

"Never claimed to be."

Allison didn't move. Instead, she stared out the balcony door, as if she might be able to step into the past and find a clue they'd overlooked or correct a perceived mistake. "Maybe we should have arrested Cradduck and Grant when we had the chance. We could have done it when I put the surveillance device on the balcony door."

"We had nothing on them then. And if we had arrested them at that moment, we wouldn't have become aware of Emmanuel Ortiz. Now we have another piece of the black-market puzzle."

"Great."

"You're grumpy because you're hungry."

"I'm not grumpy. I'm pissed off. I'm extremely frustrated that we're no closer to knowing what they plan to do."

"Yeah." Donovan's tone turned suddenly serious. "That's bothering me, too."

They walked out of the suite, down the hall, and past the library area to the elevators.

"Hang on a minute," Allison said. "I have an idea, though I'm not sure it's a good one."

Donovan followed her as she backtracked to the library. The same older woman they'd seen several other times was seated in the chair in front of the balcony that opened out onto the promenade far below. Another woman, approximately the same age, also with an accompanying walker, sat beside her.

"Good evening, ladies."

Two white heads had been bent close together, discussing

something in low whispers. Now they turned and considered first Allison, then Donovan. They didn't speak. Instead, they waited. Donovan had the strange feeling that they were being assessed. By two octogenarians. This cruise just got stranger and stranger.

"I'm Allison, and this is my friend, Donovan."

"I'm Anna Lee," replied the woman who had been in that same seat every night.

"And I'm Mary Beth. Isn't this boat just wonderful?" Mary Beth smiled broadly as if tickled to have met new friends.

"We've noticed this seems to be your favorite spot."

"It is." Anna Lee nodded. "You can see a lot from here."

Mary Beth's white hair bounced in agreement. "It's more interesting than television."

"Are you able to get off this floor and enjoy the cruise?" Donovan asked.

"Oh, sure." Anna Lee motioned toward her walker. "I get around. I saw you two at the seventies gig last night, though I noticed neither of you were dancing."

"I'm not much of a dancer," Allison admitted. She moved in front of the women—probably so they wouldn't have to crane their necks, which meant she had her back to the promenade. Donovan stayed where he was, listening intently but also monitoring everything around them.

"There are two people we're looking for. I was wondering if you'd seen them." Allison held out her phone.

Anna Lee took the device in her hands, swiped left, then right, shrugged, and handed it to Mary Beth. "Can't say I've seen them. Friends of yours?"

Allison ignored that question. "We need to speak with them and were wondering if you could help us."

"Help you how?" Anna Lee scowled.

Mary Beth was immediately on board, though. "We'd love to help. What can we do?"

"Do you both have a cell phone?"

"Of course." Anna Lee looked offended that Allison would

ask. "We're old. We're not dead. Doesn't everyone have a cell phone?"

Allison's gaze flicked up to Donovan, and he tried not to laugh. Whatever she'd expected from these two, he was pretty sure it wasn't for them to talk smack to her.

"Great. I'll AirDrop you these two photos. AirDrop means—"

"We know all about AirDropping," Mary Beth assured her. "My grandkids taught me. And Anna Lee, she's always been good with technology."

"I'm also sending my contact information, as well as Donovan's. If you see either of these people, let us know. It would be a big help."

"Now, wait a minute." Anna Lee frowned at Allison, giving her a straight-on stare. "Why would we do that? Who are you two? Are you employees of the ship?"

"No."

"Are you related to these people?"

"No."

"Then who are you?"

Allison again looked at Donovan, who shrugged. Her move. Her decision. They weren't exactly undercover here. They were trying to keep their presence low-key. He didn't see these two ladies posting on social media about two agents from the federal government who had attempted to draw them into a complicated operation. Though, in effect, that was what they were doing.

Donovan moved beside Allison, squatted so that he'd be eye-to-eye with Anna Lee. "You're right to ask. I work with the FBI. Allison is with Homeland Security." He pulled out his identification, and Allison did the same.

"All right. You could have said that from the beginning."

"We're trying to maintain low visibility." Allison put emphasis on the second word.

"Are these two people dangerous?" Mary Beth asked.

"They could be. Yes." Donovan pocketed his ID. "Don't

approach them. If you see them, text Allison or me. We'll take it from there."

Anna Lee was still frowning. "If they're dangerous, why haven't you arrested them?"

Allison rubbed her hands over her face, then stood and stalked off to the elevators.

"She's hungry," Donovan explained. "Thank you again for your help."

"We haven't helped, though," Anna Lee said.

Mary Beth added, "At least not yet."

Donovan took the time to shake both women's hands, then jogged to catch up with Allison.

"Might have been a bad idea," she reiterated.

"Maybe, or it might have been a smart move. We depend on technology a lot in our field, but as we know better than anyone else, technology can be manipulated. Those two back there. . ." He jerked a thumb back and up. "I suspect there isn't much that gets past them."

They ate in a far corner of the main cafeteria. The place was buzzing with people. The music was loud. The mood seemed festive. Donovan was surprised to see so many families. Had there been a Kids sail free special? It bothered him. Adults could be trusted to take care of themselves, but children were just that. Children shouldn't be placed in the crosshairs of a terrorist.

They finished their meal in silence, each of them studying the report from the Kids that Kendra Thomas had forwarded. When they'd finished, Donovan hopped up, scoped out the dessert bar, and came back with chocolate pastries for them both, plus two cups of coffee.

Allison rolled her eyes, but she dug in.

Finally, they pushed away from the table and walked out of the restaurant and onto the deck. The sun had just touched the horizon—a giant orange ball that sent rays of purple, orange, and yellow fanning out across the ocean. The breeze was pleasant. The water like glass.

"Calm before the storm," Allison said.

"Yeah. Probably."

"How do we protect all of these people, Donovan?"

She turned to look at him, and he saw the misery and weight she was carrying. Sometimes, the sheer responsibility of this job was enough to drive good agents to their knees.

"It's not too late." Her voice was practically a whisper, her words directed to herself as much as to him. "We could call in the Coast Guard. Send everyone to their quarters. Search cabin to cabin."

She didn't glance away. She waited, and Donovan realized again just how much he cared about this woman. Somewhere between Seattle, the Grand Canyon, and the great Gulf of Mexico, she'd come to mean something to him.

He pushed her brown curls back from her face and let his hand linger there a moment. "Not our call. Thomas is up to date on this situation."

"I guess." She turned away, turned back toward the waters of the Gulf. "Reading about a thing isn't the same as experiencing it. Reading the Kids' list of possible items in that small brown envelope wasn't nearly as alarming as watching Cradduck back away from it. The man was terrified."

"Yeah."

"What would terrify a terrorist?"

He shook his head. He didn't know. He didn't want to guess.

Allison sighed and squared her shoulders. "Let's check out the pool deck."

"Why?"

"I don't know. I just want to see it again."

The sun had set by the time they climbed the stairs and walked out onto the deck. The place was thrumming with people. Folks swimming in the pools, chilling in the hot tubs, climbing the rock wall, playing miniature golf, gathering around the bar, or dancing to the beat of the band.

People.

Everywhere.

He nodded toward the front of the ship—the *bow*. He'd learned that term as a teenager when his father had decided to buy a boat. They'd spent weekends on the lake. The memory should have been a sweet one, but Donovan had caught Allison's sense of impending doom. Would the children he was watching at this moment grow up to spend time with their fathers? These terrorists they were chasing . . . how far were they willing to go?

How were he and Allison going to stop Cradduck and Grant?

They walked to the bow of the ship and stood looking down at the helipad. The deck had been painted green with a large yellow circle in the middle. In the middle of the circle was a large, white letter H. It was a rare thing for a helicopter to land on a cruise ship. Medical emergencies had been the only instances that he had found in his research.

"It's there if we need it," he said.

"Yeah, but there's a storm coming." Allison didn't look at the horizon. She looked at him.

"I know."

Donovan didn't share with her the premonition that gripped him in that moment. The momentary flash of pain and blood and terror. Instead, he pushed that image down, locked it away, and shook his head. "Let's go back. We should grab some rest while we can."

They'd barely walked into their suite when Allison pulled out her phone and stared down at it. She glanced up at him, then back at the phone.

He checked his. Nothing.

If it had been an operational update, he would have also received whatever she was staring at.

Allison shook her head, then walked to him and held out the device. The message was simple and short.

> Mayan ruins. Ten a.m. Bring Steele if you want.

. . .

No signature.

The number had been blocked.

Instead of increasing his dread, the message produced the opposite effect. Something was happening. They were no longer in a holding pattern. So he looked up at her, smiled, and said, "Run, little rabbit. Run."

Chapter Sixteen

Cozumel was the polar opposite of Costa Luna. Freshly painted buildings stretched out from both sides of the docking area. Taller buildings, at least ten stories high, rose in the distance. Communication satellites perched on the roofs. It wasn't a city, not quite, but it was commercially developed—at least this area was. Allison counted eight industrial cranes. Construction and activity and cleanliness gave the area an overall tone of hopefulness.

"I had to pee over a hole in Costa Luna."

"What?" Donovan looked at her as if she'd been in the sun too long.

"After I'd left the jeep with Pat and Charlotte, I stopped by the restroom. No seats on the toilets, and the hardware—such as it was—didn't connect to any plumbing." She shrugged. "Compost—I hope."

"Who would steal toilet seats?"

"Exactly."

Like Costa Luna, Cozumel's docking area teemed with vendors and folks selling booze at eight in the morning, but Allison didn't see any children approaching tourists with a bundle of cheap goods. She also saw fewer stray dogs.

Donovan nodded toward the "Excursions Meet Here" sign, and they followed it to a concreted area with a thatched roof that provided shade. Brightly colored chairs and four top tables dotted the space. Music played softly through a state-of-the-art speaker system. Fans and misters hung from the ceiling. The misters sprayed them with light droplets of water, reminding Allison of the vegetable section back home at her local grocer.

She found she didn't mind being misted like a head of lettuce. The day wasn't hot yet, but it would be.

She walked past Pat and Charlotte. Pat's face brightened, and she opened her mouth to speak. Charlotte reached out, clutched the woman's arm, and said loudly, "Strange that we don't know a single person here. Right?"

Across from them sat two other women. Allison suspected it was the friends who were supposed to be on the jungle jeep excursion with Pat and Charlotte. What were their names? Robin and Debbie. At Charlotte's seemingly random outburst, the one with curly hair stared at her friends and asked, "Have you two been drinking already?"

"Great idea." Charlotte popped up and walked toward the bar area, which was serving margaritas, cold beer, and mixed drinks.

Allison snagged an empty table and pointed the women out to Donovan. He tried to hold his laughter but didn't quite manage it.

"What's so funny?"

"I'm trying to imagine you in a jeep with those two."

"Actually, they kept their wits about them, even when I was hanging out the jeep's window pointing my weapon at Cradduck and Ortiz and his dogs. I was kind of proud of them." She grinned, leaning back in her chair and enjoying the moment because she knew the day was only going to get worse. This might be her one and only chance to pretend to be a tourist and enjoy Cozumel. "That jeep, though. If I had the time, I'd go back and kick that guy's ass for renting such a piece of crap."

"How do you really feel about it?"

She opened her mouth to answer, but then their tour was called, and they queued up to board the bus. Allison was relieved when Charlotte and her friends didn't join the line. She didn't want those women in harm's way. She didn't want any of these people in the path of whomever they were about to meet.

They'd discussed who might have sent the message over breakfast, but they didn't have any answers. Of course, they'd forwarded the message to the Kids, but they had reported back that they hadn't been able to crack the sending address. "Whoever did this has some experience with cyber security and probably with hacking as well. Be careful." The Kids didn't usually add words of exhortation to their messages. Allison had taken that as a sign that the task force was growing increasingly concerned, as they should be.

She and Donovan boarded the bus and chose a seat at the back. They didn't have to fight anyone for it. These people were sitting near the front, eager to embrace their day in Isla Cozumel. Everyone seemed in high spirits, ready to see the legendary Mayan ruins.

Luis was their tour guide. He wore what looked like a Lands' End shirt—collared, peach colored, with two pockets on the front and a Mexican flag on the left sleeve. He spoke well, had a sense of humor, and answered their questions with just the right amount of detail. He was professional and pleasant.

As they trundled out of the docking area and down the well-paved roads—no giant potholes like she'd encountered on the jeep trip—Luis told something of the history of the area.

An older man in the third row asked about the well-being of tourists. "Should we watch out for cartel people?"

Luis assured them that Cozumel was very safe.

"We are a municipality of Quintana Roo," he explained. "Our governor, Mara Lezama Espinosa has been in office since 2022. She is the first woman to serve in that position, and the residents here are very satisfied with the way she has governed Cozumel.

Mara Espinosa has done much to update, upgrade, and improve Cozumel for both its citizens and its tourists."

A baldheaded man near the front raised his hand. "Can you give us an example?"

"Absolutely. Throughout the island are CCTVs so that *Policía* can maintain security. The roads are good, and your cell phone will work throughout the island. The emergency number, should you find you need it, is 066. The call will be answered by operators who speak Spanish as well as English. But stay with me, and that won't be necessary."

"So, there's no cartel here?" the woman sitting next to the man asked.

"No."

"Why is that?"

"First and foremost, Mara Espinosa is a very good governor. An honest politician, if you can believe that. Also, Cozumel is an island. The only way on or off is by water ferry, of which there are only two, making it very easy to monitor who comes and goes."

"No bridges?" the woman asked.

"No bridges. The water surrounding the island is too deep. Plus," Luis's eyes sparkled and he waited a beat, ensuring he had everyone's attention. "There are only five gas stations on the island. It's pretty easy for the *Policía* to catch someone if they need to."

Allison believed him. Cozumel appeared to be intent on modernizing and raising the standard of living for its people. And yet, she still saw *Policía* holding machine guns at the ready outside a bank, next to a shopping center, beside a hotel. More of Espinosa's attempt to ensure the safety of tourists? And if so, was that from an over-abundance of caution or because of something that had happened in the past? Or possibly something that had happened recently?

She realized, again, that she had no basis for what was normal here.

Rain began to fall softly as they pulled into the parking area for the Mayan ruins. The last off the bus, Allison and Donovan trailed a few feet behind everyone else. They walked through a courtyard lined with brightly colored tiles, a sundial sitting in the middle, benches and luscious plants, and a few iguana blinking their large eyes as they stood frozen in place.

Luis was at the front of the group, watching over them like a teacher with a class of kindergarteners under his care. He maintained a light tone, gave just enough historical information to interest but not bore, and kept the tour moving.

"He's a natural," Donovan said.

"I read that tour guides here are in training for two years. They pretty much earn the equivalent of a history degree."

They continued walking, pretending to listen, constantly monitoring the area around them. But there was no sign of their mystery contact. Allison glanced at her watch. Two minutes after ten. Where was he? Or she?

The jungle encroached on the site from all directions. Allison suspected that if she tried to step more than a few feet off the official trail, she'd need a machete. Luis confirmed that when he told them the story of a tourist who was an avid bird watcher. He'd walked into the jungle hoping to snap the perfect photo. The man didn't walk out of the jungle for two weeks.

"Fortunately, he had only minor injuries, including severe dehydration. Not knowing what was and wasn't poisonous, he was afraid to eat anything he found in the jungle, so he was also quite malnourished. Moral of the story is—stay with the group."

Allison and Donovan exchanged a glance.

The last thing she wanted to do was chase a terrorist into the jungle. Was that about to happen? Had Craddock sent the text? Why now? Why at all?

No doubt, she would have enjoyed touring the ruins at any other time. She found it fascinating that the ruins dated back to 100 B.C. and were thought to have been a holy site. She would have loved to walk through and snap photos and chat with the tour guide.

But she and Donovan weren't on vacation. They were here to meet a contact. They'd left the ship, left Cradduck and Grant on the *Harmony*, with only security guards and Price and Lilith to monitor their moves. Had that been the right thing to do? Allison's doubts grew as they finished the Mayan tour and were given thirty minutes in the shopping area. She didn't need jewelry or tequila or food. She needed answers.

"Maybe this was a trick to get us off the ship," Allison said.

"Or maybe we missed him somehow." Donovan scanned the site.

The rain had stopped, but the clouds continued to press low. Allison and Donovan stood at the edge of the shops. Across the parking area, one man held a ladder while another climbed to the top to trim a twelve-foot-tall bougainvillea. Its foliage was an impossibly bright shade of pink. Allison's Aunt Polly had one just like it on the veranda in San Saba, Texas. Most people thought the paper-like leaves were blossoms, but actually, they were bracts. Leaves. The actual flower was hidden within.

Hidden.

What had the message said exactly?

Mayan ruins. Ten a.m. Bring Steele if you want.

She turned and studied the scene behind them, the tourists, the vendors, and the sundial in the middle of the shopping area.

Ten a.m.

She strode across the brightly colored tiles.

Donovan jogged to keep up with her.

He didn't ask any questions. Allison appreciated that about him. Her mind flashed back to Malik Elliott, her partner-in-training that she'd left in Dallas. There was a time for that. A time to answer questions and train the newer agents.

But this wasn't that. She was grateful that Donovan Steele was at her side.

Reaching the sundial, she stopped and studied the waist-high device. It seemed to be a replica of something ancient and storied. She circled the device slowly until she came to the ten o'clock marking. There was nothing there. What had she expected? An arrow pointing to where they should go? A cell phone number penned in Sharpie on the face of the dial?

It was Donovan who reached underneath and pulled out the note taped there.

"Chocolate factory. Mural."

Whoever they were about to meet was being very careful, which meant that they were also experienced, professional, and, more likely than not, dangerous.

Donovan was in favor of one of them hanging back once they reached the next stop in the tour. A quick google search told him that the place was owned by Aviomar Adventours, one of the largest tourism companies in all of Mexico. He wasn't sure exactly what to expect, but he didn't like the idea of both of them walking into a trap.

Allison could meet this person, and he could hang back and cover her with his firearm. He'd feel better with a rifle, but the Sig would have to do.

Allison thought any such move would spook the contact.

He acquiesced with a short, tight nod, but he had a nearly overwhelming urge to check his weapon.

The tour bus was driving down a less populated part of the coastline now. The water sparkled like a diamond on their left. Its color was a pristine, crystal-clear blue. He thought again of his father and of those Saturdays on the boat. He'd go home after this op. He'd take his pop fishing.

Luis told them a few more local stories. Tourists snapped pictures from the bus's windows. Allison locked eyes with Donovan, then looked away.

They pulled into another parking area. Luis reminded everyone to stay close. The first thing they saw were yellow letters in green shrubbery—The Mayan Cacao Company. To the right of the signage was a brightly colored parrot. More than two feet tall, with a curved beak, it boasted bright red, yellow, and blue plumage. The bird sat on a perch underneath a small thatched roof the size of a dinner plate.

"Follow me, please." Luis stood smiling, waving the group down a trail that turned and twisted through the property. "We'll start first at the *baños*, and when everyone is finished I'll tell you the story of this magnificent mural."

After the group had taken care of their toiletry and regathered near the mural, Luis told them its history. As he was ushering them to the first stop on the chocolate tour, Donovan approached the man and spoke with him. Luis looked skeptical, but he nodded once and proceeded without them.

"What did you tell him?" Allison asked.

"That you were winded and needed to rest a moment."

"I'm not winded."

"Which he seemed to notice, but he let it pass."

They didn't have to wait long. Two couples moseyed by, chatting excitedly and snapping pictures. Finally, an older man with a salt-and-pepper beard approached them. He wore a large, floppy tourist hat and looked to be in his sixties, physically fit, and American.

He assessed them quickly, then spoke in a calm and pleasant voice. "Thank you for meeting me. My name is Edgar Burch. I worked with your father."

Donovan couldn't help noticing that Allison didn't respond to that. She simply stared at the man—her expression frozen, her body frozen, probably the very blood in her veins had frozen at his odd introduction.

"You don't believe me. I get it." Edgar shook his head, sighed, then stepped closer. "His name was Arthur Quinn. He was born in 1958. Worked for the CIA, cyber division before most people knew what *cyber* meant. He was married to—"

Allison held up a hand to stop him. "Anyone could know those things."

"His dark web name was Frodo."

At that, Allison looked too stunned to respond. Donovan thought he should step in. He needed to buy some time and give her a chance to recover. "Why are you here? What do you know about the current attack on the *Harmony*? I assume you do know something if you've tracked us this far."

Edgar glanced at Donovan, nodded, then refocused on Allison. "I'm here to warn you. I'm here because I made a promise to your father."

That pulled her from her reverie. "What promise?"

"To watch over you. Which hasn't been an easy thing to do. Arthur never even considered you'd go into the same business he'd dedicated his life to."

"I work for Homeland Security, not the CIA."

Edgar put out a hand, wiggled it back and forth. "Tomato, tomahto."

A young couple with two small children walked down the trail, peered over at them, then waved merrily. "Beautiful day to taste chocolate," the mother called.

Donovan waved back. After the couple had passed, Allison, Donovan, and Edgar stepped deeper into the shadows.

"You haven't answered my questions," Donovan said, crossing his arms and scowling at the man. He wasn't sure he bought the guy's story. Could he really have known Allison's dad? He certainly looked old enough to have worked with him.

"As I said, I'm here to warn you, Allison. This attack on the *Harmony*, it's serious. The AT hopes to catch the world's attention. They're not playing around. But the catalyst of the attack is you. Someone in middle-earth is targeting you, and I think I know who it is."

"Middle-earth?" Color had flooded back into Allison's face, and she looked ready to tackle a troll if necessary.

"It's the name for their hideout, compound, whatever you want to call it."

"And you know where that is?"

"I don't. I've hacked into their ancillary communication."

"Their what?" Donovan shook his head. This guy was sounding more and more unhinged.

"The boss won't allow any of the workers to have phones on site, but some of the hackers have them. They keep them hidden in the woods or a post office box in the local town. One person keeps his hidden behind a stack of encyclopedias at the library. Anyway. Those communications I have been able to hack."

"You're that good?"

"I am. Your father trained me, after all. He trained me when I first joined the CIA, and then we were partners." He didn't blink, didn't look away from Allison. "And then they killed him."

"What do you know about that?"

"Not enough. I know you were there—camping amongst the redwoods with your father. I know it was a man who did the actual shooting, but someone higher up in the organization ordered the hit."

"Why?"

"Best guess..." Edgar's hands came out to his side, palms up, and his shoulders lifted—the universal sign for *who knows*. "He got too close. Arthur was very good at what he did."

"And you've been following them? Since 1996?"

"When I could. When I wasn't on an active op."

"You're still with the Agency?" Donovan thought that this was at least one aspect of the guy's story that he could verify.

But Edgar shook his head. "Not for years, and I had a different name then. Look. I have to go. Even reaching out here is risky—for both of us."

"You think the Anarchists for Tomorrow have bugged the jungle?"

"I think they have a mandate from on high to catch and kill Allison Quinn. If that means sending drones into a jungle, then sure. They'll do that. Now, I really have to go."

"That's it? A warning to be careful? You didn't have anything else that you wanted to say to me?" Allison looked wary but also somewhat disappointed.

"Look." Edgar tugged his floppy hat lower and peered left, right, then back at Allison. "What they're planning, their great flashy finish, will happen on the return trip. It'll be big. Dustin Cradduck and Eloise Grant have been ordered to stop you—whatever it takes."

"Then I'll get off the ship."

"I thought of that too, but you have to get back home somehow. Fly? They'll make sure that plane never lands. Sail on another ship? You'll be putting the same amount of people in danger. Just different people."

"You think their influence extends that far?" Donovan's anger was percolating, about to boil over, and he honestly didn't know if his target would be the terrorists on the cruise ship or the man standing in front of them.

"It does—unfortunately. There are three operatives on the ship. At least three. Not two. You're aware of Cradduck and Grant. I don't know who the third one is. If I figure it out, I'll be in touch."

Allison cocked her head to the side. "How could you possibly know that?"

"And one more thing. Your task force has someone on the inside. I don't know who, but they've been there a while."

"That's impossible," Allison said. "We would know."

But Donovan wasn't so sure. Not if the person was in deep. Not if sharing that information would put the agent in danger. "There have been rumors," he admitted.

Edgar nodded. "Remember the call you received when the Grand Canyon op first started?"

"The anonymous tip." Allison's voice was softer, smaller.

"The reason we knew about the guy killed outside the park." Donovan flexed the fingers of his left hand. "We were never able to trace down where that came from, but it's how we knew about the guy who was supposed to hike down to Phantom Ranch."

Edgar stuck his hands in his pockets, seemed to weigh something in his mind. Finally, he said, "Mr. Harris. That call came from one of the devices I've been monitoring. It came from inside middle-earth."

"This is a lot," Allison said. "You're asking us to believe you, to base our next move on your information, and we don't even know who you are."

Edgar shrugged. "I'm asking you to be careful. Do it for your old man."

He turned to go, then pivoted back toward Allison, walked closer, and lowered his voice to a near whisper. "Arthur would be proud of you, Allison."

Then he was gone.

The parrot back at the entrance began to squawk, and more tourists walked by, and Donovan wondered if he might have possibly just hallucinated the entire thing.

Allison turned to look at him. Her expression was filled with misery, regret, fear. "I'm the reason. I'm why all of these people are in danger."

"That's not true." Donovan stepped closer. He'd learned that Allison wasn't a touchy-feely kind of person. She didn't allow herself to lower her guard in that way. But he also understood that she'd just been dealt a terrible blow. He reached out with both hands and gently placed them on her arms.

"Look at me, Allison." He waited for her to comply. When she did, he said softly, calmly, "You are not responsible for what these people do. They are insane, unhinged, homicidal maniacs. If they weren't targeting you, they'd be targeting someone else. They would be intent on killing people and bringing down the system whether you were in the picture or not."

She glanced away, swallowed, then looked back at him, some of the old laughter back in her eyes. "Terrible motivational speech, Steele."

"Yeah?" He grinned, looped his arm through hers, and they

went in search of Luis. They needed to get back to the ship, and Luis would know the quickest way.

It was imperative that they be on board before whatever was about to happen was set into play. Once it had been, it might be impossible to reverse. It might be too late—for those on board the *Harmony* and for Allison. Donovan wasn't going to let that happen. He didn't know what it would take to stop this diabolical plan. Hell, he still didn't understand the plan. But he would apprehend the people behind it.

He'd taken a vow to defend the Constitution of the United States against all enemies, and the AT definitely fell into that group. One way or another, this would end before they reached port in Galveston.

Chapter Seventeen

Kate understood that the next thirty-six hours would be difficult. She had a tried-and-true system for rotating her people off two at a time in three-hour shifts. It did no one any good to have a team member falling asleep in front of their terminal. Even hackers needed REM sleep. Without it, they were one keystroke away from a disaster.

She'd sent Julio and George off to catch some winks.

Mike was monitoring any on-ship communications.

Chloe was preparing for the night's fireworks—literally.

Jocelyn monitored and reported on Cradduck and Grant.

Fortunately, for the moment, both John Howard and Stella Gonzalez were in their own private lairs. Kate didn't need them underfoot. She should probably be sleeping herself, but at some point in the last forty-eight hours, things had changed for her. She couldn't eat. Couldn't sleep. Couldn't decide if now was the time to run.

Why now?

She was simply feeling the pressure of the operation. She needed to stay where she was and do her job. She needed to get a grip on her runaway emotions.

Kate walked behind Mike and asked him to scroll back to a

previous transcript between two security guards. The conversation confirmed that the guards aboard the Harmony were on alert to watch for Cradduck and Grant, but Kate knew they wouldn't find those two. They'd disappeared like the sun behind a cloud, and they wouldn't re-appear until they were needed.

Currently, they weren't needed.

The code they'd inserted into the ship's onboard systems allowed for middle-earth to see, and control, every aspect of the *Harmony*. The crew of the ship, Quinn, and Steele didn't understand just how deeply they'd infiltrated the ship's automation. They certainly had no idea that every aspect of the onboard systems had been corrupted. The AT now controlled virtually everything from who heard which coms to what they saw on their screens to how their various systems responded to commands.

In addition, the AT had set off minor operations on a half dozen other ships. It should keep the people at the joint task force headquarters busy. Should keep them distracted.

Kate murmured, "Good work" to Mike, who sat up a little straighter and nodded.

Her team was motivated and ready for the events of the next twelve hours.

They'd prepared for every possible scenario.

"Show me the current location of that storm, Chloe."

"Aye-aye." The team had really picked up on ocean-faring terminology. It was one small way they lightened the tension in the air. If they'd been attacking a corporate entity in New York, they'd all be speaking with a nasally twang.

Chloe threw the live weather feed onto the big screen. The storm approaching the Gulf showed as a long, curved, green monster sporting threatening blobs of red and yellow. It wouldn't actually tip over the *Harmony*, but it would give her crew and guests a helluva ride. And the best part? They'd never know what was coming at them.

"You're absolutely sure they're not seeing this?"

"Correct. We've overlaid their current feed with a previous one. All they're seeing is clear sailing."

"Excellent. And Coast Guard warnings?"

"They won't receive them. On board the *Harmony*, screens are showing a *system temporarily down* message, but the Coast Guard thinks those same messages are going through."

Kate nodded appreciatively. It was amazing what they could change by altering the systems. It wasn't as if they were changing reality. They couldn't create a storm out of thin air. But they could change what the captain and crew perceived to be the weather. Until the storm was close enough to be spotted, they'd have no idea it was barreling their way.

Next, she moved behind Jocelyn, expecting to see two dots on her screen that indicated Cradduck and Grant. Instead, there were three dots.

Three.

Jocelyn tapped her left forefinger against the desk—one, two, three times. Then with her right hand, she clicked the mouse. The third dot disappeared. "Our two cyberbugs are sleeping off a hard night's work," she said almost gaily.

"Good. They've earned the rest."

Despite her words, nothing about what Kate had just seen was good. Did they have three operatives on the ship? And if so, why didn't she know about it? Why would Howard keep something like that from her?

And what did it mean for the people on board the *Harmony*?

That extra dot meant that there was more going on here than what she'd been told. It meant that there was an aspect of this operation she wasn't privy to.

"I'm stepping out for some fresh air." Kate walked casually out of the room, down the hall, and to the front portico, aware that the cameras which were mounted everywhere showed her taking a stroll. Outside the front entrance was where they smoked. Where she pretended to smoke. The portico was something of a joke. It wasn't as if they received visitors at middle-earth, but it was important that the huge facility be made to look like a wealthy person's residence. That, in turn, required a covered entrance for guests.

The Montana sun was setting. Night birds called to one another. A cool breeze sent a shiver snaking down her spine.

What had she seen on Jocelyn's terminal?

John Howard had always been paranoid. He'd prefer to operate his group of terrorists like a Middle Eastern terrorist cell —each group unaware of the other. Kate had insisted that wasn't necessary or pragmatic. Their people operated as a complicated, choreographed machine. Their people needed to know about one another.

John had initially waved away her concerns. It was Brett Lindstrom who had convinced their boss that operational isolation wasn't smart.

But Brett had been killed by Stella.

Kate was on her own here.

Her stomach churned, and her hand shook as she lit her cigarette. The smell only served to nauseate her more, but she inhaled nonetheless. Put on a good show for the cameras. Throughout all of middle-earth there were cameras. John could be watching her now. She needed for him to see a woman badly in need of a smoke. She inhaled, held it, and slowly blew out the smoke. Closed her eyes as if in satisfaction.

Her mind went back to the Grand Canyon op.

John had inserted operatives as backups to his backups. Operatives that he hadn't told her or Stella about. Was it possible that he'd done the same thing again?

And if so—why?

What was he actually planning?

Just as importantly, what could she, Kate Jackson, do about it? She'd been in the room when Brett was murdered. Stella operated on instinct alone, and the woman was as quick and dangerous as a viper. Kate would need to move very carefully now if she hoped to outsmart Stella and John.

Over four thousand people.

Surely he wouldn't . . .

But even as she stubbed out her cigarette, then picked it up and dropped it in the *BUTTS* receptacle, she knew that he would. If he thought it would bring him one step closer to *Freeing the People* (always spoken in capital letters and with italics) from the tyranny of their government and the oppressiveness of technology. If he thought that was possible there wasn't a single thing he wouldn't do.

She forced her heart rate to slow as she fingered the pack of cigarettes, hopefully looking as if she were contemplating just one more.

There were very few things she could know for certain, but she could make an educated guess. A third operative meant that there was some aspect of this op she wasn't aware of. Some aspect John didn't want her aware of, which meant he thought she'd push back.

He planned to kill them. He planned to kill all of them.

She couldn't know that for certain, but it felt correct.

Now the question was how he intended to do it.

Kate needed to know that before she could stop him. If she could stop him. If she even dared to try.

Chapter Eighteen

Allison and Donovan attempted to contact Kendra Thomas, but they were patched through to her assistant.

"We're ninety-five percent certain this is a multi-ship event now. She's receiving reports and coordinating."

"Have her call us as soon as she's able," Donovan barked. Then added, more civilly, "Please."

"Will do."

Allison walked out onto the balcony.

Donovan joined her.

"We need to find the third person," she said.

"Agreed." Donovan leaned his forearms against the railing. "The question is, do we tell Captain McKinley and Becca Price what we think we know?"

"What do you think?"

He blew out a breath, then stood up straight. "I say no. Until we have more to go on, they couldn't do any type of search."

"Agreed."

"And it's always possible that McKinley or Price is the third person."

"Hard to imagine."

"Indeed."

They spent the next three hours searching for Cradduck and Grant. Find the two terrorists they knew about, and odds were they'd also find the third. They checked every corner of every lounge on the ship, stopping at the piano bar to check in again with Jeremy. Checked the pool deck. Checked the dining areas. There was no sign of either one of the terrorists. The ship's computer system showed they had not deboarded at Cozumel, which meant nothing since Eloise could erase any records as soon as they were made.

But they wouldn't leave the ship now.

Not before the big event.

How did they expect to get off afterwards? Jump in the waters of the Gulf and swim away? Be picked up by a water taxi? Allison's questions only multiplied as the day went on.

After speaking with Price and Ferguson, Donovan confirmed that nothing untoward had happened while they were in Cozumel. All systems were up and running as they should.

"Almost like we imagined it," Allison growled as they made their way back to the room.

"Except we didn't."

They changed into jeans and clean shirts for the evening's festivities, which Allison hoped would include finding and apprehending two—maybe three—terrorists.

Allison and Donovan had paused beside the bank of elevators when Allison looked over to where Anna Lee and Mary Beth sat.

The older women were waving their arms, not up high but in front of them at waist level.

Being covert?

Being careful.

Anna Lee held up her left hand as if to block prying gazes and pointed across the deck, across the open area that dropped to the Promenade. She pointed at a man who must have just walked past her and then continued on to the opposite side of the semicircular balcony. He stood there now, staring at his phone. His

AGAINST ALL ENEMIES

demeanor was calm. Cool. Deadly. Finally, he looked straight up, tilting his head back, smiling.

It was Dustin Cradduck. He was completely preoccupied with something connected to his phone. Allison looked up, then reached out for Donovan's arm. Cradduck was maneuvering a drone at the top of the massive open area in the middle of the ship.

Cradduck must have sensed their gazes on him. He shot a glance across at them, saw Allison and Donovan, and smiled.

"Go left. I'll go right." Donovan sprinted down the hall.

Allison dashed back to the library and past the ladies who were shouting, "Hurry. Get him." Guests hopped out of the way as she tore toward the balcony area and came to a sudden stop.

Cradduck was gone.

She stood there, trying to logically decide his most likely route of escape, when booms and blasts echoed through the ship. The lights shut off, plunging them into darkness. Suddenly, colored starbursts and streamers filled the interior of the ship.

Cradduck had set off a spectacular fireworks show.

The guests and crew pointed and cheered and oohed and ahhed and applauded. On every deck, where the halls and libraries and elevators looked down onto the promenade, people crammed together, pointing up, cheering at the fireworks.

Donovan pushed in beside Allison and said in a low voice, "Laser light show."

Red, white, and blue beams danced and soared over the passengers. Cradduck had also activated a haze machine, which gave the entire display a misty, ethereal feel. No fire alarms went off because there was no fire. It was all sleight of hand. But what was the point?

People cheered even more loudly as a bass drum kicked up a beat. Bruce Springsteen's *Born In the U.S.A.* was suddenly pumped at full volume through the ship's sound system. The crowd went wild. Clapping. Singing. Stomping their feet.

And then the show stopped, as suddenly as it had begun, and

a single line of text was displayed throughout the ship—sometimes stationary and splayed against a wall, sometimes twisting and turning, sometimes enlarging then shrinking back down.

They all said the same thing.

The same single line.

You deserve to be free.

And next to those five words, branches of a tree, roots that turned into a sword, Elvish writing—the entire thing reminiscent of Tolkien. A master writer's symbol that had been adopted by the Anarchists for Tomorrow.

The lights came back on, and the people began to disperse like a flock of birds—chattering to and with and over one another.

"They're all on their phones," Allison said. "They're all posting to social media and emailing friends and sending pictures to family. They're spreading the AT's message."

"Farther and wider and faster than the AT ever could."

Allison and Donovan made their way back to the library group, which was now a group of seven—Anna Lee and Mary Beth, Charlotte and Pat, Robin and Debbie, and another woman they hadn't met. The group stopped talking and froze when Allison and Donovan approached.

The new woman, holding on to a blinged-out walking cane broke the silence. "I'm Ava. That was something. Better than the Fourth of July celebration back home. But I have a feeling this wasn't a celebration so much as it was a warning of some sort."

"You didn't catch him," Anna Lee said.

"We were so hoping you would." Mary Beth twisted her hands together. "He's a wily one."

"What is this all about?" Robin glared at them both. "Why would you ask my mother to help you locate someone?"

And then they all began talking at once.

"Ladies, if you'll just . . . Ladies." Donovan raised his hands for quiet at the same moment that Allison let out a shrill whistle.

"Stop talking and listen." Allison had the terrible feeling that this was all spinning out of control.

"We want to know what's going on," Debbie said.

"And we will tell you," Allison said. "We'll tell you what we can, but not here."

They relocated to a back corner of the library. Allison explained about seeing Mary Beth and Anna Lee sitting in front of the balcony, about their need to find Cradduck and Grant, and about her idea that possibly they could help.

"A cruise ship has a lot of surveillance. Literally hundreds of cameras. But you asked my mother to help instead." Robin looked as if she was about to report them to the captain. She'd pulled out her phone and was tapping her forefinger against it. "I want to know what's really going on, and what the ship's crew is doing about it, and who you two really are."

Donovan held out his hands, patting them downward as if he were pushing against a rising tide. "I understand your concern, but—"

"Do you have a mother on this cruise ship? I didn't think so. Then don't say you understand my concern."

Mary Beth smiled broadly at her daughter.

The other women looked on with something like a mixture of admiration and solidarity. This was a tight group. Allison realized in that moment that while they couldn't be sure about any of the crew members or even most of the guests, this group was definitely not part of the AT network. No way. Huh-uh. She'd bet Aunt Polly's ranch on that.

"They're cyberterrorists," Allison explained. "Usually, their methods are limited to hacking into companies or government entities. But this group . . . they take it farther. They take it to the real world."

"And now they've taken it to our cruise ship," Debbie said. "I was kinda bored with playing bingo and watching shows anyway. Maybe we can help."

Allison glanced at Donovan, who shrugged and then nodded.

"Anna Lee and Mary Beth, do you still have the photos we AirDropped to you?"

Both women held up their phones.

"Share them with the group as well as our cell phone numbers. If you see or hear anything—"

"See something. Say something." Pat nodded so vigorously that her earrings jostled.

"And pray. We need to be praying about this," Charlotte added.

"Contact us immediately if you do."

"Unless we can stop them," Debbie said.

"No. Absolutely not." Allison tried to quell their enthusiasm with a steely glare. It was less effective than she hoped.

Donovan cleared his throat, and they turned as one to look at him. He checked to make sure no one else was within earshot. "The fireworks did not constitute the attack. That was merely the AT getting everyone's attention. If the real thing happens, you can bet that all communications will be jammed."

"What do we do then?" Anna Lee demanded.

"Stay out of harm's way. Lock yourself in your cabins if you need to. Tell those around you to do the same."

"If it's a cyber-attack, then they could unlock all the cabin doors," Robin pointed out.

"Then we'll put a chair under the door handle," Debbie said. "I'd like to see them cyber their way through that."

"The AT is trying to make a point," Allison said. "They have no reason to hurt the guests or the crew on this ship. They have no reason to turn this into something violent."

Her mind flashed back on the two bodies in the freezer. Collateral damage—she hoped. "They also have no scruples. Be careful. Be vigilant. Be smart."

"You could be a recruiter for whatever agency you work for," Debbie said and laughed nervously. "I'm ready to sign up for Team Allison!"

"What do we do in the meantime?" Robin asked. "Before the coms go down."

"Other than be careful and vigilant and smart, which I might add we always are." Ava tapped her cane against the floor for emphasis.

"Go about your normal activities. If you do happen to see something—"

"Say something," they replied in chorus.

The group of women formed a sort of circle, and although they wore expressions of concern, Allison thought they also looked excited. Of course, they were. To them, this must have been like having three minutes in a scene of their favorite police drama.

But Allison knew it was more than that.

Despite what she had said to them, she had the terrible feeling that this particular op would bridge the gap between the cyber world and the real one. She had a dreadful certainty that this was about to *get real* in a very grim sort of way.

One by one, the seven women put their right hand in the middle—one on top of the other, like some sort of all-girl, senior-citizen, football team.

"Well," Mary Beth looked up and smiled. "You're with us, right?"

So Allison and Donovan added their right hands on top of the others.

"On three," Debbie said. "Team Allison. One, two, three . . . Team Allison!"

Donovan and Allison walked to the stairs in silence, thumbing through messages from the crew.

"The fireworks were not ours." ~Price

"All systems are functioning normally." ~Ferguson

"I can't find any evidence of the program you wrote." ~Lilith

"What the hell is happening?" ~Captain McKinley

Allison stuffed her phone into her pocket and turned to Donovan. "Do you have anything from Thomas?"

"I do not."

"Odd."

"More than odd, though we can't really know what's happening on other ships."

"Right."

They made their way to a quiet spot across from the main help desk. Allison could hear people congratulating the ship's personnel on the fireworks display. She didn't expect the celebratory mood would last long. She was certain they hadn't seen the last of the AT's handiwork.

Donovan thought maybe they needed to be more pro-active. He thought that up to this point, they were simply responding to the AT's provocations. It was time to be offensive not defensive.

When he said as much to Allison, she rolled her eyes. "Another football analogy? Really?"

He only shrugged and waited.

"You're right, of course. Tell me what you had in mind."

"There are two good-sized theaters on this ship. The main theater is where they do the comedy show and music shows. It's called the Starlight Pavilion." He nodded toward the bow of the ship. "It holds the largest number of guests. Five stories from the orchestra pit to the domed ceiling, plus backstage dressing areas."

"Okay."

"The Winter Wonder Showcase is at the other end." He jerked

his thumb toward the stern. "It holds half as many, but still quite a few. Most shows, they have to turn people away."

"How do you know all this?"

"Read the brochure. Plus, I used to—"

"Cruise a lot. With the cruise girlfriend. Got it." Allison stretched her neck to the left then the right. "Both places have a captive audience."

"Exactly."

Allison sighed and rubbed her hands over her face.

"You okay?"

"Fine. Just frustrated."

"Same."

"Walking around randomly isn't working."

"Agree."

She stood and scowled in the direction of the front of the ship, then toward the back, then directly at Donovan.

"Ice show starts in ten minutes."

"Let's go."

Donovan took one side of the theater. Allison took the other. As he'd predicted, the place was packed. Every seat was filled. They couldn't possibly scan the crowd and pick out Cradduck or Grant. But then Donovan didn't think they'd be sitting in the crowd. He thumbed a text to Allison.

"I'm going up to the lighting booth."

"I'll head backstage."

Either location would be a perfect spot to launch an attack from, but they didn't find the two terrorists in either place.

As the lights went down and the spotlights came up and the music swelled, they walked out of the theater.

"Not ice show fans, I guess."

"Which leaves the Starlight Pavilion." As they walked to the other end of the ship, Donovan thought back to his previous cruise vacations. Cruising was something that he probably wouldn't have done on his own, but his girlfriend at the time—Danielle—had loved cruising. So he cruised. It wasn't a huge sacrifice to make. He'd sat through many a show and had always found them to be entertaining. The large number of talented entertainers on a cruise ship had always fascinated him. He supposed it was a pretty good gig.

Room and board—covered.

Food—all you can eat.

Drinks—probably comped.

Off time—spent sunning on the deck.

No responsibilities or traffic jams. Send your dirty clothes down to the ship's laundry.

They walked through the center pair of double doors, and Allison stopped in her tracks. You could read about a thing, but it was different when you saw it in person. The Starlight Pavilion was huge. Red velvet seats fanned away from the stage and up toward the rafters. The place was packed. The tourists in rousing good spirits after the surprise fireworks show. The mood was one of giddy anticipation.

"They'll do it here." Allison's voice was a whisper, her words a reaffirmation to herself. Then she glanced at Donovan.

"Do what?"

"I wish I knew."

The energy of the crowd was contagious. Allison stood straighter. Her gaze scanned the people slowly, carefully. She was in the zone. It came off of her like ripples from a rock tossed into a vast sea.

And he felt it too. That quickening of the pulse. A prickling sensation at the base of his neck. They had both been trained well. Hell, they'd been trained to be the best. And they were. But this? What was happening now? This was pure instinct. Donovan realized that Allison was spot on. Whatever was next, it would happen here, in this theater, in the midst of these guests.

He stepped closer. "Should we evacuate?"

She shook her head. "They'd still do it, and we have no idea where their backup location is. Plus, we could be wrong."

"We're not wrong."

"Nope. I'll go right." And then she was gone, weaving through the rows of seats.

Donovan went left.

The lights came down and the music swelled. Tina, the cruise director, strode out to thunderous applause. The spotlight followed her to the center of the stage, where she entertained the guests with a little self-deprecating humor and several cruise jokes.

"Where do sick cruise ships go?" Three-second pause. "The dock." A rimshot from the drummer in the orchestra pit followed. The crowd groaned, then laughed.

"How small are the showers in cruise cabins?" This time a whisper of laughter flowed through the crowd before she shared the punch line. Tina laughed, stepped closer to the orchestra pit, and said, "Good crowd tonight."

The drummer was joined by the bass player—just a short rift that anteed up the energy level a bit more.

"Cruise cabin showers are so small, it's easier to soap the walls and spin." She raised her voice to be heard above the laughter and applause. "And now for tonight's performance by the *Harmony*'s fabulous orchestra and dancers. We hope you enjoy this performance of Timeless Rockin' Rhythms."

The theater was plunged into darkness, colored lights came up, and fourteen people appeared on the stage. The first number was *Johnny B. Goode*. By the time Donovan reached the end of his section, they'd moved into *Roll Over Beethoven*.

Donovan scanned the crowd, the orchestra pit, the stage. He spotted Allison on the opposite side of the room. The floor vibrated from the stomping of the crowd, the rhythm of the orchestra, and the dancing on the stage. The Chuck Berry song moved seamlessly into *Great Balls of Fire*.

He looked back toward Allison, but she had moved. For one heart-stopping second, he couldn't locate her. Then he saw that she was climbing a ladder attached to the back wall. At the top of it was a platform, a dancer, and a cable that stretched to the far side of the stage. The singer, who had been positioned there, launched himself off the platform and smoothly glided across the stage, singing and spreading his arms wide to *Rock Around the Clock*.

Donovan wouldn't have thought the crowd could grow louder, but it did—clapping, whistling, hollering as the beat went on. He pulled out his phone, texted.

"What are you doing?"

But Allison didn't answer. He watched in horror as she stood on the platform, wrapped what looked like a hand towel over the cable, and hurled herself toward the stage.

He didn't call out or gasp or cover his eyes.

Donovan wanted to do all of those things, but in that moment, his training as an agent overrode his instincts as a man. He pulled his weapon, pointed it toward the area of the stage that Allison was approaching, and assumed a shooter's stance.

She was moving toward something.

She was moving toward someone.

She'd perceived a threat and was intent on stopping it. Cradduck? Most likely. Donovan didn't see Grant making such a bold move. No, Grant was the techie of this pair. So maybe it was Cradduck. Or the third terrorist.

No one noticed him standing there with his weapon drawn.

No one was paying the least bit of attention to him.

Their eyes were on the performance. They'd applauded enthusiastically as the dancer swooped across the stage. When Allison slid down the cable—dressed in her distressed blue jeans and blingy top, brown curls bouncing, eyes locked on the far side of the stage—they went berserk. Calling out. Cheering. Applauding.

The dancers looked up in surprise, and the orchestra continued to play *Jailhouse Rock*, no doubt unaware of the scene that was playing out above them.

Donovan heard the unmistakable sound of a gun being shot.

He couldn't see Allison.

He couldn't tell who had fired the weapon or if anyone had been hit. He holstered his Sig Sauer and took off at a sprint. Down the aisle. Past the guests. Up the stairs. Finally, he bolted onto the stage. Scanned from right to left and spotted Allison, crumpled in a dark corner, as the dancers danced and the musicians played and the crowd continued to applaud.

Chapter Nineteen

Allison fought the powerful urge to pull her weapon and wave it at the people around her. They were here to help. She understood that. But she needed them to step back and let her do her job.

"You're sure it isn't broken?" Donovan asked.

"Her shoulder slipped out of the socket. It should feel better now that I've popped it back in place." Dr. Mbachu peered at her as if she were a human lie detector. "Does it feel better, Allison?"

"Feels fine. Now let's go and get Cradduck."

"Hang on a minute." Donovan positioned himself in front of her. He literally blocked her exit.

They were in a small changing room that barely held the three of them. She could feel the thump of the orchestra through the floor, hear the crowd singing Little Richie's *Tutti Fruitti*.

"Tell us again what happened," Donovan said.

She didn't know if he was testing her memory, worried she'd suffered a concussion, or was simply stalling. Pacifying him would be quicker than arguing with him. Donovan had to be one of the most stubborn agents she'd ever had the misfortune of working with.

"I saw Cradduck. He had a gun. I couldn't very well just yell *gun*, now could I? With that crowd?" She nodded toward the audience, still enjoying Timeless Rockin' Rhythms. "I looked up, saw the dancer on the platform, figured if he could do it then so could I."

"Where did you get the towel?" Donovan scowled at her, plainly not satisfied with her story.

"Before I climbed up the ladder. Took it off one of the servers who was walking by with a tray of drinks. Look, Donovan. I'm fine. I didn't hurt my hands." She held them out, palms up, as proof. "When I saw that he was going to shoot, I pulled up my knees, let go of the towel, dropped, and rolled."

"And dislocated your shoulder."

Donovan's words should have been a shout. She could have handled a shout. But instead, they were a plea. Allison saw that. Saw the worry and the fear. She understood that somewhere on this op, their distant yet at times strangely compelling relationship had morphed into something else. They weren't merely co-workers. They were partners.

And possibly more.

"Donovan's point, which I think is a good one, seems to be that you could have been shot, Allison." Dr. Mbachu tsked, even as she closed up her medical kit. "If it swells, put ice on it."

"You heard her." Now Allison did push past him. "If it swells, I'll put ice on it."

"Wait," Donovan said. "How did he miss you? If he was aiming at you—"

"He wasn't. Not at first, anyway. When I saw the gun it was pointed toward the side of the stage, in the direction the cruise director walked off."

"Tina?" Mbachu shook her head in surprise. "That would make quite a statement, to kill the cruise director on stage."

"Okay. You think he was aiming at Tina, you scamper up the ladder, which must have taken thirty seconds—"

"I'm faster than that."

"Say twenty then. Plenty of time for Cradduck to get off a shot."

"Maybe the dancers were in the way," Mbachu said. "Maybe he was waiting for the perfect moment."

"He spies you coming toward him." Donovan turned as if he could see the setup of the stage, which he couldn't. There were costumes and stage props and walls between them and the show. "You're a clear target. All he has to do is change his focus, move the sight of the gun a few inches, and take you out."

"That's why I pulled my knees up," Allison admitted. "To make myself a smaller target."

"What aren't you telling us?"

Allison's frustration peaked. "I clocked him. Okay? I clocked him with my feet and the gun went off. You'll probably find the bullet up in the ceiling. Then I let go of the towel, landed on my shoulder, rolled, and when I got up, he was gone."

"Why didn't you say that to start with?"

"Because my job is to stop him, Donovan. And I failed. Now can we just get on with this?"

"Yeah," he said. "Let's go get this guy, and when we do, I get a shot at clocking him."

"Or shooting him. You could do that."

"I just might."

They were out of the theater and nearly to the piano bar when Allison skidded to a stop and did an about-face. "Where's Price? Where's Captain McKinley?"

"Huh?"

"A gun went off in there." She waved her hand toward the theater. Those folks were true believers of the show must go on. Because it was. Literally. Going on. "Why has no one followed up on that?"

"Maybe they're not aware."

"Mbachu was there."

"In the audience. In case any of the dancers twisted an ankle. She said she attends when she's able."

"You know a lot about her."

"I asked while you were out."

"I wasn't out."

"So you remember the conversation?"

"No. I guess I was out."

They both pulled out their phones. Nothing. No messages. No missed calls. No texts.

"No service," Allison said.

"How's that possible?"

And then their eyes locked. So it had begun—this time in earnest. This time was the real thing. Allison didn't know how she knew that, but she knew. Everything that had happened up until then—the intrusion at the 70s disco dance, the lights out, the elevator problems, the fireworks show, the computer glitches. It had all been leading to this.

Donovan stuck his phone in his pocket and strode toward the piano bar.

"We really don't have time for a drink."

Jeremy nodded hello, held up a finger without missing a note, and finished his song, which was aptly Billy Joel's *Piano Man*. "Back after a ten-minute break, folks." Immediately, smooth jazz flowed from the overhead speakers, and the folks in the bar upped the volume of their conversations.

Jeremy picked up his iPad and motioned toward a booth. The three of them piled into the semi-circular seats. Jeremy on one side. Allison and Donovan on the other. Raquel brought a glass of ice, his bottle of whiskey, and two waters.

"Join us?" Jeremy snagged her hand, held it in his.

"Can't. I'm working, but eventually I need to meet these new friends of yours." Raquel winked, then walked back behind the bar.

Allison drank down half the glass of water.

"What's wrong with you?" Jeremy stared at her and waited.

"What do you mean, what's wrong with me?" She put all the hostility she could muster into the question.

"You're holding your shoulder funny."

"Am not."

Jeremy glanced at Donovan, eyebrows raised as he took another sip of the whiskey. "Okay."

"Have you seen our guys? Guy and gal?" Donovan asked.

"Nope."

"You're sure?"

"I'm sure." He tapped his temple. "Memorized their features."

"Our phones are out." Donovan glanced around the bar.

Allison did the same. At least half of the patrons were on their phones. "Is yours working?"

The piano man pulled it out of his jacket pocket. Allison had noticed that he was quite the nappy dresser. She supposed it was the only expense of his job. Other than the iPad.

"Seems to be," he said.

"And your iPad. Is it working?"

"Yup."

"You're sure?"

"I'm sure. But here, look for yourself..." He pushed it across the table to her.

She tapped and scrolled and refreshed. "He's right. It's working."

"So they're targeting our phones," Donovan said.

"They have our numbers."

"Yeah. Which means they've probably cracked the software lock too."

Allison and Donovan were silent, trying to envision what that meant. What information had the AT harvested from their phones? And how would they get in touch with Kendra Thomas?

"Thomas has probably already answered our message," Allison said. "They're diverting our texts."

"She'll notice when we don't respond."

"Unless they respond for us."

"How can someone respond for you?" Jeremy asked, refreshing his drink and then offering the bottle to Allison and Donovan, who both declined.

Donovan pulled in a deep breath, again scanned the crowd, and said, "Pretty easy with all the AI programs available. Feed in our past messages, then tell AI to answer in the manner that we would."

"It can do that?"

"Sure. We thought we were struggling against disinformation with the rise of social media." Donovan tapped the table. "Deception and misinformation have always been hard to separate from the truth. AI will make it exponentially more difficult."

At that point, a twenty-something guy who looked like he spent way too much time in the gym jogged into the bar area. "Something's happening outside. Something big. You have to see this." And without another word, he dashed away.

Allison and Donovan were out of the booth before the guy finished talking.

Donovan turned to Jeremy. "You coming?"

"Nope. Think I'll stay here and finish my drink."

"Keep your eyes peeled."

"Will do."

By the time they reached the doors that opened out onto the deck, quite the crowd had built up.

"What's happening?" Allison asked the couple beside her.

"Big storm," the man said.

And when he said that, Allison became aware of a slight tilting in the ship. Or was she imagining that?

A woman near the front grimaced. "I guess it came up all of a sudden. One of those rogue storms you hear about."

"Stay inside, and you'll be fine," Donovan said.

The word *fine* had barely left his mouth when all of the monitors, and they seemed to be everywhere, switched to a view of the pool deck. The lounge chairs were held in place by a long cable snaking through them. It helped during a storm, but its primary purpose was to keep people from moving the deck furniture around. That cable was no match for the wind and the waves. As they watched, one lounge chair was buffeted to the left and right, then snatched away. With the cable broken, the rest of the chairs sailed across the open area, then disappeared into the darkness.

A few passengers had been caught outdoors unaware of what was barreling toward them. Now they tried to walk toward the doors, but the wind pushed against them. They leaned into it, and suddenly a piece of debris struck one of the men. He staggered, then dropped to his knees. Several people in the crowd where Allison and Donovan were standing gasped. A few tried to call the ship's emergency number with their phones.

Allison was sure those calls were blocked.

The AT wouldn't let them call for help, and the AT, for the moment, were the ones calling the shots.

"We need to get up there," Donovan growled.

They hit the stairs at a run. Five minutes later, they turned the corner on the correct floor and jogged toward the front of the ship, where the pools were, where the video was being shot from, and where the captain's bridge was located.

Donovan had no trouble pushing through the crowd. He was a big guy, and Allison was suddenly grateful for that. She would have found a way to plow through, but it wouldn't have been easy. Allison was the quarterback, and Donovan was the center, clearing a path for her.

Good grief. She was thinking in football analogies.

Maybe she'd been around Donovan too long.

Dr. Mbachu and two of her medics had beat them to what looked like a triage area.

"Anyone else out there?" Donovan asked.

"Yes. A mother and father. They're trying to reach their child." Mbachu never looked up from her patient. The man had a large gash on his head that was bleeding profusely.

The doctor's manner was calm, her voice matter of fact. "Toward the bow. Starboard side."

They had no trouble making their way to the doors that led into the pool area. All the passengers on this deck had moved away from there as if afraid the storm would push its way through the doors to the interior of the ship. The monitors continued to play a live feed, but Allison didn't pause to look at it.

She thought she understood what they were headed into.

And she didn't hesitate to go where she was needed.

Then they stepped in front of the sensor, the automatic doors swooshed open, and she was hit with the fury of the storm.

Donovan was an expert swimmer, thanks to his training as well as all those days on the lake with his dad. He had great respect for the water but no fear of it. He'd never been frightened by storms —atmospheric disturbances that sometimes included dangerous amounts of rain, high winds, hail, and plummeting temperatures.

Plummeting temperatures—like the night he'd spent on top of a mountain in Washington State. Trapped in a snowstorm. Cut off from all communication. Allison injured and drifting in and out of consciousness.

They stepped onto the deck, and that moment bled into this one.

He had to look at Allison. He had to confirm that there was no blood running from her shoulder. That she was alive and vibrant and at his side. She gave him a thumbs up, and they pushed out into the storm.

The wind was like a hand intent on shoving them back.

The rain fell so hard that he quickly lost sight of everything except Allison. She'd pulled one of the bright orange lifebuoys from the wall and held it to her chest. They fought their way forward. Pressed on toward the bridge and the starboard side of the ship. They were soaked to the skin. The temperature must have dropped twenty degrees. To think that only hours before, they'd been walking through the balmy streets of Cozumel.

They weren't in Cozumel anymore.

They were in the middle of the Gulf—six hundred thousand square miles of water that at its deepest was over fourteen thousand feet. They were surrounded from top to bottom and side to side by water.

Waves crashed over the boat with the fury of a tempest intent on destruction. The deck rose and dropped beneath their feet. Still, they staggered forward. And then, over the wind and the waves, he heard it—the terrible scream of a mother. The agonizing cries of a father. And below all of that, the sobs of a small child.

The parents didn't look surprised to see Donovan and Allison appear out of the storm. Perhaps they'd been waiting on help. Maybe they were in such shock that a leviathan rising out of the water wouldn't have baffled them.

The father shouted to make his voice carry over the storm. "She's at the top of the water slide."

They had obviously been trying to reach her, but had been pushed back by the storm again and again. The father's arm hung limply at his side, quite obviously broken. Perhaps he'd been struck by one of the airborne chairs. Maybe he'd slipped on the deck and crashed hard against it.

The mother looked to be six months pregnant. She screamed her child's name repeatedly. "Nevaeh. Nevaeh." Her voice was ragged. Her face, a mask of terror.

Nevaeh.

Heaven spelled backwards.

The sheer agony of her scream was a sound that Donovan feared would follow him into his dreams.

Allison didn't even hesitate. She plunged forward toward the water slide.

Donovan had wondered about Allison's weight before. Not

aloud, of course. His mother had raised him better than that. He wasn't sure that she topped one thirty. The waves could easily push her over.

"I'll go," he shouted.

But Allison was already gone. Clawing her way around the swimming pool, heading for the stairs of the giant slide that must have looked like paradise to a young child. The stairs seemed as if they could touch the stars if there had been any stars to reach.

Donovan caught up with his partner, pulled her back, pulled her close, and pointed toward the covered slide. She nodded, and they changed direction.

The slide itself was curved and orange, and the rain was pouring down it like a fast-running river. But once they climbed inside, the wind stopped buffeting them. He could hear the cries of the child more clearly now.

"She's inside it," Allison said.

"At the top." Donovan had to work to keep up with Allison, who scampered up the slick surface as easily as a monkey climbs a tree. He could hear her talking to the girl before he rounded the last corner. And then he was there with them. Allison held a trembling and frightened Nevaeh in her arms. The girl had thrown her arms around Allison's neck.

"I need you to let go, honey. So I can put this around you. It's a lifebuoy. It'll protect you."

The girl was having none of it. She clung to Allison like Allison was the life preserver, not the orange ring.

"Hang on." Donovan squeezed up so that he was just below them. The noise of the storm was terrific, the wind and rain threatening to tear the slide from its mooring. He prayed it would hold. A few more minutes was all they'd need. Once he was as close as he could possibly get, Donovan took the ring from her. "Hold her close."

One woman. One child. One lifebuoy. It would have to be enough. He snugged the ring around the two of them. Pushed it down far enough that both Allison's and Nevaeh's arms could pop out and over the ring.

"Good?"

"Yeah. We're good."

Two large, round, brown eyes stared at Donovan. "I'm scared."

"Yup. Me, too. You're Nevaeh, right?"

"Yeah."

"Good to meet you, Nevaeh. I'm Donovan. That's Allison."

The girl nodded, tears still streaming down her face.

"Your parents sent us to get you."

"My mom and dad?" The girl's eyes widened even more.

"Yup. Your mom and dad are waiting. We need to go down this slide and across to the doors."

Nevaeh shook her head, then began crying again.

"Honey, I'm not going to let anything happen to you." Allison tightened her arms around the girl.

"Allison's going to hold on to you, and I'm going to block the wind. Sound good?"

"I guess." The girl rubbed her nose with the heel of her palm, then patted Allison's hand.

Allison looked at him and rolled her eyes as if to say, *what's a person to do?* And he knew then. He knew they'd be all right. They'd fight their way back across the deck. Reunite Nevaeh with her mom and dad. Get the entire family inside to Mbachu's triage center. Then, he and Allison were going to find Cradduck and Grant and kick some ass. The AT didn't create the storm, but they damn sure messed with every monitoring system on board the ship.

They put the crew and the passengers in danger.

They put Nevaeh in danger.

It was time that this particular cyber operation ended.

He fought to control their descent, which was no easy thing to do inside the slide's protective shell, a torrent of water running under them. He pushed his arms and legs against the plastic of the slide's cover at every turn, waiting to feel the presence of Allison and Nevaeh before moving on. It took a lifetime. It took less than a minute.

When they popped out at the bottom, the storm had intensified. It was as if they were in the center of a monsoon. The wind was behind them now, so he moved Allison and Nevaeh in front and did all he could to temper the force of the wind and the rain.

More than one piece of deck furniture slammed into his body. He was bruised, soaked, exhausted. He was pretty sure he'd wake up the next day sore in places he hadn't been sore since high school football. And none of that mattered.

It was worth every bit of pain and discomfort when he saw the expression on Nevaeh's face. When he saw her parents shout, then weep. When they were finally back inside the ship, and he pulled the lifebuoy off of Allison, and Nevaeh literally threw herself into her parents' arms. He felt that rush of satisfaction of knowing that this day, for this moment, he and Allison had made a difference.

They handed the family off to Mbachu. She paused long enough to say, "Captain McKinley wants to see you on the bridge."

"Good." Allison squeezed water out of her hair. "Because that was our next stop."

There was a private staircase and elevator that led to the bridge. They chose the stairs, which required a card swipe to gain entrance. Once there, they jogged down the hall, swiped their way onto the bridge, and skidded to a stop at the total chaos that greeted them.

The storm, if anything, was more startling here than it had been when they were out in it. Because here, in this room with floor-to-ceiling windows to the port, the bow, and the starboard, a person understood the big picture.

And it was terrifying.

Monitors on the wall were blank except for a message which read:

We Will Be Free.
AT

The wind pummeled the windows, and the window's wipers —like a car's but much larger—were no match. Lightning occasionally slashed across the sky, revealing waves larger than the boat, rain falling in torrents, and a vast expanse of water with no sign of any other vessel.

Donovan knew at a glance that all systems were down.

Weather radar—off.

Dynamic positioning system—off.

Satellite navigation system—off.

Ballast control, bow thrusters, propulsion—all off.

The bridge was literally full of people. Captain McKinley, two deck officers, two able seamen, several of the security crew, and the staff captain. A frenzy of activity permeated the space, but the men and women were stoically going about their tasks. No one on this bridge was panicking.

Captain McKinley was speaking with the lookout, who peered through a pair of binoculars even as he explained that he couldn't see a thing. When McKinley looked up, Donovan saw the weight and the fear that the man carried.

The lives he was responsible for.

The sense of failure.

Donovan jerked his head to the right, and the Captain met them near the sitting area. No one sat. No one spoke—at first.

McKinley ran a hand around the back of his neck. "I don't understand how this happened. Our radar was clear. Coast Guard sent us nothing. Other ships, again, nothing."

"They looped in old footage on your radar. And they've blocked communication from the Coast Guard as well as other ships." Allison lowered her voice. "I suspect they've even sent responses, represented themselves as you. That way the Coast Guard wouldn't come looking."

"They can do that?"

"They can, and they have. This isn't your fault, Captain. This is the AT's fault, and they are the ones responsible."

"No. I'm responsible. Don't you get that? I am responsible for every man, woman, and child on this ship." His gaze went to the windows, to the behemoth surrounding them. "I'm responsible, and there's not a damn thing I can do right now."

"Actually, there is." Donovan worked to keep his voice calm but forceful. McKinley wasn't used to taking orders from anyone. At the same time, the man looked as if he'd jump at any chance to ensure the safety of his crew, passengers, and ship. "Move everyone to the center of the ship—away from windows, balcony doors, anything that might break."

"And put them where?"

"In the halls," Allison said. "Interior rooms. Libraries. Public areas."

"Then ride it out. This ship is heavy. It was built to withstand a storm."

McKinley nodded in agreement. "It may tilt. It is tilting. But you're right. We won't capsize."

Donovan nodded toward the other crew members. "You have a solid crew here. Is your bearing repeater still functioning?"

"Yes."

"Then navigate manually."

"That's what we've been doing. The problem is that we don't know which direction this storm is going."

"You can make an educated guess," Allison said. "The wind is coming from the north. I know that because we were on the pool deck and could barely walk to the bow of the ship."

"Rescuing a child. We saw you." For maybe the first time, there was a note of respect in his voice.

"The waves are higher on the starboard side. Nearly washed us off the deck." Donovan waited for McKinley to meet his gaze. "Maintain a northern heading. Navigate into the storm and ride it out. When did this start?"

"Forty-five minutes ago."

"Then it will be gone in another forty-five, an hour at the most."

"You don't know that."

"I don't. We work with the information we have. Right now, we don't have a hell of a lot. You can't outrun it. Steer into it."

"Okay." McKinley walked over to pick up the bridge phone, cursed, and slammed it back down. "Parker. Get over here."

A young man looked up in surprise, then hurried toward the captain.

"All guests and crew to the middle of the ship," McKinley barked. "Hallways, interior cabins, public areas. Our entire onboard communication system is out, so I need you to get the word to key people who will carry out the process."

"Yes, sir." And the man was gone.

Allison and Donovan moved back toward the door.

"Where are you two going?" McKinley bellowed.

"To help spread the word, Captain. To put your people in the middle of this ship."

They were halfway down the hall, lurching to the right and left with the waves, when Allison stopped, hand on the wall.

"You okay?"

"Yeah."

"But—"

"But the AT did not cause this storm. They saw an opportunity, and they took advantage of it to disable this ship."

"Correct."

"Which brings me back to the question that I had the very first day. Back even farther than that. Back to the disabled vehicles in Dallas."

"Why?"

"Exactly. How does this further their cause?"

"I can't see that it does," Donovan admitted.

"But it must. There's something else that they have planned."

"A one-two punch."

"Right. And you can bet the second punch is going to be harder and deadlier."

"We'll deal with it when it happens."

"Yes. We will."

For the moment, the best that they could do was to move everyone to the middle of the ship.

Chapter Twenty

K ate worried a thumbnail as she stared at the monitors. The storm was incapsulating the cruise ship, as they'd hoped. April storms were infrequent in the Gulf, but this one had arrived at precisely the time they'd needed it—in other words, during the *Harmony*'s return trip. She was aware that John had a backup plan for sending the cruise ship into chaos, but the weather and their hacking abilities had rendered the backup plan moot.

Or so she thought.

Stella and John walked into the room at the same time. John stood at the back, as was his habit during the most critical moments of an operation. He liked to think of himself as an overseer. Perhaps an overlord. Kate thought overlord fit him best. She'd actually looked it up the night before when she couldn't sleep.

An absolute or supreme leader.

One having great power or authority.

Yup. That described John to a T. As for Stella, she was simply a lunatic.

The lunatic of the group walked to the front, right up to the monitors, and waved a manicured hand at it. "Can't we get better images than these?"

No one dared to answer.

John explained, "They're in the middle of the storm. We can't fly a drone through that weather, so the best we can do is hack into the on-board cameras."

Stella sniffed. "And are *they* seeing this? The passengers?"

Kate knew that question was for her. "We have the live feed playing on monitors throughout the ship. Also, they can look out the windows and glass doors and see what's happening. From the texts we've intercepted, and there are quite a few, people are beginning to panic."

Stella clapped her hands. "Excellent. I love to hear that. Allowing them to post to their pitiful little social media feeds works in our favor. After all, we want the word to get out." She said the last with gusto, as if she were announcing that the circus was coming to town.

"What about that other thing, John? Where do we stand on that?"

John glowered at Stella. Kate's crew averted their eyes, pretending to be busy with their monitors. The fact that John didn't answer made Kate think the question was, in fact, directed toward her.

"I don't know what you're talking about. What other thing?"

"You know...the chemical/biological substance. What's the point of stranding a cruise ship in the middle of the Gulf unless you're going to do something with it? Something truly dramatic. Something that will catch the entire world's attention."

No one spoke.

John had his gaze locked on the ceiling. As if the answer that Stella was expecting might be there.

Had she said *chemical*? *Biological*?

A trembling spread through Kate's limbs. The sound of her heartbeat thumped kaboom, kaboom, kaboom in her ears. Her skin felt suddenly clammy. She feared she might be sick.

John sighed and moved to the front of the room. "What Stella is referring to is a biological attack that is being prepared even now. I gave the greenlight forty minutes ago. A few of you helped me with the details, though you might not have known exactly what you were doing."

When no one spoke, he added, "Kate, I'm sorry that I had to leave you out of this. I wasn't sure you had the . . ." He cocked his head and looked at her quizzically. "The stomach for it."

Kate didn't answer. She didn't trust her voice. It would tremble. Or crack. She might attack him. She might be shot exactly like Brett Lindstrom had been.

"We are a team," he continued. "And as members of that team, you all deserve to know. In approximately ninety minutes, our operatives inside the ship will launch a biological attack. I can't accurately predict how many will die, but I can assure you that we'll have the attention of the entire world. We'll finally receive the consideration we deserve."

No one was looking at their monitors now. Everyone had their eyes locked on John Howard—even Stella, who was actually beaming.

John seemed out of words though, so Stella jumped in.

"You've all done a fine job of hacking, invading, corrupting, and even disabling components of the world's cyber infrastructure. Now we have a chance to let everyone who has been held captive know that we mean business. We will not stand idly by while the world, our very existence, is threatened by AI and orbital satellites and unlawful surveillance. We will no longer tolerate governmental and business overreach."

She might have been expecting applause.

No one spoke. No one moved.

If Kate had been in possession of her firearm at that moment, she might have shot them both. They were willing to kill hundreds, even thousands, in order to forward their agenda. What was next? Release smallpox on the general population? Taint the water supply? There were over eighty-four thousand dams in the

U.S. alone. Would they seize control of those and release their waters? Would they flood a nation?

Stella clapped her hands, pulling Kate from her reverie. "Things are going to get exciting! I suggest anyone who needs a break take it now. Tonight will be an all-hackers-on-deck event."

Stella moved closer to John and spoke in a hushed voice.

George and Jocelyn and Mike and Chloe and Julio returned to business as normal. Or they seemed to. Perhaps, like Kate, they were thinking over how to jump off this sinking ship.

Kate ran through her mental checklist, the one she'd kept since being assigned to middle-earth. She had wondered, from the very beginning, when it would be time to leave. She'd worried, for more than two years, that she wouldn't recognize the moment.

This was that moment.

She needed out, and she needed out now.

But first, it was imperative that she warn Steele and Quinn. The lives of every man, woman, and child on that ship might depend on it.

Chapter Twenty-One

Allison and Donovan spent the next thirty minutes spreading the word. Everyone away from the windows. Rooms with balconies were to keep doors closed. Guests were to remain in the hall, go to an interior room, or wait in a public area.

The top decks took the brunt of the storm. A few windows were broken from flying chairs. Several balcony doors shattered.

"If that's the worst of it, we got off easy," Donovan said.

"I doubt that will be the worst of it."

The lower decks had problems with water seeping in through the doors, which shouldn't have been able to happen. But very few things were completely waterproof. Turned out that an exterior cabin on a cruise ship was not.

Most people were quick to follow instructions.

A few tried to hide their fear behind bravado.

"What's going to happen if I stay in my room? Think I'll get swept out to sea?" This from a twenty-something blonde who was upset that the bars had been temporarily closed. "I paid for that drink package. How can they close?"

"Yes, you could get swept out to sea. How would your family back home feel about that? And your answer is that you want to drink right now? Seriously?" Allison looked at the woman with such derision that, for a moment, the blonde was speechless.

For a few seconds.

"I'm calling my travel agent. In fact, I'm calling CNN. Wait until they see what's happening here."

"Good luck with that," Donovan muttered.

By and large, though, people helped one another. The lounge areas on the promenade deck were full. People had repositioned the chairs so they were away from the windows. And the middle of the promenade, the area that was open to the top of the ship, the area that Anna Lee and Mary Beth held court over, was deserted. Several pieces of hanging art, metal sculptures, and signage had fallen due to the beating that the ship was taking from the storm.

"But she's holding," Allison said.

"Who's holding?"

"The *Harmony*." Allison studied Steele, grateful he was here. Grateful she was going through this op with him. "Why are ships always female?"

"It's a vessel, not unlike a womb."

"Eww."

"Also there's female deities to consider."

"I'm not up on my ancient history, Steele."

"Gods and goddesses were associated with navigating the sea. Aphrodite. Venus."

"I'm sorry I asked." But Allison was feeling better about things. The bridge had suffered no damage at all. Surely they were nearly out of the storm. She was feeling optimistic, and she knew that was dangerous.

"We need to find something to eat and we need to hydrate."

"What?" She turned on her partner, completely bewildered by his suggestion. "We're supposed to take a lunch break?"

"We didn't have lunch. In fact, I don't remember the last meal we did have. You might run on adrenaline and fury, but I need calories."

They walked into one of the guest stores, which surprisingly was still open. Bottles of water were free, but people were loading up on snack food. Allison grabbed two protein bars, and Donovan settled for a large bag of trail mix.

Allison shook her head in mock dismay. "You realize that's mostly sugar."

"It's healthy."

"It has chocolate candies in it."

"And nuts and raisins." He wagged the bottle of water back and forth. "Plus, I'm washing it down with this."

The cashier wrote down their cabin number, since the computers were down. Walking out of the store, Allison realized the interior of the ship was pretty dark, but people took turns using their phones to provide a little lighting to the areas where they sat.

"They might want to save that phone power."

"Yeah. Except the phones don't work."

They both slumped into chairs that were empty owing to the fact that they were too close to the windows and not easy to move. In fact, they seemed to be bolted to the floor. The windows provided no clue as to what was happening. All Allison could see was her reflection—hers and Donovan's. The darkness pressed in as if its intent were to smother them.

No stars.

No lights from other ships.

Only the periodic tilting of the boat and the crash of waves.

Allison sipped her water, accepted the fact that you never knew what moment might be your last, and plunged into the emotional pool she usually avoided. "I don't know that I properly thanked you."

Donovan raised his eyebrows, scooped out a handful of trail mix, and waited.

"Washington State?"

"Ah."

"I could have died up there, Donovan."

"I wouldn't have let that happen."

"And the Grand Canyon."

Donovan closed the bag of trail mix, set it on the table, and leaned forward, elbows on his knees. He didn't speak until she looked at him. Allison thought she saw regret in his eyes, but given the near darkness, she couldn't be sure.

"I failed you on that op—in the Grand Canyon. What you went through there should not have happened."

"The hell you did. It was . . ." She shook her head and fiddled with the protein bar. "Sometimes the bad guys get lucky."

"Nope. You should not have been undercover on your own. And after I met you up top, after I told you how dangerous Blitz was . . ." Words seemed to fail him for a moment. He sighed heavily, his shoulders heaving forward. "I should have inserted someone with you. Hell, I should have gone myself."

"You couldn't do that." Her voice was low, trembly, and she hated that. She hated that when she thought of that hike into the canyon, the storm, the terror, and the bodies . . . she hated that she still had an emotional response to those memories. Her agency-mandated shrink said it was completely normal, which didn't make her any happier about it.

She cleared her throat, breathed in and out. "I didn't answer your calls for several reasons."

He waited. Oh, how she appreciated a man who didn't feel a need to jump in and fill a silence.

"I was upset. Not at you as much as at myself."

"A little at me."

"Okay. A little. Only when you questioned my decisions." She shook her head, stared at her reflection in the window, wondered what else was out there. "Every step of the way, the decisions I made seemed like the only decision I could make. I've been over and over it, and I don't see how—"

"You did great, Allison. You have to know that."

"I did?"

"You're becoming a legend."

"Whatever." But she appreciated that he was trying to lighten the moment. Now wasn't the right time to talk about the past. But when was the right time? They were only together when they were chasing terrorists.

"Maybe we should hang out together," he said.

"What?"

"You know..." Donovan poured another handful of trail mix into his palm and held it out for her.

Allison rolled her eyes but accepted the offering. It did taste better than her protein bar.

"Go hiking or something."

"Seriously?"

"What's wrong with hiking?"

"Nothing. I guess. I'm not great with high places, as you know."

"I'm kinda glad you're not perfect."

She threw the unopened protein bar at him. He caught it, grinned, and stuck it in his shirt pocket. And then she said something that she hadn't even realized she was thinking. "You could come to Aunt Polly's."

"The famous ranch in west Texas?"

She waggled her hand back and forth. "Sort of west Texas, more like western central Texas. Anyway. It's a great spot. You wouldn't believe how peaceful it can be."

Donovan opened his mouth to ask a question, or tell her he wasn't interested, or ask her when. She'd never know what Donovan was going to say in that moment. Because a shot rang out. Allison might have thought she'd imagined it. The storm was loud. People were talking. The shot had to be a long way off.

But she hadn't imagined it.

Donovan was already up and moving in that direction.

And Allison was only two steps behind.

Donovan knew the direction the sound came from, but he didn't know exactly where the shooter was. Judging it to be farther rather than closer, he jogged down the promenade. Allison easily matched his pace. When they were three-quarters of the way down, he slowed and directed her to the opposite side of the hall. Once she was in position, they proceeded forward, toward the casino, past the gaming area which was dark and deserted, and into the piano bar, where they could make out the plaintive sound of someone sobbing.

Jeremy was on the floor next to the piano.

A pool of blood spread out around him.

Raquel clutched his hand, sobbing and pleading with him to hold on.

Donovan knelt beside Jeremy and felt for a pulse.

"How's he doing?" Allison called. Her weapon was still drawn, and she was maintaining a 360-degree surveillance. Certainly, no one could come at them from the windows at their back.

"Weak. Looks like a contact wound. Make that multiple wounds."

"Jeremy. Jeremy, look at me." Raquel pressed both of her palms to his cheeks. "Look at me, darling. I love you. Please look at me."

Jeremy's eyes lingered on her for a moment, and then he turned his gaze to Donovan.

"What happened, Jeremy?"

"Surprised them."

"Surprised who?"

"They were . . ." He licked his lips. "I'm thirsty."

Allison was there, handing Donovan a bottle of water. He uncapped it, raised Jeremy up ever so slightly, and held it to his lips.

Raquel was weeping and pleading. Kissing his hand, his face, his forehead.

"Three of them," Jeremy managed to whisper.

"We know. We know there's three. Was it Cradduck or Grant?"

Jeremy closed his eyes, and Donovan thought that was it. The man had passed. He sat back on his heels feeling sick and angry and frustrated. How had this happened? Why hadn't he been able to stop it?

"Crew," Jeremy whispered.

The single word brought Donovan out of his reverie. "What?"

"Crew."

And then he was gone.

Raquel's wails intensified, and somehow, miraculously, Dr. Mbachu pushed through the small crowd that had gathered. She felt for a pulse, considered the injury, evaluated the amount of blood on the floor, and shook her head.

One more tally on the AT's scorecard.

Donovan put a hand on Raquel's back and said, "I'm sorry." Then he stood and strode away from the lounge area. He was headed toward the outer doors, needing fresh air, needing a moment outside of this enclosed space that was filled with danger and tragedy and far too many people, when Allison caught up with him.

"No, Donovan. No." She tugged on his arms and turned him toward her. "You can't go out there."

Then she stepped even closer, slipped her arms around his waist, pushed her forehead into his chest.

And for a moment, it felt as if *she* were holding *him*. Allison Quinn, agent extraordinaire who was five inches shorter and easily half his weight, shouldered the burden of his pain.

Chapter Twenty-Two

Kate had excused herself with a migraine, claiming she was going to her room to fetch some meds and that she would be back shortly.

She wasn't going back—ever.

She knew that the moment that John had uttered the phrase *chemical/biological substance*. Her stomach churned, her eyes stung, and her heart felt as if it was going to pound through her rib cage.

This simply couldn't be happening. She'd been too careful. She'd been aggressively vigilant. It wasn't possible that John Howard had so completely blinded her to what was actually happening on board the *Harmony*.

And why would he?

Did he suspect her?

She used her keycard to access her room which included a sleeping area, private bath and small living area complete with a mini-kitchen. Her hands shook as she filled a glass with water and drank it down. "Five deep breaths," she muttered but only made it to three when her phone dinged. The message appeared for less than seven seconds.

If she hadn't picked up immediately...

But she did.

Portico. South side. Now.

As she stared at the words, they disappeared completely from her device. She couldn't retrieve it, couldn't re-read it, couldn't recover it.

But she hadn't imagined what she'd seen. *Portico. South side. Now.*

Kate didn't pack. There wasn't a single thing she needed from this life. She paused long enough to sit casually at her desk, careful to hold the tablet in a direction that couldn't be seen from the camera mounted in the corner of her room. Hopefully, it would look like she was working. If John had access to her tablet—and she assumed he did—he would see an email image with random typing.

What could he have seen in the past weeks?

A note to her granny, who didn't exist.

A follow-up with an old economics professor at a college she'd never attended.

He wouldn't have seen anything. She'd been careful.

Now she activated the clean sweep program the Kids had written—essentially deleting any cloud records, then melting the circuits on the tablet.

Her phone.

She had to swipe her phone.

But first, she had to tell someone what was happening, and if John had hacked into her phone . . .

If he'd found her previous encrypted messages to Reid Clark, he'd be able to reroute this one. He'd be able to cancel this one.

She couldn't risk that.

Instead, she keyed in two phone numbers she'd memorized long ago and sent the text. Then she activated the clean sweep program on the mobile device. Sitting on the side of her bed, she bent down as if to slip off her shoes, then tossed the phone under the bed. It was all she could do not to look up at the camera mounted in the corner of the room. Instead she reached for the pack of cigarettes on her nightstand, picked it up and hurried down the hall toward the portico. South side.

It was where they smoked.

Kate was not and had never been a smoker.

But smoking was the only plausible reason for standing outside. John called it a "nasty little habit," but allowed that every person had a vice, and this was apparently hers.

The south side of the portico was where the rain from the gutters hit against a paving stone. Nice and loud. Too loud to be heard, though they'd be seen. She didn't know of a single place in middle-earth that wasn't included on a surveillance feed—even the bathrooms. Hell, she'd helped to set them up.

But it was possible that whoever was watching would simply see two women stepping outside for a smoke.

Jocelyn was already there.

Jocelyn? Was Jocelyn Green working for the task force? No way. Not possible. Kate would know if Reid Clark or Kendra Thomas had sent someone in to back her up. But Jocelyn had obviously written the text as well as code to erase all record of that text. Now she stood at the edge of the portico, rain splashing her boots, holding a lit Pall Mall, and staring out at the rain. Kate attempted to light her Marlboro, but her hand was shaking too badly.

All four thousand, two hundred crew and guests.

Dead.

Bile rose in her throat, and the panic that lurked at the base of her brain nearly broke through.

Jocelyn flicked her Bic and held it toward Kate's cigarette.

"He knows you're a plant." Her voice was low, barely a whisper. She met Kate's gaze, though not for long. Maybe long enough to convey an apology. To express regret.

"He doesn't know the details." She leaned against the brick of the portico column and took a drag on the cigarette. "I'm to report back to him in fifteen minutes."

"He'll see us."

"He'll see what he wants to see. Me having the upper hand, enjoying a smoke with a woman I'm about to destroy."

"And are you? About to destroy me?"

Jocelyn dropped the half-smoked cigarette on the pavement, ground it with the toe of her shoe, picked it up, and placed it in the *BUTTS* receptacle, practically beaming at the camera as she did so.

"I'm giving you a head start, Kate."

"Why?"

"Because this—killing thousands—it's not what I signed on for."

She turned to go back inside, and Kate said, "Be careful."

"Yup. You can count on it."

Jocelyn walked back into the building with all the attitude of a model gracing a fashion show's runway.

Kate's mind flipped through her options, which were few.

Going back inside would get her killed.

Breaking into a sprint wouldn't work. She'd be shot in the back before she reached the woods.

So instead, she patted her pockets as if in search of something. If John or his goons were watching, he might think she was still looking for the migraine meds. He didn't know that she knew. He would still be feeling superior.

She looked out toward her parked vehicle and checked her pockets again, finally pulling the car's key fob from her pocket. She'd kept it on her since arriving at middle-earth thirty-one months ago. She'd kept it in her pocket in case she had to run, but now she understood that John's surveillance capabilities had exceeded even what she knew about. The car would have been tagged with a tracker. If she managed to get out of this, it would be on foot.

John would see her walk toward her vehicle.

Would he buy the act she was presenting?

Would he look away, just for a second?

Shaking her head and swearing, she stepped into the pouring rain and walked toward the Volkswagen Beetle parked at the back of the paved lot. It was a newer model, but she'd had it specially ordered so that there were no computers onboard. No backup camera. No dashboard GPS. No satellite radio. She thumbed the unlock button on the fob, opened the door, and bent down as if to look inside.

And then something happened that she couldn't have hoped for in her wildest dreams. The parking lot lights blinked out.

Jocelyn?

The Kids?

She didn't bother to figure out who or why. She dashed toward the woods. Ran north. Didn't waste a single minute looking back.

If he came after her, and she suspected he might, there wasn't anything she could do about it.

She had no weapon.

No way to call for help.

All she had was her training, and it would have to be enough. How many nights had she lain awake wondering if she should run, how she could run, where she would run?

The information that she had provided the task force was critical to every op involving John Howard and the AT. But she'd known she couldn't stay undercover forever. Reid Clark had said those very words to her the last time she'd seen him—just shy of three years ago.

"This isn't the age of Cold War espionage, Katelyn. With the advent of tracking technology, drones, and artificial intelligence, every covert operation has a time clock. You can't stay undercover forever. Stay as long as you're effective. The minute you're not, the minute you're in danger, come home."

Come home.

Those words pulsed with the erratic beating of her heart as she made her way into the woods that surrounded middle-earth. If she were very lucky, she had a fifteen-minute start on John's security goons. Best not to count on luck, though. Luck came in both good and bad forms. Luck could get her killed.

She picked up her pace, jogging through the pouring rain, not bothering about whether she left a trail. She would leave a trail. Everyone did, and John's guys were very good at search and retrieval missions.

Allison and Donovan were standing on the bridge when their phones binged.

Captain McKinley sent them a sharp look. "I thought all communications were down."

"They are." Allison pulled the device from her pocket. Coms were down. They'd confirmed that. No one was even able to post on social media anymore. Apparently the AT was satisfied with the ripple they'd thrown into the world's instant communication pond. If someone was able to get through, to get past the wall the Anarchists for Tomorrow had placed to block all communications, it meant that either they were a Class A Hacker or a member of the AT. Or both.

She stared down at the screen, her mind struggling to accept what she was reading.

> Biologic weapons on board. Move everyone out on the decks. Mission clock T-28 minutes.

A chill descended over Allison. She looked at Donovan who was tapping his device as if he could make it tell him more. She turned her attention outside to the raging storm. They were in the middle of it now, or she hoped they were in the middle. Halfway through and they could possibly hold on. She didn't want to think about conditions getting worse out there. Who knew how big or dangerous this storm was? Who knew where they even were in the vast waters of the Gulf?

Lightning cracked across the sky.

Giant waves splashed over the deck railings.

Wind gusts continued to toss around deck furniture.

And though it was four in the afternoon, the sky was as dark as midnight.

Donovan had moved from disbelief to action. He was already setting the countdown clock on his watch. Allison did the same.

"We need to move all passengers and crew out onto the deck," Allison said.

"What?" Captain McKinley's voice was explosive. "We just moved everyone to the center of the ship."

Donovan showed him the text, and McKinley's entire body froze. His hands stilled, his eyes locked on the screen, even his breathing seemed to pause . . . as if he could hold this moment. As if he could keep them from careening forward into the abyss.

Allison felt real sympathy for the man. He was having to process a lot of information and a whole slew of threats, in a very short period of time. No doubt, he was still fighting the idea that all they'd endured, all they'd been through, could have been avoided.

She no longer thought so.

This plan was so bold, so beyond anything the AT had attempted before, that she had no doubt they had backups to their backups. What was happening to them was bound to happen to someone.

McKinley looked up at them. "Coms are out. How can we—"

"Price can send the security team," Donovan said. "Two people to each deck. They can relocate everyone to their muster station. Word will spread among the passengers. We can do this, but it needs to happen fast."

"I'll get word to Price. You two . . ." His eyes no longer held irritation or condemnation. He was pleading with them. He, like Allison, was scared. And not just for himself. For the souls under his care.

Donovan and Allison were running by the time they burst out of the bridge and into the hall. They didn't wait to confirm that McKinley would do what had to be done. He would. There was no other option.

They had to get to engineering and stop this attack. If it was biological, and the AT planned to disperse it, they would do so through engineering, probably through the boat's ventilation system.

They sprinted down the hall.

Raced down the stairs.

Passed deck after deck of folks clustered in the center areas of the ship. Families sitting together with their backs against the interior walls of the halls. Interior rooms with doors open, showing they, too, were crammed with people. The library areas held groups huddled together, voices low, eyes darting back and forth as if they might be able to see the danger coming at them.

They wouldn't see biological weapons.

They wouldn't even know what had happened to them.

Mbachu joined them on deck three. "What's happening?"

Allison and Donovan didn't slow. "It's not just a cyberattack. It's a biological attack too."

Mbachu fell in next to them, easily matching their pace.

"Probably anthrax, then."

"Probably."

"We need to contact the CDC. They'll send help."

"All coms are out," Donovan said. "We need to stop them before they release it."

And then they hit the engineering floor, sprinted around the corner, and came face-to-face with the inner sanctum of a ship in crisis. Various alarms were sounding. Red strobe lights flashed their warning. Crew members dashed from one workspace to another.

Allison noticed that no one was in a panic, though. Scared? Of course. But still doing their job. She and Donovan and Mbachu bounded into the main engineering room—no guards were there to stop them. And maybe that was what the AT wanted as well. To throw so many hurdles at the security team, the captain, and the engineers that they were spread thin. Anyone could have walked into the main engineering room and killed everyone there before they were even noticed.

But their goal wasn't to kill the crew.

Their goal was to kill all persons aboard the *Harmony*.

Brock Ferguson was barking orders at his staff. "I want that weather feed up now. We need to know what we're headed into."

Of course, they didn't know. Couldn't know. All the cameras were down, and they were stationed in a windowless room in the center of the bottom of the ship. The ship's designers hadn't prepared for that scenario. Ferguson was fighting a tempest he couldn't even see, and it was about to get much worse.

A crewman went to Ferguson and said, "Wind gusts look to be over sixty miles per hour, plus heavy rain and lightning."

Allison headed to Lilith. For the first time, the young woman looked as if she feared she was out of her depth.

"Nothing's responding. They've taken complete control, and I can't even . . ." Lilith's face was etched with misery. She looked at Allison and waited for an answer. But Allison didn't have answers. She only had several bad options.

"Forget the system. The AT is releasing a biological weapon."

The room went suddenly quiet as precious seconds ticked by. Allison was in the zone now. She understood what was happening. Understood that these people in this room needed to be on board with what happened next. An op that threatened high civilian casualties had to be handled very carefully. To say that every second counted was not an exaggeration. But rushing forward headfirst wouldn't help anyone and could result in an even worse scenario.

She mentally counted to ten, giving them as much time as she could, then explained, "We're sending all crew and staff to their muster stations."

"You can't do that," Ferguson said. "We have to stabilize the ship, get an accurate weather forecast, and keep those people inside until we do."

"Anyone who stays inside will be dead," Mbachu said. "I've seen firsthand the effects of biological weapons. Those people are better off outside, facing the storm."

Allison turned to Lilith. "Take over Ferguson's station. Try to bring the feeds back up. Try to find where the AT has infiltrated the ship's systems and repel them."

"Okay. Right. On it."

Ferguson stepped away from his station, eyes wide, pupils dilated. His adrenaline was spiking, but he managed to say, "What do you need from me?"

"Show us where the ship's ventilation system is." Donovan joined them at the center table. "They'll disperse it through there. It's the only way to cover an area this large other than dropping a bomb on us."

Ferguson blanched at the word *bomb*.

"There are still operatives on this ship, Brent." Allison kept her voice low, steady, but emphatic. "Their employer is not going to drop a bomb, because those operatives would be killed, too. At this moment, they're donning personal protective equipment— gloves, gowns, gas masks. We don't have any of those things to distribute among the passengers or the crew. We need to stop them, and we have . . ."

"Nineteen minutes," Donovan said.

Allison echoed, "Nineteen minutes."

Ferguson nodded, went to a shelf, and pulled down several rolls of blueprints. Mbachu and Allison cleared off the center table as Ferguson and Donovan rolled out the plans.

"We updated the system after Covid, integrated advanced filtration systems that would capture smaller particles."

Allison looked at Mbachu who shook her head.

"It won't filter anthrax," Mbachu said. "The spores are too small."

Donovan swept his hand over the blueprint. "If you wanted to put something into the system, where would you do it?"

Ferguson didn't hesitate. "Here." He stabbed a spot in the center of the ship.

"One deck below," Donovan said. "Let's go."

Ferguson called after them, "Should I—"

"Stay there. Help Lilith."

And then they were sprinting down the hall to the stairs that Allison had never noticed before because she hadn't thought to check out the very bottom of the ship. She had assumed that the AT would limit their attack to the technological side of things.

Her heart hammered. Sweat dripped down her back. Her thoughts were hyper-focused on the present moment, and at the same time, racing through every possible scenario they might be about to confront.

Donovan stopped abruptly at the bottom of the stairs.

Allison skidded to a stop behind him and pulled her weapon. She checked right then left, surprised to find Mbachu still with them. Why had the good doctor come along? She wasn't armed. She had nothing to defend herself with, let alone stop a terrorist. Allison was about to tell her to go back, to go up top and see if any of the passengers or crew needed her, but she never did that because Donovan stuck his head around the corner, and that was when the shooting started.

Chapter Twenty-Three

K ate moved quickly through the trees, heading in what she hoped was a northerly direction.

She was betting that John would expect her to go south, toward the town of Whitefish, toward the road where she might be able to catch a ride.

So she did the opposite of that. She moved north, deeper into the woods. The rain continued to fall in sheets. She tripped in the mud but caught herself before going down completely. She checked her watch. Fourteen minutes until the biological agent would be released on board the *Harmony*. She suspected John had opted for anthrax. Bacillus anthracis was easily found in nature. It could also be produced in a lab. Dustin and Eloise could release it into the ship's ventilation system without anyone knowing. It was both odorless and tasteless.

The passengers and crew wouldn't know what had been used against them until their symptoms began appearing—fever, chills, shortness of breath, headache, tiredness, and body aches. They would most likely initially brush away those symptoms as having to do with the stress of being on board a ship caught in the middle of a storm. They'd return home, disperse across the United States, and it would take a week to two months before they realized something was still wrong. If they sought medical attention early enough and the doctors diagnosed it correctly and quickly, fifty-five percent of those infected would survive. Without treatment, inhalation of anthrax was always fatal.

It wouldn't come to that, though.

She'd sent the message to Quinn and Steele. They would warn the authorities.

If the message went through.

If Quinn and Steele were still alive and onboard.

If they could find a way to contact the authorities.

Kate stopped, wiped the rain from her face, and took stock of her location. She'd traveled at a good pace and covered a lot of ground. But she could still make out the roof of middle-earth in the distance. Despair pulsed at her throat, tore at what little energy remained.

She wasn't James Bond.

She was a woman with an excellent grasp of how to code, program, and analyze. She had an undergraduate degree from DePaul University, a graduate degree from MIT. She'd been trained by Homeland Security. She would not be brought down by the likes of John Howard.

She would make it out of these woods alive.

And then she'd warn the authorities.

She'd be in the room when John was cuffed and dragged from middle-earth. John and Stella. They were narcissists in save-the-world clothing. They were frauds, and they were dangerous. She hoped they'd spend the rest of their lives behind bars, far from any computer terminal.

That thought cheered her a bit.

She pushed on.

Three times she heard drones flying over her location, which meant John had reassigned part of the IT people to search for her. She counted that as a good thing. It meant he was worried—as he should be. It also meant there were fewer eyes helping Dustin Cradduck and Eloise Grant. There was even a chance that Jocelyn had flipped sides. Given enough chaos among John's programmers, she might have a chance to stop what was happening on board the *Harmony*. If it could be stopped.

She needed to believe it could be.

But she needed to do more to distract John Howard. The man had an ego that was larger than a hot air balloon. He'd want to catch her. He'd consider it a matter of pride. It might become more important to him than the operation on board the cruise ship. An informant in his midst? He'd be furious. He'd be hell-bent on revenge.

As she approached a clearing, she waited in the woods, staring at the sky, needing to time her dash across the clearing at the perfect second.

When she heard the high whine of the approaching drone, she stepped into the clearing. Moved quickly, but not too quickly. She wanted it to snap a good picture of her. The drone flew closer, its buzzing now right behind her.

Surely he hadn't found a way to arm the damn things.

If he had . . .

She slipped into the woods on the far side of the clearing.

Turning to look back, she saw that the drone had been joined by two others. They hovered six feet off the ground, and all three shone a bright light into the woods. Kate dashed for a clump of vines that was growing up and over and through a stand of dead trees. She dropped to her knees and crawled into the cover of the vines, continuing until everything was completely dark, until she could no longer see the light of the drones.

Donovan pulled back as the bullets whizzed past him. "Eloise is manning the machine gun. Dustin's climbing to the top of the ventilation shaft."

"I'm a better climber," Allison said.

"I'll take the girl." He had already pulled the Sig Sauer P320 from his ankle holster. Patting his pockets to assure himself he had the two extra clips, he nodded at Allison, who took off toward the far side of the room at a sprint. Donovan poked his head around the corner, saw Eloise turn toward Allison, and ripped off two shots.

Eloise let loose with a string of bullets from the machine gun, haphazardly aimed in his direction. The girl had obviously not been taught how to conserve her ammunition. She had the machine gun on full automatic. As long as her finger was on the trigger, the bullets kept coming. He figured she'd be out of ammo pretty quickly. He could also tell she wasn't accustomed to using the weapon. The recoil had caused the weapon to jerk up, which resulted in most of the bullets flying over Donovan's head.

"I'll go the opposite way, try to draw her attention away from Allison." Mbachu was gone before he could argue with her.

Presented with three separate targets, Eloise sprayed the remaining bullets in a circular pattern to cover the entire room, then dropped the machine gun and sprinted for the emergency exit. Donovan stepped out, aimed, corrected for her speed and the objects between them, then fired three shots in a tight pattern. He missed her chest because Eloise chose that moment to jump for one of the hanging ladders as if she could climb her way out of the room.

One or more of the bullets entered her lower calf, and she fell to the floor like a deflated balloon, screaming and clutching her leg.

Donovan pivoted toward Allison. She was halfway up the ladder. Dustin was perched on the top rung and was leaning over the shaft. He had managed to pry off the lid. He was wearing a splash suit which included coveralls, gloves, and a full-faced hood-style mask with a respirator.

Interesting that Eloise had worn none of that. Did she honestly think she'd be safe from the spores because she was twenty feet below the drop point? Dustin wore a sling carrier across his chest, which he was reaching into. He'd completely ignored the gunfire as well as Eloise's cries for help.

Donovan adjusted his position to get a clean shot.

Allison reached for Dustin's leg, but he kicked her away, landing a solid jab to her head. She shook it off, reacquired her grip with her left hand, and pulled her Glock with her right. If she shot him . . .

If he fell and dropped whatever contained the spores . . .

"Stop!" Dustin's voice was commanding, steady. In one quick move, he pulled off his mask, tucked it under his left arm, reached into the sling carrier, and pulled out not a vial but a small brown envelope. Not large. Approximately the size of the palm of his hand.

Donovan's heart sank.

Mbachu had been right.

Anthrax.

This idiot had been carrying around anthrax on a ship full of people for the last twenty-four hours.

"I'll do it," Dustin said. "It'll kill you and your partner back there. It'll kill everyone."

"Including Eloise," Allison said.

"She's willing to give her life for the cause."

Eloise did not voice agreement. She had taken off her sweatshirt and was attempting to wrap it around her bleeding leg—alternately crying and shouting, "I've been shot, Dustin. It's over. Just give it to them. It's over."

And then Dustin did something Donovan did not anticipate. Seamlessly, as if he'd practiced it a thousand times, he put the brown envelope in the grip of his left hand, the hand that was holding onto the rim of the ventilator shaft. With his right, he pulled a weapon and shot Eloise.

Center of mass. Three shots.

She fell back on the floor.

He pointed the gun down at Allison. "Now. Move back down the ladder, or you will be next."

He was apparently aware of Donovan. He'd glanced Donovan's way as he'd pulled out the envelope, but his attention was now focused completely on the closer threat—Allison, still perched just a few rungs below him. He wasn't aware of Mbachu ascending the ladder on the other side of the shaft.

Donovan stepped out into the open, weapon raised and sighted.

Dustin Cradduck might drop that envelope of anthrax, exposing them all. But Donovan was damn sure the man wasn't going to walk away from this room. He would take him out before he had a chance to put the hooded mask back on. And surely he wouldn't release the biological agent while he himself was still exposed.

Later Donovan would think back on this moment and wonder if Dustin was somehow aware of what he was planning to do. Did he know that his life was about to end? Did something in his subconscious warn him about a third danger creeping up on his location? Did he sense Donovan's concentration?

Whatever the reason, Dustin finally turned his attention away from Allison and toward Donovan, met his gaze, and raised his firearm. And that was when Mbachu slammed the ventilator lid down on his hand. The lid must have weighed several hundred pounds, and Donovan suspected it severed Dustin's fingers at the joints.

He screamed as he fell, landing on the floor in a silent heap.

Allison had pivoted toward the inside of the ladder, narrowly missing being dragged down with Dustin.

Mbachu was still at the top of the ventilator shaft. She screamed, "Behind you."

And then Donovan felt the bullet slam into his body.

Chapter Twenty-Four

Allison stared at Price, unable to believe what the woman had done.

"Come on down, Allison. I wouldn't want you to fall."

She hesitated. She was trying to process what had happened, what her eyes were telling her—that Donovan was down, possibly killed. Her mind couldn't accept it. He couldn't be dead. She would not lose a partner on this op. She would not lose Donovan. She couldn't. But he wasn't moving. Hadn't so much as groaned when he'd crashed to the floor.

Price motioned with her gun, motioned toward Donovan, who remained immobile.

"You, too, Dr. Mbachu. Those metal ladders can be slippery, so be very careful."

Allison and Mbachu climbed down their respective ladders and stood side-by-side, three feet from Donovan. Mbachu made a move toward him, but Price shook her head and motioned with her weapon. "Stay close to Allison, where I can watch you both."

Allison felt a hot anger bloom in her that she'd known only a few times in her life. When Nina had almost killed Zack. When Blitz had told her that her father was one of them. And this moment—with Donovan motionless on the ground and Price pointing a gun at her.

She tried to tamp down the rage. She needed to engage with Becca Price. She had to create a space where she could outmaneuver this woman. "You're going to kill us, so what difference does it make where we stand?"

"I might not." But her smile confirmed the lie.

"You were willing to kill everyone on this ship, and we're supposed to believe you might let us walk out of this room?"

Price laughed. It was a mirthless, wicked sound. "I suppose you're right. But the truth is that I need your help."

"Why would we help you?" Mbachu had pulled herself up to her full height and looked for all the world like a warrior princess.

"Any number of reasons. You might be under the illusion that you can get a hand up on me—save the day. Or perhaps you think that you could survive an anthrax attack. Keep it together until the Coast Guard and the CDC arrive."

"Maybe I want to stay alive long enough to kill you," Allison said.

And it was true. Her adrenaline had spiked. Dustin was dead. Eloise was dead. Donovan was bleeding out three feet from her. And suddenly, all Allison wanted was revenge.

She wanted . . .

Nope. She *needed* to wipe that smug look off Price's face.

"Allison, I've always liked you. I like your spunky attitude."

"Let me help him," Mbachu said. "Just let me check the wound."

Price cocked her head, as if she were a cat, sitting inside a home and observing a chickadee on the window ledge. "Tell you what. Allison, you go and check Dustin. See if he fell on the package. Show it to me."

"I'm not touching that stuff."

"Do as I say, and I'll let the good doctor see to your friend."

Donovan had landed face-down with his left arm trapped underneath him and his right splayed at his side. At Price's words, his right index finger moved up, then down. A signal? A sign? A warning for her not to fall for whatever Price was up to or a go-ahead signal telling her to play along?

"All right." Allison held up her hands, palms out.

"Leave your weapon. Remove it from your ankle holster. No, Allison." She waited until Allison met her gaze. "Use two fingers of your left hand. Drop it on the ground. Now, kick it away. Good."

Allison stepped toward Dustin.

Mbachu knelt beside Donovan.

"Move slowly, Allison. That's right. Now just push him over. Let's see what's underneath him."

The brown envelope. Still sealed, though she wasn't sure any seal could protect them from the deadly agent inside. Her mind wanted to dart away, to bring up the details of the 2001 anthrax letters sent to Congress. To calculate their odds of survival. But that would have to wait. What happened an hour or a week from now would take care of itself. She needed to focus. She needed to create a space.

"Pick it up."

"I'm not touching that."

"Don't worry. It's securely sealed—an envelope within an envelope within an envelope. Military-grade protection for military-grade weapons. Quite ingenious, really. Stella acquired it at considerable expense. *No expense is too great*—I believe those were her exact words. She was quite proud of the entire plan and especially pleased that John was able to make sure that you were on board."

Allison wasn't buying it.

She wasn't about to touch that envelope.

"If it's so safe, why was Dustin wearing PPE?"

"Dustin was a bit paranoid. He couldn't really grasp the science of it all. Now hurry up. This storm will be past us in the next few minutes, and I want to be as far from here as possible when the weather clears."

As if she had a helicopter waiting to whisk her away.

She probably did.

No expense is too great.

Allison glanced at Mbachu, who averted her eyes toward Donovan, who was looking directly at Allison. He didn't move his lips. Didn't say a thing. But she knew him that well. She understood what he was trying to tell her.

This was it.

This was the moment. The one they'd talked about. The one they'd both felt approaching.

So she knelt as if to pick up the envelope, aware that Price's eyes were locked on her. How could she look away? This was the AT's master plan, their destiny, their coup de grâce, their deathblow.

She reached for the envelope, and that was when Mbachu pulled out the weapon that Donovan had been lying on. She pulled it free, stood, pivoted, fired.

Then fired again and again and again.

Allison sprinted over to her and placed her hand on top of the weapon. "She's dead."

Mbachu met her eyes and nodded once. She slowly released her grip on the weapon, and allowed Allison to take it. Then the doctor dropped back onto the floor. "He has a chest wound. I need something to seal it."

And at that moment, Allison was aware of Donovan's struggle for air, of the sucking sound his chest made as he breathed in and out. She wanted him to open his eyes, to look at her again, to tell her they'd done it—hell, yeah.

The good guys had won. Again.

But he didn't do any of those things.

He lay there, eyes closed, blood pooling beneath him.

"There's a first aid kit on the wall near the door we came in through."

Allison sprinted across the room, located the first aid box, opened it, and stared at the contents, not comprehending what she was seeing or what Mbachu might possibly need.

"Gloves, sterile dressings, and tape," Mbachu called.

Allison's hands were shaking, her adrenaline finally coming down. She pocketed the first aid tape and two packages of nitrile gloves, snatched at the box of dressings, dropped it on the floor, picked it up, and raced back to Mbachu.

The doctor had already pulled away Donovan's clothing. "Let's confirm it's a through and through." She tore open one of the packages and snapped on a pair of gloves.

Allison did the same.

"Help me roll him. Toward you. Gently—"

And still, he didn't wake. It occurred to her that he might not. He might die on this floor in the bowels of a cruise ship. But he had been conscious. She hadn't imagined the look he'd given her. She hadn't imagined the concern in his eyes.

He couldn't die now. That couldn't happen. Allison could not envision a life where he wasn't teasing her, challenging her, supporting her.

And her mind slammed back into the memory she'd worked so hard to forget—being shot, bleeding into the snow, wondering if this was how it would end, wondering why she couldn't feel the pain of the wound, wondering if this was how she'd die.

Donovan had been there. Had he felt the despair then that she was feeling now? As Allison had lain in the snow on a mountain in Washington State, bleeding from a shoulder wound, had he panicked that they might never have a chance? But they'd barely known each other then. He couldn't have . . .

He couldn't have cared for her then.

Not like she cared for him now.

"Entry and exit wounds are clear." Mbachu motioned for them to gently lie him back down.

"We're going to seal this wound with the packaging those sterile pads come in. Tear them open, then place them over the wound. I'll tape as you hold them in position. One at a time.

Inside of the package will go against the wound. That's it. Two should do it. Good. Now we need to roll him over and do the same on his front."

"The . . . the bottom." Allison's voice sounded as if it came from a very far distance.

"We leave it untapped."

When they'd finished, they both stayed exactly where they were. The storm, no doubt, was still raging. Eloise was dead. Dustin was dead. Price was dead. Allison and Mbachu watched Donovan closely.

His breathing evened out.

The sucking sound stopped.

Color returned to his face.

"Will he make it?" The words were a whisper. A prayer.

"Yes." Mbachu didn't even hesitate. "But I'm going to remain here and watch for signs of a collapsed lung. You need to go and update the captain."

Allison glanced over at Dustin. "Do you want his PPE?"

"No. If the anthrax has already been released, it's too late. If it's not released, if the anthrax really is packaged as well as Price believed, then we don't need it. Go. I'll stay with Agent Steele."

***

Forty minutes later, Allison stood on the deck on the *Harmony* next to the helipad, as the Coast Guard rescue copter landed. The storm had abated while they'd been locked in battle with the AT. The heavy rains were now visible in the distance, the Gulf water almost calm. A hint of sunshine was attempting to break through the cloud cover.

Mbachu was standing next to Donovan. They'd put him on a stretcher, hooked up an IV, stabilized him, and moved him out on the deck. He'd need surgery to repair any interior damage, but he'd survive.

Allison jogged over before they could load him on the copter.

As if he sensed her presence, he opened his eyes.

He had a dreamy look on his face, smiled at her, reached for her hand.

"Must be some good stuff they put in your I.V."

"Why's that?"

"Because you're smiling, Steele. You've been shot in the chest, and you're smiling."

"I'm smiling at you." His grip on her intensified.

"Thank you," he said. And there was something captivating in the way he said those two simple words. Maybe it was his vulnerability because he was strapped to a stretcher, too weak to make a break for it. Or perhaps she was hearing the sincerity that acknowledged he would be dead if it weren't for her and Mbachu. Or possibly Donovan was voicing their comprehension of what they'd averted, of how great this tragedy might have been.

Whatever emotion it was that filled his voice, it caused tears to sting Allison's eyes.

She did something then that she'd never have imagined doing five years earlier when she'd first met him. She leaned over and kissed his cheek, inhaled the smell of him, remembered how his arms had felt around her. Then she stepped back, or tried to because he still had a pretty good grasp on her hand. The man was freakishly strong for someone teetering on death's doorstep.

"You saved me," he said.

"Just returning the favor."

"Your hair is beautiful in this wind."

It wasn't wind per se but rather the downwash velocity created by the rotation of the helicopter blades. Allison rolled her eyes, but she smiled. How could she not smile at Donovan Steele cracking jokes as he was being loaded into a helicopter?

The pilot gave a signal, and she stepped back from the chopper, stood there on the deck as they loaded him. It lifted off. Allison stood there a minute, then two—watching it race across the Gulf waters. Finally, she turned and walked toward Captain McKinley and Dr. Mbachu.

McKinley held out a hand, and she shook it. "I'm sorry I gave you such a hard time. It seemed like . . . It seemed like we were handling this all wrong, and so I resisted every suggestion you had. Good suggestions that saved the lives of these people."

"You were looking out for your crew and passengers."

"Right." His eyes darted away, then back to hers. "If we hadn't set sail from Galveston, they would have released the biologic somewhere in town, right?"

"Possibly. Probably. The AT was going to use the anthrax to make a statement one way or another."

"CDC personnel have already done preliminary swabs," Mbachu said. "There were no signs of anthrax around the ventilator shaft. They'll run more tests once we dock and, of course, confirm if it was actually anthrax in the brown envelope.

"It's real," Allison said. "The AT is just that crazy."

"I best get back to it." McKinley shook her hand again, thanked the doctor, and then walked across the deck and into the ship. Perfect posture. Dressed for inspection. No nonsense.

But a bit wiser, probably.

Allison thought he was now aware that the world was running by different rules. The entire nature of the enemy had changed since McKinley served in the U.S. Navy. Their opponents—whoever they were—no longer limited their attacks to military targets. They didn't hesitate to involve civilians. They often weren't from other countries. The enemy was among them, and they were willing to do whatever it took to win.

Mbachu sighed. "Guess it's back to treating motion sickness and hangovers for me."

Allison turned to study her.

"What?"

"You did well in there."

"I suppose I fell back on my training. Chicago experience and all that."

"We could use someone like you on the task force."

"No. Thank you." Mbachu's smile was wide, revealing beautiful teeth. Though she must have been exhausted, her eyes said plainly that she could still appreciate the good things in life. Dr. Mbachu seemed to Allison like a person whose soul was content with the choices she'd made.

"I had quite enough of that life over the last twenty years," Mbachu admitted. "This trip has made me realize it might be time to settle down. Find a quiet place in the country—maybe somewhere in the heartland—Iowa or Ohio or Indiana. One of those vowel states. Buy a house. Sounds nice, right?"

Allison nodded in agreement, though honestly, she couldn't imagine doing such a thing. What would she do all day?

They spent the rest of the evening setting the ship to rights, assuring passengers that the danger had passed, enjoying the quiet trek home. Allison checked in with Pat and Charlotte, Debbie, Robin, Mary Beth, Anna Lee, Ava. They were holding court in the library. Someone had found cold sandwiches and warm cokes. She thanked them for their help. Stayed and ate with them when they insisted. And shook her head as she walked away at the unlikelihood of those women aiding a JCTF operation.

Life was strange at times.

She filled out her reports and removed the surveillance device from cabin 784, though she was careful to wear gloves. The rooms would be dusted to confirm that only Dustin, Eloise, and Becca had been there. It would also be checked for any trace elements of anthrax.

Finally, finally, she sprawled across her bed and fell into a dreamless sleep.

Kate poked her head out of the tangle of vines. Darkness. Nothing but darkness. She let her eyes adjust. Focused on her senses. What could she hear? Nothing.

Nothing and no one.

She concentrated on her breathing. Listened.

Night birds. Water somewhere nearby.

Nothing else.

But she knew that John would be out there. He or his goons. She moved away from her hidey hole slowly, placing each foot down as carefully and quietly as possible. Her vision adjusted to the night. She was able to make out leaves collected in piles, decomposed under the winter snowpack, now saturated with the recent rains. Twigs and limbs and piles of rotting wood lay every few feet. Branches from the towering trees that had broken in the wind or under the weight of heavy snow. When possible, she walked on top of the larger logs. Maybe it would obscure her footprints. John would have trackers out in the morning. He'd probably have dogs too. She'd never be able to outrun dogs.

Focus on what you can do.

Reid Clark had overseen her training. It had been the most difficult thing Kate had ever attempted. Grueling. Exhausting. Nearly impossible. She'd doubted her abilities, her motivation, her strength and resolve.

Forget what you can't do. Focus on what you can do.

It was a common refrain on the task force. Play to your strengths and hope someone else could cover your weaknesses. The biggest obstacle to her survival, as she saw it, was that John Howard had the best surveillance technology available.

Biometric surveillance. He had her fingerprints. Her DNA. Facial recognition and iris scans and voice recognition. Those things had been necessary for access control, but they could just as easily be used to track someone. If she made it to town, if she appeared on any of the traffic light cameras or even private CCTV he would hack in and find her.

The woods . . . the woods were an advantage.

Yes, he would have thermal and night vision drones.

But the acreage around middle-earth was large. Even someone like John Howard had limited resources. Those drones couldn't be everywhere at once. They'd fly a grid pattern. They'd use AI to map out likely hiding places.

Focus on what you can do.

Her heat signature wouldn't be that different from a large animal, and there were large animals in these woods. They'd caught grizzlies on the monitors more than once—seen them and laughed because they were watching the live feed from safely inside the fortress. Grizzlies could weigh nearly eight hundred pounds. She had no desire to cross one, but she was comforted by the fact that they were in the area. That they might draw the drones away from her for even a short time.

Moose also roamed the woods. They were actually the largest animal in the area at fifteen hundred pounds.

She wasn't the only mammal beneath these trees.

That was to her advantage.

But it would be foolish to simply wander. She would succumb to dehydration or exhaustion long before John Howard admitted defeat.

She walked into a small clearing, stopped, glanced up, and forced her heart rate to slow and her mind to analyze what she was seeing. The rain had cleared and the night sky seemed to be washed clean. Easy enough to find Polaris—the North Star. Next, she looked for Orion. She turned in a circle, blinking and cursing and knowing in her head that it was there but fearing that she was misremembering her orienteering course.

Orion's belt. Three bright stars, close together, in an almost straight line.

There. Betelgeuse—Orion's right shoulder and Rigel—Orion's left foot. It was coming back to her now. The time she'd been blindfolded, driven into the desert, and left. Alone. Forced to use her training to find her way back. Forced to survive.

She'd done it then.

She'd do it now.

And there was the sword of Orion, which pointed south.

She knew where she was in relation to the stars. But which way should she go? Which direction should she choose?

Northeast of middle-earth lay Glacier National Park. It

encompassed more than one million acres. A girl could get lost there, but she'd have to get past John's perimeter fence. She could do that. She would do it if that was her last resort. But it wasn't her first choice. The only way past the fence was through it, and John would be on her in minutes. It would be a race, one that she was ill-equipped to win.

Northwest lay US-93, which led to Grasmere, British Columbia. Again with the perimeter fence problem. Plus, it was seventy miles. She couldn't hike seventy miles without supplies.

She closed her eyes.

Envisioned the aerial map of middle-earth.

And suddenly, she knew. Directly south lay county roads. The perimeter fence was weakest there because it had to pass over several streams. The forest between where she was and where she needed to go was dense. It wouldn't be easy. She'd have to move quickly, carefully. She'd have to stay alert. Avoiding the drones would be critical.

She could do it.

She could slip under the fence.

The last of her terror fled as training and reason and confidence bolstered her spirit. Middle-earth was large, but it had boundaries. John Howard would expect her to go west, intersect US-93, and hitchhike into Whitefish. Kate had no intention of showing up in the small town of eight thousand. First, she suspected he'd hacked his way into every governmental and private security system. Second, she did not want to draw John's attention to Whitefish. She did not want to put those people in danger. For all she knew, he had an extra supply of *Bacillus anthracis*. She wouldn't put it past him to use it. He'd already done so with the people on the *Harmony*. John Howard would consider Whitefish to be a bonus round to his diabolical plan.

She'd go south.

She'd cross where the stream passed under the security perimeter—lie on her stomach and crawl through the water if she had to.

And then she'd hitchhike toward one of the many fishing lakes. From there, she'd borrow a phone and call the task force.

She knew more than coding and hacking and subterfuge.

Reid had prepared her for far more than that.

He'd also trained her to never give up.

Chapter Twenty-Five

Before the *Harmony* docked at Galveston, Allison made one last visit to the engineering room. Brock Ferguson had definitely been changed by the incident, and not in the way that Allison might have predicted. Instead of being intimidated by the events of the last five days, he'd developed a quiet resolve.

"I want to work for corporate."

"What would that entail?"

"Coming up with plans that would harden our systems, protect us against the likes of what we experienced on this cruise. It's time to become proactive instead of reactive."

"I can't think of a single ship's engineer who could do a better job."

"Do you know any other ship's engineers?"

Allison smiled, shook his hand, then took a seat beside Lilith Maguire. The girl was still all attitude. She wore a Pink Floyd tee. She'd somehow found the time to do a French braid with her red hair. Her green eyes were rimmed with purple eyeliner, but they still danced when she looked directly at Allison.

Lilith had risen to the challenge. She'd started this cruise as a top-notch programmer hiding out on a cruise ship, enjoying the drink package and watching the parade of tourists. She was ending it with the skills of an ethical hacker. It was hard to go back to your previous life once you'd seen the dark side. Once you'd been challenged by it. Lilith struck her as someone who had been shaken from her sleep.

Allison crossed her arms and leaned back in the chair. "Interested in a job with the task force?"

Lilith stared at her with a deadpan look that tried to convey she wasn't interested. It failed.

"Your talents are wasted here. What you were able to do while I was dealing with Dustin and Eloise and Price . . . You got the message out, Lilith. You had the Coast Guard and the CDC here before Dustin's body was cold. Probably while Price was shooting Donovan."

"I still can't believe that last one."

"Wolf. Sheep's clothing. You know." Allison wasn't merely appealing to the girl's ego. She was among the best Allison had ever seen—and she'd accomplished much while under the imminent threat of a terrorist event. "Lilith, you managed to get through to the Coast Guard while the AT's program was still running. I'm not even sure the Kids could have done that."

"The Kids?"

"Tech geniuses. Saviors of the task force. Bunch of geeks, basically, but we love them."

"Would I have to wear lame clothes like yours? No offense."

"None taken, and no."

"Would I get to carry a gun?"

Allison shrugged.

Lilith swiveled her chair right, then left, then back toward Allison. "Tell me more."

Yeah. Lilith Maguire would fit right in with the Kids.

As for Allison, she thought she might put in for a week's leave from the task force. They would dock in Galveston in a few hours. Galveston to San Saba was just over three hundred miles. She could be at Aunt Polly's in time for dinner.

And she could take one more swing at her father's old computer. This time she'd search for the name Stella. Something told her she would find a connection. She was more convinced than ever that this op had been designed to draw her into it. What was it Price had said? *She was quite proud of the entire plan, and especially pleased that John was able to make sure that you were on board.*

Allison would get off the ship in Galveston, put in a call to the task force, then head to Aunt Polly's. It wouldn't be a real vacation. But something told her that Kendra Thomas would approve her request. She'd be allowed to file what remaining reports were required remotely and to do the debrief via Skype. Thomas had been after her to take a vacation for months.

She'd try to call Reid Clark.

Confirm that he was still in charge of the DHS side of things.

Check in on Donovan.

And research the name Stella. If she had any luck at all, it would bring her one step closer to her father's killer.

Dawn streaked the sky when Kate stumbled out of the woods. She'd huddled at the edge for hours. She was soaking wet from her crawl under the perimeter fence. Wet leaves clung to her clothes and her hair. The gash on her left leg from a pointed branch continued to bleed.

She was hungry and thirsty and weary all the way to her bones.

Still, she crept forward carefully. Watched. Assessed.

Confirming whether they were still looking for her. Twice she'd heard the drones dip close and then zoom away. Once, she'd heard men's voices. That had been hours ago.

She wanted a shower. A tall glass of water. Sleep.

She startled at the sound of a vehicle coming down the narrow county road. Old. Beat up. Safe . . . maybe. A pick-up by the sounds of it. Not a Suburban. Not one of John's fleet of vehicles.

Kate stepped out into the road for a better look. The truck was a Ford, its paint job long ago faded to an indiscernible color. The front bumper had suffered a blow on the passenger side and was now held up with bailing wire. Both windows rolled down. A man's arm propped on the sill.

The car approached, slowed, stopped.

The man driving was an old guy—white beard, thinning hair, rheumy eyes, bib overalls. A gray-muzzled hound dog sat on the seat next to him, staring out the front window as the man allowed the old truck to idle.

Kate and the man looked at each other for a full moment.

Finally, he broke the silence. "Need a ride, miss?"

"I do."

And then she heard it—the sound of a drone. She must have flinched because the old guy reached behind him and snagged a rifle from the gun rack that ran along the back window. Quicker than she would have thought possible, he was out of the truck and taking aim. The drone was losing altitude. Someone on the other end, someone directing it, wanted a front image.

"I wouldn't—"

The rifle's report broke the peacefulness of the morning.

The drone fell to the ground in front of them—all wires and circuits and metal. Its rotors silent. Its communication ability shattered.

"Can't abide those things," the old man said. He remounted the rifle, then turned toward her. "Name's Gerald. Gerald Davis."

"Katelyn Ballou."

He held out his hand, and she shook it.

Calloused. Dirt beneath the nails. This guy had to be the real deal. Old dog on the front seat and a Winchester rifle in the gun rack. One of John Howard's guys couldn't look this authentically blue-collar if he spent a week trying.

"Nice to meet you, Katelyn Ballou." Gerald nodded toward

the passenger side. "We best get going. I had Hank out before sunrise to fish, and he's ready for breakfast."

She got in, allowed Hank to sniff her hands, then buckled her seatbelt.

Gerald pushed the gear shift into drive and slowly, intentionally, drove over the remnants of the drone. A smile broke across his well-lined face, and he laughed.

She wanted to join him. She wanted to believe that this day had started new, fresh, without the dangers of the day before. But that wasn't true. And the wreckage of the drone behind them proved it.

"Do you mind if I..." She motioned toward the radio.

"No. Go ahead. Only get AM stations out here, but you should be able to find something."

Static.

Rock and roll.

Country music.

The news.

"The cruise ship, the *Harmony*, which docked at Galveston early this morning was said to have experienced a software glitch which caused the vessel to drive into, rather than out of, the storm last night. Dream Sail Cruises issued a statement that all 5,148 crew and passengers arrived safely back in port. In other news . . ."

Kathryn turned the dial again, found a golden oldies station, and set it to low. Which seemed to suit Gerald and Hank just fine.

Two hours later, she was picked up by a task force helicopter. Seeing the Montana countryside from the sky, she felt immense gratitude that she was leaving it all behind. She'd been in the heart of the AT long enough. It was time to go home.

The End

Enjoy **FREE** bonus scenes and novels when you join my mailing list. Plus, get updates on new releases, deals, and more from Vannetta Chapman. Click on the newsletter tab at

vannettachapman.com

Already a subscriber? Provide your email again so we can send you the FREE Allison Quinn bonus scene. You will also continue to receive exclusive offers in your inbox.

Thank you for reading, *Against All Enemies.* I hope you enjoyed the story. If you did, please consider rating the book or leaving a review at Amazon, Bookbub, or Goodreads.

Keep reading for a preview of *Veil of Mystery*, the prequel to my Kessler Effect series.

An Excerpt From

Veil of Mystery
    prequel to The Kessler Effect Series
    June 6, 20~~
    Alpine, Texas

The first anomaly occurred on Tuesday morning at fourteen minutes after ten. Keme Lopez noted the time, confirmed that his back-up system had taken a screenshot of all open windows, and replayed the video that had appeared on Twitter. There wasn't much to it—a mere fourteen seconds from start to finish. Already it was at the top of his Twitter feed.

He sat back, trying to understand what he'd seen. Trying to come up with a better explanation than the Twitter universe had. Slowly, cautiously—as if playing the video might cause some danger to befall him and his family—he again clicked *play*.

A woman with short blonde hair sobbed as she recorded live. He could see the *Recording Live* button at the bottom of the screen. The video definitely represented something that had happened in real time. From the looks of the people in the background, what he was seeing had actually occurred.

As tears streamed down her face and in words that were nearly incoherent, she told her husband that she loved him.

Keme paused the video.

He zoomed in on passengers in the background. Some huddled together, heads bowed, praying. A mother in the next row rocked her child back and forth. Many passengers had their hands over their faces, and about a third sat in the classic "prepare for crash" position. Several men stood, though the nose-down angle of the plane obviously made that difficult. They seemed to be looking out the window.

When Keme zoomed in more, he was able to see clear blue skies. So this plane crash—if that's what it was—was not weather-related.

Mechanical failure? But there was no smoke that he could see. No holes in the plane. It seemed to be simply falling from the sky.

A soft rap on his open door jerked him back to the present—a June morning in Alpine, Texas.

"I'm headed outside to work in the garden," Lucy said.

Keme's wife was a professor of literature at Sul Ross University. She was five foot, four inches with a curvy figure and brown hair—the tips dyed with turquoise streaks. Keme had married up, and he realized that anew every single day.

"What would make a plane fall from the sky?"

"Excuse me?"

"Mechanical failure, a bomb exploding, maybe a pilot who had a heart attack..."

"Not the last one." She moved into the room and stared at his screen, then reached past him and clicked *Play*. She watched the video in silence, then played it again. Finally, she stepped back, leaning against the doorframe and staring up at the ceiling.

He waited.

Finally her brown eyes met his.

"That's awful. Is it real?"

"Seems to be. Why did you say '*not the last one*?'"

"Because that's what a co-pilot rides along for, and I think...I think a plane switches to automatic pilot if something unusual happens."

"Probably so."

"When was that video recorded?"

Keme glanced at the time on his computer. "Almost fifteen minutes ago."

"Anything on the news sites?"

He clicked to a different tab and unmuted the window.

"The video was apparently taken aboard a direct flight from London to Austin just a few minutes ago. According to the FAA—"

The screen abruptly went to a plain blue background with *Please Stand By* displayed in a large font. Beneath it was a banner which read *We are experiencing technical problems at this time.*

"What happened?"

"I don't know." He again noted the time—10:30. "They've just stopped streaming."

He clicked over to two other news stations, but they both displayed the same blue screen with the same disclaimer.

"Is the internet down?"

"Doesn't seem to be." He clicked back to Twitter.

Top story—#Planecrash
Second story--#newsoutage

"An EMP?" Lucy crossed her arms, frowning at the screen.

"The internet is still up. I guess it could be a localized EMP, but the odds that it would affect all news outlets seems...impossible."

Lucy squeezed his shoulder, then kissed his cheek. "Let me know if anything else bizarre happens."

"Where are you going?"

"To weed the garden."

Which was exactly like Lucy. She was somewhat unflappable. A nuclear bomb could be headed their way, and she'd say, "I certainly can't stop a nuke. Might as well weed the garden." She was very big on ignoring things out of her scope of influence. Maybe not ignoring, but she certainly didn't spend hours worrying over it. He envied her that, even as he watched her walk away.

His eyes scanned the shelves in his office which held a wide variety of items that he thought of as simply—*my history*. There were water sticks, deer antlers, arrow heads, and rocks. The collection represented his Native American heritage. His mother was one quarter Kiowa. His father was Hispanic, and it was from his father that he'd inherited his handiness. For his Pop that meant farm equipment. For Keme, it meant computers.

A long workspace counter stretched along two walls of his office, and it was filled with computers. At the age of forty-two, he managed to make a pretty good living fixing people's computers. Alpine was only six thousand folks. Given their remote location in the southwest corner of Texas, computers were how they remained connected to the rest of the world.

He turned his attention back to his monitor.

For the next twenty minutes he browsed the world wide web, but there was no consensus as to what had happened. Definitely no official statement.

Then he clicked back to Twitter and saw that the plane crash had been bumped down to the number two spot. In its place was the hashtag #stockmarketcollapse.

Keme no longer invested his money in the stock market, but he did stay apprised of the general situation. There'd been a lot of "collapses" in the last few years. It usually meant the market dropped ten percent then rebounded twelve to fifteen percent the next day. He was pretty sure the market was manipulated so that the ups and downs made the rich richer and kept everyone not in that group out.

Just another of your conspiracy theories, Lucy was fond of saying.

He clicked on #stockmarketcollapse and scanned through the posts.

As he watched, the ticker went from a seventy-five percent loss to an eighty percent loss.

The DOW had dropped eighty percent? That wasn't possible. Circuit breaker rules had been put in place in 1988 to protect companies against panic selling. He tried clicking over to another site, but now his machine seemed frozen. None of the sites would refresh. He leaned back in his chair to check his modem. Red lights blinked back at him.

It wasn't unusual for the internet to go down in Alpine. They were, after all, in a rural part of Texas. Keme picked up his cellphone and stared at the icon in the upper right. No internet signal at all. Furthermore, when he tried to place a call, it wouldn't connect.

So the internet was down, as well as the cell towers?

Pocketing the device, he grabbed his hat and stepped outside.

Lucy was squatting in front of the tomato plants. Sitting back on her heels, she asked, "Any answers?"

"Nope."

"More questions?"

"Yup. Internet is out completely and so are the phones."

"Huh."

Keme glanced north toward Alpine. "The stock market crashed just before the internet went down."

"By how much?"

"Eighty percent."

Lucy wiped away sweat from her brow. "I didn't think that was possible."

"It shouldn't be."

She stood and brushed at the dirt on the back of her jeans. Walking over to him, she cocked her head and studied him. "You're worried."

He shrugged, then admitted, "Yeah."

"Akule is fine, honey. She's right there..." Lucy jerked a thumb toward Alpine. "We can go check on her if you like."

Their daughter had recently moved back to Alpine, but their son, Paco, lived with his wife and children in the Dallas area. If something big was happening, Keme would like to have his family close.

"Have you called Tanda?"

He smiled, kissed her forehead, and pulled her into his arms. "Phones are out. Remember?"

"Oh, yeah." She snuggled against him. "Sounds like you won't be fixing anyone's computer this morning. How about you and I go inside and—"

At that moment there was an explosion that caused the ground to tremble.

"What—"

"Look."

A cloud of smoke was rising on the horizon. Something had exploded. The scream of emergency vehicles immediately followed. Whatever was happening, it was happening in the middle of Alpine.

You can purchase *Veil of Mystery in ebook or print,* exclusively from Amazon.

Also by Vannetta Chapman

FOR A COMPLETE LIST OF MY BOOKS, VISIT MY website
vannettachapman.com

Contact the Author

Share Your Thoughts With the author:
Your comments will be forwarded to the author when you send them to
vannettachapman@gmail.com.

Submit your review of this book to:
vannettachapman@gmail.com
or via the connect/contact button on the author's website at:
VannettaChapman.com.

Sign up for the author's newsletter at:
VannettaChapman.com.

Printed in Great Britain
by Amazon

59223044R00158